It was truly a hail of bullets, like something out of a sci-fi movie.

"This is certainly the best Frame Gear I've ever piloted. But it's still rather slow to handle..."

In Another World With My Smartphone

Patora Fuyuhara
illustration·Eiji Usatsuka

Luli

The fourth of Touya's summoned Heavenly Beasts. She is the Azure Monarch, the ruler of dragons. She often clashes with Kohaku due to her condescending personality.

Kougyoku

The third of Touya's summoned Heavenly Beasts. She is the Flame Monarch, ruler of feathered things. Though her appearance is flashy and extravagant, she's actually quite cool and collected.

Sango and Kokuyou

The second of Touya's summoned Heavenly Beasts. They are the Black Monarch, two in one. The rulers of scaled beasts. They can freely manipulate water. Sango is a tortoise, and Kokuyou is a snake. Sango is a female, and Kokuyou is a male (but he's very much a female at heart).

Kohaku

The first of Touya's summoned Heavenly Beasts. She's the White Monarch, the ruler of beasts, the guardian of the West and a beautiful White Tiger. She can create devastating shockwaves, and also change size at will.

High Rosetta

Terminal Gynoid in charge of the Workshop, one of the Babylon relics. She's called Rosetta for short. Her Airframe Serial Number is #27. For whatever reason, she's the most reliable of the bunch.

Francesca

Terminal Gynoid in charge of the Hanging Garden, one of the Babylon relics. She's called Cesca for short. Her Airframe Serial Number is #23. She likes to tell very inappropriate jokes.

Mochizuki Moroha

The God of Swords. Claims to be Touya's older sister. She trains and advises the knights of Brunhild. She's gallant and brave, but also a bit of an airhead at times.

Mochizuki Karen

The God of Love. Claims to be Touya's older sister. She stays in Brunhild because she says she needs to catch a servile god, but doesn't really do all that much in the way of hunting him. She's a total pain in the butt.

Pamela Noèl

Terminal Gynoid in charge of the Tower, one of the Babylon relics. She's called Noel for short and wears a jersey. Her Airframe Serial Number is #25. She sleeps all the time, and eats laying down. Her tremendous laziness means she doesn't do all that much.

Preliora

Terminal Gynoid in charge of the Rampart, one of the Babylon relics. She's called Liora for short and wears a blazer. Her Airframe Serial Number is #20. She's the oldest of the Babylon Gynoids, and would attend to the... personal night-time needs of Doctor Babylon herself. She has no experience with men.

Fredmonica

Terminal Gynoid in charge of the Hangar, one of the Babylon relics. She's called Monica for short. Her Airframe Serial Number is #28. She's a funny little hard worker who has a bit of a casual streak. She's a good friend of Rosetta, and is the Gynoid with the most knowledge of the Frame Gears.

Bell Flora

Terminal Gynoid in charge of the Alchemy Lab, one of the Babylon relics. She's called Flora for short and wears a nurse outfit. Her Airframe Serial Number is #21. A nurse with dangerously big boobs and even more dangerous medicines.

Doctor Regina Babylon

An ancient genius from a lost civilization, reborn into an artificial body that resembles a small girl. She is the "Babylon" that created the many artifacts and forgotten technologies scattered around the world today. Her Airframe serial number is #29. She remained in stasis for five-thousand years before finally being awakened.

Atlantica

Terminal Gynoid in charge of the Research Lab, one of the Babylon relics. She's called Tica for short. Her Airframe serial number is #22. Of the Babylon Numbers, she is the one who best embodies Doctor Babylon's inappropriately perverse side.

Lileleparshe

Terminal Gynoid in charge of the Storehouse, one of the Babylon relics. She's called Parshe for short and wears a shrine maiden outfit. Her Airframe Serial Number is #26. She's tremendously clumsy, even if she's just trying to help. The amount of stuff she ruins is troublingly high.

Irisfam

Terminal Gynoid in charge of the Library, one of the Babylon relics. She's called Fam for short and wears a school uniform. Her Airframe Serial Number is #24. She's a total book fanatic and hates being interrupted when she's reading.

Character Profiles

Elze Silhoueska

One of Touya's fiancees.
The elder of the twin sisters saved by Touya some time ago. A ferocious melee fighter, she makes use of gauntlets in combat. Her personality is fairly to-the-point and blunt. She can make use of Null fortification magic, specifically the spell [Boost]. She loves spicy foods.

Yumina Urnea Belfast

One of Touya's fiancees.
Princess of the Belfast Kingdom. She was twelve years old in her initial appearance, and her eyes are heterochromatic. The right is blue, while the left is green. She has mystic eyes that can discern the true character of an individual. She has three magical aptitudes: Earth, Wind, and Darkness. She's also extremely proficient with a bow and arrow. She fell in love with Touya at first sight.

Mochizuki Touya

A highschooler who was accidentally murdered by God. He's a no-hassle kind of guy who likes to go with the flow. He's not very good at reading the atmosphere, and typically makes rash decisions that bite him in the ass. His mana pool is limitless, he can flawlessly make use of every magical element, and he can cast any Null spell that he wants. He's currently the Grand Duke of Brunhild.

Sushie Urnea Ortlinde

One of Touya's fiancees.
She was ten years old in her initial appearance. Her nickname is Sue. She is the niece of Belfast's king, and Yumina's cousin. Touya saved her from being attacked on the road. She has an innocently adventurous spirit.

Lucia Leah Regulus

One of Touya's fiancees.
The Third Princess of the Regulus Empire, she's Yumina's age. She fell in love with Touya when he saved her during a coup. She likes to fight with twin blades, and she's on good terms with Yumina.

Kokonoe Yae

One of Touya's fiancees.
A samurai girl from the far eastern land of Eashen, a country much like Japan. She tends to repeat herself and speak formally, she does. Yae is quite a glutton, eating more than most normal people would dare touch. She's a hard worker, but can sometimes slack off. Her family runs a dojo back in Eashen, and they take great pride in their craft. It's not obvious at first, but her boobs are pretty big.

Linze Silhoueska

One of Touya's fiancees.
The younger of the twin sisters saved by Touya some time ago. She wields magic, specifically from the schools of Light, Water, and Fire. She finds talking to people difficult due to her own shy nature, but she is known to be surprisingly bold at times. Rumors say she might be the kind of girl who enjoys male on male romance... She loves sweet foods.

Paula

A stuffed toy bear animated by years upon years of the [Program] spell. She's the result of two-hundred years of programmed commands, making her seem like a fully aware living being. Paula... Paula's the worst!

Sakura

A mysterious girl Touya rescued in Eashen. She had lost her memories, but has now finally gotten them back. Her true identity is Farnese Forneus, daughter of the Xenoahs Overlord. Currently living a peaceful life in Brunhild, and she has joined the ranks of Touya's fiancees.

Leen

One of Touya's fiancees.
Former Clan Matriarch of the Fairies, she now serves as Brunhild's Court Magician. She claims to be six-hundred-and-twelve years old, but looks tremendously young. She can wield every magical element except Darkness, meaning her magical proficiency is that of a genius. Leen is a bit of a light-hearted bully.

Hildegard Minas Lestia

One of Touya's fiancees.
First Princess of the Knight Kingdom Lestia. Her swordplay talents earned her a reputation as a 'Knight Princess'. Touya saved her life when she was attacked by a group of Phrase, and she's loved him ever since. She's a good friend of Yae, and she stammers a bit when flustered.

IN ANOTHER WORLD WITH MY SMARTPHONE: VOLUME 11
by Patora Fuyuhara

Translated by Andrew Hodgson
Edited by DxS

Original Japanese edition published in 2017 by Hobby Japan
This English edition is published by arrangement with Hobby Japan, Tokyo

Find more books like this one at www.j-novel.club!

President and Publisher: Samuel Pinansky
Managing Editor: Aimee Zink
QA Manager: Hannah N. Carter
Marketing Manager: Stephanie Hii

ISBN: 978-1-7183-5010-6
Printed in Korea
First Printing: August 2020
10 9 8 7 6 5 4 3 2

Contents

Map of the World

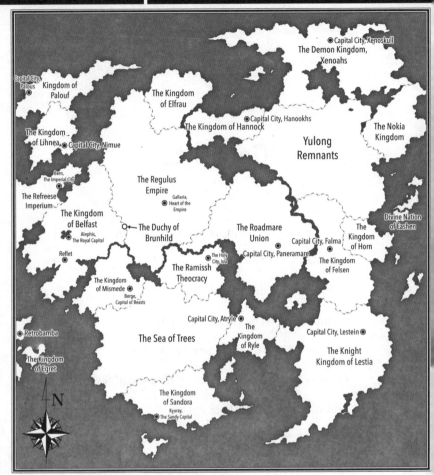

Capital City, Palous
Kingdom of Palouf

The Kingdom of Elfrau

The Kingdom of Hannock

Capital City, Hanookhs

Capital City, Xenoskull
The Demon Kingdom, Xenoahs

The Nokia Kingdom

Yulong Remnants

The Kingdom of Lihnea
Capital City, Nimue

Bern, The Imperial City

The Refreese Imperium

The Regulus Empire
Gallaria, Heart of the Empire

The Kingdom of Belfast
Alephis, The Royal Capital

The Duchy of Brunhild

Divine Nation of Eashen

The Kingdom of Horn

Reflet

The Roadmare Union
Capital City, Paneramare

Capital City, Falma

The Kingdom of Felsen

The Holy City, Isla

The Ramissh Theocracy

The Kingdom of Mismede
Berge, Capital of Beasts

Retrobamba

The Sea of Trees

Capital City, Atryle

The Kingdom of Ryle

Capital City, Lestein

The Knight Kingdom of Lestia

The Kingdom of Egret

N

The Kingdom of Sandora
Kyuray, The Sandy Capital

The Story So Far!

Mochizuki Touya, wielding a smartphone customized by God himself, has made a name for himself in the new world. He is now Grand Duke of Brunhild, a nation formed of territory from both the Kingdom of Belfast and the Regulus Empire. Having rightfully inherited the ancient legacy of Babylon, Touya now commands a fleet of enormous humanoid mechs known as Frame Gears. Using his power, Touya has unified many nations of the world and created a collective defense force to repel the Phrase, monstrous invaders from another world. But still... North, East, South, and West... Trouble brews in all directions, and there are still many that have their eyes on his prize.

"The world boundary, hm...?"

"Do you know any way to fix it up?" God quietly pondered as he munched on a rice cracker. They were a specialty in Eashen, so I'd brought them up to him as a gift. We were sitting in the ever-familiar little room amidst a sea of clouds. You guessed it, we were in the realm of the gods.

It would've been fine to consult him over the phone, but I didn't want to be rude. That's why I brought him a gift and came to see him in person.

"Well, you certainly could fix it, yes. A high-ranking god would be able to do it with little effort at all. But you know how it is by now, don't you my lad? We cannot interfere with the lower realms. Although if a wicked or renegade God were responsible for the damage, that would be an exception." God Almighty sipped his tea and heaved a sigh.

"The barrier was repaired five-thousand years ago, right?"

"Indeed it was. But that was not my doing. There are species in the lower worlds that could hypothetically do such a thing, though."

Who, though...? You're being a little vague.

"What if I used the power of my divinity to do it...?"

"You may find that a most unwise act, my boy. Can you stitch a cobweb back together by hand? Using such vast power for such a precise job... Do you truly have the precision control necessary?"

11

He has a point, I guess...? At least he doesn't seem to have an issue with me using my Divinity down there, though. It'd be bad if I tried to fix it and ended up making it worse.

"Oh right, I never thought to ask but... Is there anyone that's used divinity in an evil way?"

"Of course. Well, they are not exactly gods in the same sense as us, though. Most are born in the lower worlds. If they took a dark emotion like regret, grudge, attachment, and let it pool in their being, then they could attain such a state of corrupted divinity. This is typically attained by a bad person coming into contact with something divine to begin with, though, like a Sacred Treasure. Your old world had many folk stories about this kind of happening."

"Would you interfere in those cases?"

"I do not believe it appropriate to interfere directly, even in those cases. In cases like that we would simply offer divine aid to the people of that world, like granting a sacred blade to a chosen hero or some-such. The wicked deities formed by such acts have divinity even lower than servile gods, after all."

Lower than servile gods, huh...? Well, I guess they are just imitations.

"What if the hero dies?"

"I would not interfere. The world would end, most likely. Do you think I should just give chance after chance? I would give them a single chance to remedy the danger, because abandoning a world would surely bring it to ruin. Worlds would fall if they were not watched over. Though I do have measures in place to ensure that I pay attention to them for the most part." God let out a small laugh of self-derision. I wondered how many worlds had been abandoned or ruined as a result of their failures, though.

Just as I pondered that, God raised a finger and began to speak up.

"That reminds me, the smartphone that you wield is most certainly a Sacred Treasure at this point in time."

"Wait, seriously?!" I took out my smartphone and looked from it to the old man. *This is a Sacred Treasure, seriously?*

"When you died back then, I brought this object into this realm with you. Naturally, I tinkered with it a little, as you know. That little device is truly a Sacred Treasure, one that contains the power of the gods. How do you think it can call me, my boy? How do you think it can stream information from another world?"

I mean, true... That makes sense. Still, I didn't realize it was an item of that caliber.

"Would it be possible for me to make a Sacred Treasure of my own?"

"I do not see why not. It is simply a matter of channeling your divinity into an object. But, as I told you before, wicked and evil deities are typically born through interaction with divine powers, so perhaps you might want to refrain."

"Yeah, makes sense." *So they grant Sacred Treasures to heroes to fight against evil people who obtain divine powers. But what would happen if an evil deity got hold of the sacred item? That'd be bad, right?*

God explained that he usually destroyed the sacred sword or other divine relics after they were used to defeat the villain, and then it was replaced with a fake. Now and then he'd forget to do this, and the presence of the Sacred Treasure in the world would ultimately give rise to another villain a few hundred years down the line. That certainly wasn't good news.

Still, I had come to learn that God and his ilk were not omnipotent. There were plenty of troublesome gods, apparently. Even in my old world we had myths and legends about the divine taking human form to cause mischief. Gods were just as varied as humans... As I was beginning to learn quite well.

"Ah, Touya. It is a little premature to think about this, but... Would you like to be the one assigned to the world you live in right now?"

"Excuse me?"

"Well, you see... High-ranking gods, the superior gods... Each is assigned a particular world to oversee. I thought that when you ascend to that level, you would prefer a word that you are familiar with."

Hold up. Hold up! Superior god? That'd make me a higher rank than both of my sisters, wouldn't it? Or... Is that not weird? I guess I am a direct benefactor of God's blessing, but still...

"...That means I'd have to join the pantheon of gods though, right?"

"If you do not wish for it, then I have nothing more to say. I know that many of the other gods would like it, however. It has been several thousand years since the last god was inducted. The elder ones would not mind having a younger god around so they could brag a little, you know?"

It's nice that they're supportive, but... I kinda have mixed feelings about this.

"If I joined the pantheon, would I be allowed to have children? I'm getting married soon, you know...?"

"Many gods have fathered children with other species. We do not have a policy prohibiting it. The children would have strength and capabilities beyond the standard, but they would not become more powerful than you."

That makes sense. Hercules, Perseus, Achilles, and Cu Chulainn are all examples of half-gods from Earth's legends. There are a ton more, too.

But according to the Doc, I'm having eight daughters and one son... If they all have demi-god strength, that might make raising them a little bit much...

"A-Ah, just a question but... is there a god in charge of looking after kids?"

"There is, yes... But one should strive to raise his own children when possible."

"Tsk..."

It was just a hypothetical! Of course I wouldn't abandon my kids... Man, this is annoying. Why am I getting stressed about what won't be born for ages, anyway? It's not like they'll be giving birth right after they marry me, right? Right...?

"You should take care not to rely on your divinity too much for now. Just continue on doing what you can. Consider your arrival in that world to be a blessing... Although perhaps it is not my place to say such a thing, given how I sent you there. Either way, I am proud of you. Keep working hard."

"Thanks." *I guess he's just saying to take things as they come, huh? Well, that seems fair.*

After receiving some praise from God himself, I left his domain.

"So, we're recruiting more knights?"

"Indeed. We're currently low on manpower. We're no longer a fledgling nation, so there's no more breathing room." Kousaka nodded slowly as he spoke. He had a point, we didn't even have a hundred active knights in our country. Around forty of them weren't active combatants, either, and they didn't know how to pilot Frame Gears.

Some of them served Tsubaki as intel gatherers. Others worked for old man Naito and handled formal paperwork. That's not to say they weren't capable of fighting, they'd passed the test after all, but they didn't have to attend formal training.

Our country wasn't very big or anything, so we didn't need thousand-strong armies like other nations, but bolstering our ranks a bit definitely didn't sound unwise.

"Guess it sounds fine to me."

"Indeed. Brunhild is not getting any smaller, it is not."

"Yeah, it isn't. I guess the town will be more peaceful if we have more guards around." Elze, Yae, and Hilde often patrolled of their own volition, as well as participating in the knight training. They weren't formal members of the order, but they still liked to help out. They'd probably appreciate more people being assigned to keep the general peace.

"So how many are we talking?"

"Well, hm… I would move with the aim of doubling our current pool of knights, so I'd like to see a hundred new recruits. But we should see about recruiting one-hundred-and-fifty if we include domestic patrols, office workers, and castle guardsmen."

That many...? Well, I guess that should be okay... Even though they're called the Brunhild Knight Order, they're technically financed out of my pocket so it's more like they're my personal band of mercenaries.

I get a fair bit of money from trade with Olba from Mismede, and sometimes I get to kill Behemoths, which yield heavy rewards. Sometimes I use [Search] to find missing stuff for important people, too.

"And how many of these people will be Frame Gear pilots?"

"Let's say we should aim for... a hundred in total, including the sixty we have trained for it already."

So only forty out of the new batch, huh...? The rest will end up being royal guards, town guards, and office workers. Well, that's fine. That's important work for the order too. People who'd have a problem with doing those duties probably wouldn't make it through the recruitment phase anyway.

"Then we should recruit them based on combat proficiency..." It was true that we needed people who'd handle the paperwork efficiently, but...

I couldn't afford to lower my standards just to accommodate people who might be more suited for office work. They needed to be strong, ready, and capable.

Still, I felt like throwing any of them to Moroha for special training would bring even a weakling up to par in terms of strength.

"Alright, then start setting up a recruitment panel. I trust your judgment on this part, so have anyone you think would be a good fit apply as well."

"Very well." I personally didn't know anyone qualified to join the order, so I left it to him.

I could've roped in Sonia and Rengetsu, or Lop's party, but they were adventurers, so I didn't want to restrain them. They probably made more money on their quests anyway.

I decided to post an ad in the guild. There'd probably be a lot more interested people this time around.

Yumina and the pope should be involved so we can use their Mystic Eyes to screen people, but I wonder if I can ask Doc Babylon to make a polygraph test. A lie detector would come in handy... Didn't I actually see something about that in the storehouse records?

I warped off to Babylon and headed into the Hangar. I found Monica and a mini-bot performing some routine maintenance on Gerhilde.

"Hm, where's the doc?"

"She's currently holding a meeting with Rosetta in the research laboratory. They're like, totally discussing what to do with the next Frame Gears and stuff."

"Huh..." I didn't fully get it, but I headed to the research laboratory to see what was going on. There was a miniature Frame Gear and a bunch of blueprints strewn across the Doc's desk. There was a cross-section image of a Frame Gear hanging on a nearby wall.

The two girls in the room were pointing at different parts of it, muttering and grumbling.

"Something wrong? You guys look annoyed."

"Ah, master sir! We're just... Working on Frame Gear development, sir...! We were thinking that Linze's Frame Gear would be a transformation type, and a fusion type that could combine with Elze's, sir!" As she spoke, Rosetta picked up the miniature Frame Gear and folded its arm and legs inwards; this freely allowed it to spread out wings and transform into flight mode.

Neat. That's a pretty smooth form shift.

The Frame Gear looked sturdy enough in design that it could survive atmospheric re-entry. Having a flying Frame Gear would also give us an edge in battle. I looked over the miniature figure again, wondering if we couldn't produce these as children's toys. They'd probably be popular.

"The issue is Leen's Frame Gear. Specifically, what we're doing with it. I was thinking of making it a heavy ordnance unit, with big guns installed all along its body. The Phrase resist magic, after all. So I was thinking we could load it with magic-based explosions for splash damage, or missiles for a more direct approach. Perhaps bullets, too. I thought back to that anime I was watching earlier and wondered if I couldn't make something like that Vulcan rotary cannon and Gatling gun. That was my thought process at least, but…"

That doesn't sound cost-effective at all. For starters we'd need to produce a ton of bullets or missiles that could damage a Phrase's body, we'd need something above mithril at the very least. That's the kind of thing that'd be ungodly to maintain, price-wise.

Then again, we could always arm it with Phrasium rounds… No, wait. That's a no-go. It'd be impossible to make tens of thousands of those things, it'd take the workshop's full operational capacity 24/7 to keep producing them. There's no way I can dedicate the time or resources necessary to a venture like that.

Plus it's probably limited in how much ammo it can actually take around with it. We could maybe see about making it a standing unit that constantly has ammo fed into it, but would we ever even need a sentry turret type Frame Gear?

"If you made a Frame Gear like that, let's say it starts firing all of its ammo non-stop… How long would it last?"

"It'd probably last around a minute in total."

"That's nowhere near enough." Even in anime, giant robots lost most of their power when they ran out of ammo. There was no way I'd risk it.

If it focuses fire, it might be able to last a little longer... But that's still not good. Plus there's no guarantee every bullet would land, either. It sounds like a pain. It'll just end up using up all the ammo and becoming a regular melee Frame Gear.

"How about we nix the Gatling idea and make a high-powered sniper? Something that could penetrate the Phrase Cores at long range. Don't you think that'd work out better?"

"That might be practical, sir! But... The aesthetic I was going for with this Frame Gear was more of a mobile fortress, sir! Big, bad, beastly! The kind of thing that would be equipped to mow down armies at mid-to-long range!" Rosetta collapsed with a grumble. A sniper would definitely be slower and less bombastic.

"We could always set it so it shoots out [**Fire Arrow**] barrages, or maybe [**Thunder Arrow**]. But that wouldn't help against the Phrase. The Gatling gun could use magic-based attacks, too." The doctor shrugged and smiled a bit as she spoke. Bullets wouldn't be an issue in that case, but Leen running out of magic power would be a real threat.

"...Actually, master sir! Where do you keep your ammo?"

"For my gun? Just in a pouch at my hip. There are live rounds, explosive rounds, and paralyzing rounds in there. I alternate them based on the situation." I showed her the pouch, and the three split pockets inside. There were twenty bullets of each type inside.

"...Hm. You switch these in the heat of battle? Isn't that obstructive?"

"Oh, nah. I have them load into my gun automatically. I programmed the gun with [**Apport**] so it ejects spent casing and immediately replaces the chamber slot with new rounds, then I—"

"That's it!" I wasn't finished talking, but the two of them suddenly jolted upwards and yelled in my direction.

"That's it, yessir! We don't gotta load the ammo on to the Frame Gear directly, no sir! We just need to build a huge ammo repository inside Babylon and then use [**Gate**] or [**Teleport**] to reload from there!"

"Hm... That gives us a small delay on firing, but frankly, that's not a big deal. There are more benefits to that setup than setbacks. Still, we'd need to have enough ammo produced, hm..." The two of them were just going right into it without me. I was being left behind in the dirt.

"Ah, Touya. How much of the crystal material do you have now, anyway?"

"The Phrasium? A ton. We only really use up a lot of it when we make a new special Frame Gear, so we have a lot to spare right now." I took all of the Phrasium I could find during the Roadmare and Yulong incidents. I had enough to cause a market crash if I put it all into circulation.

"So we have enough material, excellent. And we can't have the workshop tied up making bullets... I'll have no choice but to make another with an ammo focus."

"Another? Another what?"

"Another workshop, duh. I was always planning on building a second one anyways. It won't be on the same scale as the current one. It'll only be about the size of a smallish house. I'll call it the junior workshop!"

You're basically making a munitions factory! Isn't that a little much?! Well, I mean… I guess if it works just like the current workshop it could be a handy backup.

"Small or not, won't it be hard to build another workshop?"

"It'll be fine, sir! We can just make it with the workshop!"

Huh? Making a workshop with the workshop? I was stunned by what Rosetta had told me.

"The workshop is an engine of power, sir yessir! Making a smaller version of itself is a piece of cake!" Rosetta grinned and puffed out her chest.

"Should take us about two weeks, I think. We'll need to fine-tune the magic processors, as well… Well, we'll have you move it with a [Gate] afterward, Touya. It can't move like a Frame Gear, after all."

"Yeah, that's fine, but…" *Making a workshop with a workshop so we can create while we create… That's playing dirty.* It was true that it might not be able to produce Frame Gears due to its smaller size, but it would still be capable of mass producing a lot of other stuff.

"Alright! We've set our course, let's get on it!"

"Yessir, ma'am!" The two brats ran full-pelt out of the research laboratory.

I wonder if they're always this high-energy…

I looked down at the miniature model Frame Gears. Linze's with its aerial form shift, and Leen's with its Gatling arm and Vulcan rotary cannons.

This'll be interesting... An Aerial Combat Gear and a Heavy Duty Bombardier Gear, huh...?

I picked up the model of Linze's gear and stood it atop Leen's. *Heh, these are good. Oh, it's off-balance... Maybe I should see about selling these. If we made them smaller, we could put them in little randomized capsules. I could make little gacha machines and place them around... A little kid should be able to afford something like that on a basic allowance, right?*

I left the lab with the scale figurines as I pondered such thoughts to myself.

Our recruitment drive for the knight order had gathered quite a bit of attention in the end. I attributed this to posters being put up in places like the guild and busy roads.

In all honesty, the wages offered by my knight order were low. Even if an individual knight earned a promotion, there wasn't much room for job growth either. If they were after a lucrative job, they'd be better off working for another nation.

Adventurers often earned great riches by taking huge risks and fighting magical beasts. The risk was proportional to the gain. But even mediocre adventurers could probably make more than what my knights earned. I wanted to formally increase their wages once Brunhild became a bit more prosperous, but that wasn't feasible for the time being.

The advantages of working for Brunhild's knight order was that the pay was steady, and basic life necessities were covered as well. Plus, there wasn't nearly as much risk as being an adventurer carried with it. Some of them did fight the Phrase, but they were still equipped with Frame Gears, which kept them relatively safe from harm.

I thought that these circumstances would mean we'd get maybe a thousand applicants at most, but I was way off. We had over three-thousand people wanting to join up. I was amazed.

We wanted to recruit about a hundred and fifty people from this pool, as well.

There were too many people to fit in the courtyard, so we had all the prospective applicants head to a northern plain that we typically used for Frame Gear practice.

There were a lot of people here just to watch, as well. It wasn't like we were putting on a show or anything, but having the townsfolk around to see their new prospective guards probably wasn't the worst thing.

"Greetings. I am Lain Netherland, and I am in charge of Brunhild's knight order. I will be presiding over today's recruitment proceedings." Lain stood up on a platform and introduced herself, using her smartphone's speaker as an amplifying mic.

As an aside, Nikola had the family name "Strand," but Lain and Norn only had forenames due to their lack of family.

I thought a family name would be beneficial to people in their elevated positions, so I gave them the names Lain Netherland and Norn Siberia. The names come from the Netherland Dwarf Rabbits, and the Siberian Huskies, but it wasn't like the people of this world would know anything about it. They were beastwomen, so I thought those names matched up just fine.

I didn't think it was a good idea to appear in public, so I kept out of sight. More specifically, I disguised myself as a participant with [**Mirage**]. I wanted to see everything as my knights-to-be would see it, after all.

I had to disguise myself because my face was already pretty well-known at this point, and I didn't want anyone coming up to me in the middle of things.

I'd informed my knights of the plan, so they wouldn't be worried about anything I did. I also told them to treat me like any other examinee.

Plus, being on the ground level would allow me to get to know those who wished to join me. I'd already found out a few people who weren't a good fit for Brunhild's order.

I'd noticed a few people in the crowd who were goofing off and completely ignoring Lain's speech, for example. I didn't know if they were ignoring her because she was a woman or because she was a beastwoman, but either way that made them unfit for duty.

I noticed that a remarkable number of knight applicants were women. Around forty percent of the people in the area were girls, give or take. That made a bit of sense, given that most other knight orders in the world didn't recruit women, and the ones that did only recruited nobles. Word had probably gotten out about how Brunhild was a country that cared not for race, sex, or creed.

There were a lot more beastmen and demonkin, too. I couldn't help but wonder if this was the overlord's doing... Part of me suspected that he sent a bunch of demonkin to join so he could get more information on what Sakura was doing. Even for a doting father, that would be a little much... I decided to give them the benefit of the doubt and assume they were regular participants.

"Now, let us begin. Please turn around."

"Huh?" Lain pointed to the horizon and, as if on command, the sound of flapping wings overwhelmed the area. Everyone turned around to find a monstrous dragon staring them down.

"GRWAUUUUUUGH!" The Azure Dragon, Luli, reared her head and roared with bestial vigor.

H-Hey, isn't that a little much? I just told you to scare them a bit.

"Eeek?!"

"I-I-It's a Dragon! Why?!"

"Run for your life! It's gonna kill us!" The vast majority of the applicants began to head for the hills, scattering in all directions and desperate to escape. Luli did nothing but silently stare at them as they dispersed.

Those that ran were naturally disqualified. That was phase one. There was no place for cowards in our army, we needed people who would stand their ground for the innocents around them.

We lost about two-thirds of the initial crowd. Luli descended to the ground, and Lain began to speak again.

"Those who prioritize themselves over the citizens of our nation have no place amongst us. Congratulations, those that remained have passed the first test." Lain finished talking, and the crowd finally realized what had happened. There were some people who had gone weak at the knees and simply couldn't run away because of how deep their fear was. That wasn't a big deal to me, though. I had a feeling those people would be weeded out during the next few phases.

Some of the cowards came back and tried to make excuses for themselves, saying that they were running back to town in order to fortify it, or that they were swept away by the crowd unintentionally, but Norn and the others simply ignored them. There were those that refused to back down even after being rejected, so I telepathically told Luli to roar at them. They ran away again, and I knew they wouldn't come back.

Luli soared back up into the sky, having done her job. Lain began to speak again as the crowd watched Luli fly off.

"Alright, on to phase two. I'll be having everyone spend three days in the forest to the west of this plain. Water is plentiful as there's a large river running through it. But you cannot bring food inside. We will provide water canteens, however. If you leave the forest before the three days are up, you are disqualified. We're going to have several knights from our order take the role of hungering Oni, and they will hunt you down. These Oni will not kill you, but they will attempt to knock you unconscious and remove you from the woods." Lain finished up her explanation, and several examinees raised their hands as if to question her.

"Can we fight back against the Oni?"

"Yes, of course. Defeating them is completely fine. But we would ask you to refrain from killing if you can avoid it."

"Can we team up with others in the forest?"

"That's also fine, yes. But it may be easier for the Oni to track you if you're in a large group."

"How many Oni will there be?"

"I can't tell you that. There could just be one, there could be a hundred. They'll all be wearing distinguishable Oni masks, so you'll be able to tell at a glance."

"Can we use magic?"

"Magic use is prohibited for this exam. We've erected a barrier around the forest that renders magic useless, so you'll have to use your wits." I didn't want the forest burning down due to fire spells. All they had to do was avoid the Oni for three days. If they relied on magic all the time, it wouldn't say much for their survival skills.

"If you remain in the forest after three days have passed, you will pass this stage of the exam. There is no limit to how many people can pass. If everyone here is inside the forest by the end, then you all pass. We will be distributing badges to you, fasten them to your clothing. If you remove them at any time and toss them to the ground, you will be teleported back here. If you think you've reached your limit, don't be a hero. Resign if you think you can't take it. The badges will work if you leave the forest too, they'll bring you right here. You'll still be disqualified, though." We started handing out the badges we'd used last time. I ended up getting the last one.

"This goes without saying, but terrorizing other contestants into giving up their badges or leaving the forest is also forbidden. Doing so is grounds for immediate disqualification. You must act in a way that fits the image of a knight." Lain hopped down from the platform, and Nikola began to guide everyone towards the woods.

I was walking along with them when a black-haired woman next to me started to talk in a hushed tone.

"Preparations complete. We can move out any time."

"Good work, Tsubaki. Let's monitor how the first two hours go for now. I want to see what everyone does. If there are any people acting sneakily or suspiciously, have them removed. I don't have time for troublemakers."

"Understood." Tsubaki nodded subtly by my side. She was infiltrating the participants, just like me. Not just her, either. A few members of the knight order were mixed in with the other examinees. Most of them were Tsubaki's intel corpsmen.

They were going in without food, so survival was paramount. I devised this test with the idea that it'd bring out a person's true nature. I had people infiltrate the exam to investigate how people would act, but also to ensure the safety of any innocents in case of emergency.

I had a feeling there'd be dangerous troublemakers mixed amongst the hopefuls, and the forest had a few magical beasts in it as well.

Heh, I wonder if they'll run into the special traps I set...? Heheheh... I wonder if they'll be able to last the whole time in the forest...? Heh... W-Wait, that makes me sound villainous! I'm working on it, I promise! I'm a good guy!

The forest was pretty broad, and it had a lot of dense shrubbery. There wasn't much leeway for vision in there. Brunhild's territory was originally overrun by magical beasts, and I'd driven out most of them, but the woodland had slowly become somewhat of a breeding ground for the more stubborn ones in recent months.

Nobody really went all the way out there, with the exception of the odd adventurer sent on a guild quest to find certain items. The density of the forest protected the highway from magical beast attacks, but I still thought it'd be safer to wipe them all out.

As I pondered that, we reached the edge of the woodland, and Nikola began to explain the proceedings.

"The examination begins here. You'll enter the forest in order of badge number, taking a canteen with you beforehand. If we call your number and you'd like to quit now, then let us know and you can leave. If you're unarmed and would like a weapon, put in a request and we'll grant you some basic gear. Once you've entered the forest, you're free to move. The Oni are already inside, so take care. Now, Contestant One, Contestant Two…" Nikola used his smartphone to photograph every contestant as they passed by, confirming their entry.

Norn began to take photos as well and, after about thirty minutes, I was finally called upon. They didn't have to take a picture of me, but they still did.

"Have Flora and our recovery mages on standby, alright? Set the teleporter destination to the starting area, too. Oh, right… Nikola, Norn… You two are gonna be Oni too, right?"

"Right. We'll be entering the forest soon."

"Yeah, we will. But what if we encounter you or the other infiltrators while we're in there?"

"Attack us like you would attack anyone else. We'll fight back in order not to raise suspicions. At night, I'll take the role of Oni as well." Norn flashed an awkward smile towards my response.

"…Hold back, please. I'd feel sorry for anyone that fights you, Oni or contestant." She had a point.

Most members of our knight order were playing the role of Oni for this examination. Not the office workers, though. Even old man Baba and old man Yamagata were participating. The Oni were told not to disqualify anyone that displayed exemplary traits in any particular way. I didn't want the really good people failing by chance here and missing a chance to shine during the interview.

The people playing the roles of Oni were holding poles that were enchanted with [**Paralyze**], so they wouldn't be injuring the contestants. Even if they were defeated, the Oni would simply leave them lying there if they displayed some great type of skill or personal trait. If they were just bad, though, their badges would be removed, teleporting them to disqualification.

Moroha wanted to be an Oni, but I very delicately rejected her. I couldn't afford to have her doing that. Nobody would end up passing.

"Alright, I'm going in. If anything comes up, call me."

"Gotcha."

"Have fun, Boss." Nikola bowed his head toward me, and Norn began to wave and grin. I walked into the dense undergrowth.

"Alright, so what am I even gonna do in here..." I decided to get some water, first and foremost. I walked toward the river with my canteen in hand.

If I remember right, the river should be in the middle of the woodland... Flowing down from north to south-east.

I could see some other examinees in the distance as I made my way through the woodland. Seems they'd had the same idea.

Man, I can barely see... There's a ton of trees around, too. Oh, a rabbit. That's a good find, but I only have a sword on me...

Even though I was capable of using magic in here, there was no way I could. I didn't want to compromise my identity.

Every member of Brunhild's cause was exempt from the barrier's rules. But there was always the risk that someone would see me. It wasn't like I could use [**Storage**] to pull out a bow and a set of arrows.

I wonder if this basic gear'll be enough if magic beasts come attacking... Well, the trees are dense enough that I could run off without a hitch. Well, I guess I shouldn't use magic here, anyways... But man, I'm gonna end up hungry at this rate. I have food in my [Storage], water too, but I can't afford to raise suspicion. It'd be suspicious if I had water with me without even going to the river.

The current exam was to measure the proficiency of knights who would become castle guards, town guards, or spies under Tsubaki. Anyone that proved themselves capable in here would get an interview right away. That kind of left the office work department a bit behind... But whatever. We didn't need a dedicated magic squad yet, either.

It was a survival game, and only those with basic survival skills would make it through. I wondered if they'd fight or use their wits to flee. Either way, if they lasted three days in here, they'd have what it took.

I kept on walking until I heard the sound of running water.

I came out into a clearing and saw the river, its bed lined with smooth pebbles. It was about six meters wide, so it wouldn't be difficult to cross. For the most part it was shallow, too.

I filled up my canteen and chugged some of the fresh, cold water. *Man, that's good...*

I looked around and saw a lot of other examinees in the area, they were filling their canteens up as well. This place was pretty open, so it was easy to sense danger... But it was also a prime area for the Oni to find you.

If they were smart, they'd leave right after filling their water up. Some of them had the right idea and were filing off already. After all, anyone who lingered here too long was at real risk of failing the exam immediately.

I headed back into the woodland and clambered up a big tree. *Alrighty...*

"[Long Sense]." I projected my senses through the surrounding area. There were some people moving in groups, and some who had decided to kick it solo.

Oh, this guy's climbing a tree like I did... Can't really make out his face, though. He's wearing a mask, dressed in all black... Kinda looks like a ninja, heh. Huh? Is he... looking at me? No way. He's over a kilometer away, and there are obstacles, right? What... he's waving, now? I moved my body, returning the wave. The man displayed a shocked and surprised reaction. I wondered why he waved in the first place, though. Perhaps he was trying to determine whether or not I could see him as well. If he was a ninja, then it was probably one of his ninjutsu techniques, something that worked differently to magic. Either that or he possessed some kind of Mystic Eye, which wasn't out of the question either.

"Gah! An Oni! Gugh!!!"

"Hngh! Gyaaah!"

"R-Run! Run for it!" My hearing directed me toward a sudden burst of yelling, so I turned my gaze to the river once more.

Two members of our knight order, wearing their Oni masks, were making short work of some of the stragglers who still remained by the river. They were relentless in their approach, knocking contestant after contestant down with their stun rods. They were old man Baba and old man Yamagata...

They projected an air of joy around them as they gleefully knocked down their prey, swiping the badges from their fronts. They honestly seemed like ruthless bandits... A little too much like ruthless bandits, honestly. Those that were stripped of their badges vanished in a flash, teleported away to the starting line. Apparently not even one of the people there showed any kind of potential.

Other examinees in the area had heard the commotion, and their reactions were varied. Some of them fled, while others moved in to see just what had happened. Some stayed still, as if making a single move would expose them.

I turned my attention back to the tree, and the ninja man was gone. *He's surprisingly swift... Gotta be a ninja.*

The Oni duo by the riverbed made their way into the dense woodland and joined the shadows once more.

"His right eye's busted! Flank him from that side! Get him!"

Hm? What's all this, then... I projected my senses toward a group of three examinees. They were fighting against a King Ape some distance away from the river. *Wait, that's not a King Ape... It's bigger than usual. Is it some kind of mutation?*

"Go for his legs! Stop his movements!" The man barking orders looked to be around twenty years old. He had short, silver hair. He was wearing chainmail that looked weathered but surprisingly durable. His command over the group was pretty damn impressive, too. Plus, he was making full use of his companion's skills, despite having apparently just met them.

I watched them for a while, and they ultimately managed to take out the oversized King Ape. While they were fighting, the leader was keeping a close eye on the surrounding area. He was likely looking out for an Oni attack, just in case. I had instructed the Oni not to fight the examinees while they were engaged with magical beasts, but they didn't know that. I had a feeling that this guy was leadership material.

I climbed down from the tree, headed south, and eventually ran into an examinee digging in the ground.

"...What are you doing?"

"Eeek! A-Ah! Ah... F-Food... I was just trying to acquire some food." I scared him, apparently, but he quickly settled down. He must've mistaken me for an Oni to begin with.

"Food?"

"Hm? Oh, y-yeah… This vine here grows giant mountain yams. You can eat the produce that grows underground, at least during this season… After three months they'll ferment and go toxic."

"Huh, really…?"

"Th-The Oni could catch me if I light a fire, s-so I just thought I'd go foraging for stuff, you know? There are a lot of edible flowers and nuts in the area, too."

Huh, I see… So even if you catch a rabbit, cooking it isn't advised. Nobody's gonna eat a raw one, either. This guy isn't doing anything flashy, but it's still a valuable survival skill.

The young man had a lot of flowers, nuts, and fruits on his person. He basically had every kind of edible plant in the area. Evidently, he knew his stuff.

"I-If you go south, there are persimmo trees as well… I only took a few, so there should be some left."

"Hm, thanks. I'll check it out." I left the man behind to continue his foraging. He didn't seem all that interested in holding up a conversation anyway.

Then, I went in the direction he told me to go, and the persimmo trees were there. Persimmos had a pear-like texture, but they were sweet. I subtly opened [Storage] and put some inside, but kept one to eat.

Tasty… Huh? A whooshing sound came from behind me. I jumped back just in time, having noticed something flying toward me from the underbrush. It was a fist.

I just managed to dodge the punch, but I instinctively threw my persimmo away.

Whoa! The attacker stood tall, wearing a distinct black oni mask. They had long, silvery hair that shook in the wind. And it was clearly a woman… A woman I knew all too well.

"Haaah!"

"Gaaah! W-Wait! Elze, Elze! It's me! Me! Touya!"

"...Touya?" The gauntlet-clad punch was inches from my face before stopping.

Holy cow! You nearly took my damn head off!

"Did you use **[Mirage]** to join as a contestant or something?!"

"Ahaha... Something like that..." *Crap, I totally forgot... I was talking about it at dinner last night, and Yae, Hilde, and Elze said they wanted to participate... Not as participants, though. As Oni...*

"Why'd you attack me from behind when I was eating...?"

"I can't afford to show mealtime mercy, you know? You think anyone who gets caught off-guard so easily would survive your sister's training?"

She raised a fair point. Unless you had some level of talent, you wouldn't make it far under Moroha.

"Maybe dial it back a bit, though. Were you using **[Boost]** or something?"

"...No, I decided not to use it for the exam. I didn't want to cause any injuries."

What?! Those gauntlets would give anyone a goddamn concussion! Well... I guess if they get sent back, there are recovery mages on standby, but still...

"Alright, I'm gonna keep hunting enemies. Good luck, Touya."

"You too!"

Good lord... She's getting scarily strong...

I clambered up a nearby tree and activated **[Long Sense]**, keeping up my vigil. I saw some examinees being attacked by the Oni, and I saw others co-ordinate assaults against magical beasts. Seemed like none of my guys had been knocked out, either.

Some people had been disqualified, but not as many as I'd have thought. Ideally the numbers would be whittled to less than five hundred, but they were holding fast.

Gradually the sun went down, and the real fun was about to begin.

I used my smartphone to confirm there was nobody in the vicinity, then deactivated [**Mirage**]. I pulled open [**Storage**] and retrieved my mask. I put it on and changed my outfit into a jet black one. Then I leaped from tree branch to tree branch as I made my way onward.

Upon noticing a light in the distance, I projected my senses toward it. There was a large group of contestants there, gathered around a campfire. They were cooking game that they'd successfully hunted, and taking turns watching the perimeter.

Heh, not a bad idea. With that many, they must be sure that the Oni won't come for them. Taking turns eating and guarding is pretty smart, too…

They'd be a little bit harder than usual to defeat, but I was certain that my Oni could defeat them if they went all-out.

I used my smartphone to determine where the Oni were gathering nearby and swiftly moved to join them.

"Evening, lads."

"Hm?! Oh… Your Highness. You gave me a fright."

"Don't frighten me like that, squirt. Almost jumped outta my skin." The people sitting around the area all got a little annoyed by my sudden appearance.

Old man Baba, old man Yamagata, Logan, Nikola, and a few others were there. There weren't more than ten. They were all guys.

The atmosphere was pretty relaxed. Our knight order was pretty familial, after all. We had a band of brothers kind of feeling. We were all good people, too. Yumina's Mystic Eye made sure that any bad people were rejected at the interview stage.

"So, what's the situation? Found any talented people?"

"Aye, a few who'd do well if polished up."

"Indeed, I've found some promising young soldiers." Baba and Nikola nodded in my direction. That was good news. I was glad to hear that there were some real promising people in the running. I'd seen my own share, too. The ninja, the commander guy, and that plant-gathering guy were all good in my book... Though it was still possible they'd have been taken down by the Oni by now. Especially the plant guy, he seemed resourceful but physically weak.

"So what are you guys planning? Gonna attack that group?"

"Hmph... There are ten of us here, but about a hundred at their camp. It's not like we couldn't beat them, but we'd have to go all-out... Measuring individual skill in a large-scale battle like that isn't really viable, either." Yamagata grumbled slightly as his arms folded. He had a point, though. We were at a disadvantage in terms of examining them. If we went in, we'd get surrounded and we'd have to take them out fast. That would mean we wouldn't have much time at all to test their skills.

Plus, while we had a good few Oni gathered in the area, the group around the campfire was comparatively small when you considered how many other contestants were still out in the forest.

That being said, if they had such a big fire set up, it felt like they were almost goading us to attack them.

"What about you, Your Highness. What would you do?"

"Me? I think I'd show myself, scare them a bit, then run. I'd then start ambushing any of them that decided to follow after me."

"Hmph... Do you think they'd fall for that?"

"Sounds fine ta me. Anyone that charges headlong instead of holdin' their ground isn't fit fer us anyway! Defeated or not, we'd see their true colors." Baba was right. Doing that would show us the reckless idiots hiding amongst them. I used [**Long Sense**] along with my smartphone to project an image of the enemy camp into the air.

"I see... There are people watching the perimeter, so that means the people inside will be slacking, hm?" Nikola muttered as he surveyed the image. There were some nervous contestants keeping an eye on their surroundings, while others were goofing around and looking pretty relaxed. They had confidence in numbers, apparently. It seemed like they thought they could afford to relax.

Hm...? What's going on there? I looked over at a certain area in their camp, a couple of examinees showed up near the fire, and about ten of the men gathered there were trying to ward them away. I turned up the volume out of curiosity.

"No way! Beat it, damn it! There are already too many here as it is!"

"What? We're not asking for food or anything, we just wanna get some time by the fire. What's wrong with that?" The approaching group was a small team of beastmen and demonkin, two men and two women. They had a bunch of dead rabbits with them, and it seemed like they were asking permission to cook there. It was safe to cook while you were surrounded by allies, after all. Less chance of a surprise Oni attack.

"Hmm... One of the beastmen is a lion derivative, and the other is winged... The demonkin are a wardog and an arachne, respectively." Nikola gave me some context on their species.

Hm, interesting... I've seen those kinds of beastmen before, but those demonkin are definitely new to me.

Wardogs were a type of demonkin that resembled canines. Not in the wolfish sense like Norn, who appeared human with a wolf tail and ears, though. They were like anthropomorphic dog people from head to toe. They kind of resembled werewolves, shaggy fur and all. They couldn't turn into humans, though. And their features were more like household dog species than wild wolves.

The arachne stood up gracefully. Her black hair was short, and neatly arranged in a princess cut style. She looked pretty cute, honestly. There were a lot of spider legs jutting from her back, however. And also, her eyes were a piercing red.

"Beat it, you hear me?! If your type hangs around, the magical beasts in the area are gonna sniff us out and cause trouble."

"That's right. You stink like animals, so get the hell out!"

"It's fine if animals fight amongst themselves, but don't get us lumped in with it."

"You...!" The lioness beastwoman had to be restrained by the wardog male. She was about to angrily attack the people by the fire, it seemed. The woman growled slightly before lowering her arms. The wardog simply sighed and shook his head. They quietly turned around with the winged man and the arachne girl, then left.

"Tsk. What the hell are those monsters even participating for? They should stick to Xenoahs and Mismede. Who even runs this knight order? Would they let pets eat at the same table as people, too?" The man who rejected the group turned back to his fellows at the fire.

"Brunhild's a new country, so they probably just lack people with skill. It's the only reason I can think of for recruiting animal labor. Beastmen and demonkin... Gross. It's a weird country for sure."

"The commander was a beastwoman, right? If someone like that can rise so high, we'll have no trouble getting noble status in a place like this."

"Dumbass. If someone like you becomes a noble, then I'll obviously be high up in the government. I heard the grand duke here was an adventurer once, too. This knight order's just a joke, that's why they don't care who or what joins it." The group chuckled amongst themselves, quietly. But my smartphone had picked up every last detail.

"Yeah, I guess so. That's why things'll change after we get recruited, huh. Can't have a knight order with animals running around... Let's aim for the top spots."

"Hm? You wanna be the new commander, then?"

"I guess so, yeah. Once more real soldiers come in, they won't need those beasts anymore. We'll just defeat the current commander and vice-commanders in training, show how good we are, and we'll get promoted. Winners win, losers lose." The group of men began to laugh obnoxiously. They were smiling and laughing, but none of the Oni around me were so high-spirited.

"...These guys are worthless."

"Agreed." Nikola, who was himself a fox beastman, glared down at the screen. He was close friends with Commander Lain, even before coming to Brunhild, so his anger was completely understandable. I could see that his fists were clenched.

These guys clearly thought we were recruiting demi-humans out of necessity or lack of resources. That was a grave misunderstanding on their part.

Beastmen and demonkin rarely traveled outside of Mismede or Xenoahs, so the outside world generally had little experience in dealing with them.

A lot of people still saw demonkin as a subspecies of magical beast, and there was a lot of discrimination against beastmen as if they were all unruly savages or something.

Demi-humans, in general, had been historically mistreated, having been considered inferior creatures on a genetic and social level. There was even a period in the past where they were commonly used as slaves for manual labor, or other degrading duties.

After Mismede was founded, discrimination against beastmen was reduced somewhat, but it wasn't completely gone. Demonkin were extremely rare sights though, so the fear against them could also be seen as synonymous with fear of the unknown. Either way, I didn't want people who were like that in my country.

Our country was special, they were right… Our knight order might not have seemed like a proper one, but it was one nonetheless.

I didn't see the problem, though. Most of the world leaders I'd met didn't really act like stereotypical kings or emperors. All of them had weird quirks, come to think of it. If you based the idea of a 'good' knight order on some stereotypical image, then you were a dumbass.

Lain and the others had been entrusted with the knightly duties initially because we didn't have many people, that was true. But they'd endured training that would make even the most seasoned knight fight to his fullest. They *were* Brunhild's knight order. They had made it their own.

They'd been trained by Moroha herself, making them comparable in power to Yae or Hilde. People who talked big like those guys wouldn't hold a candle to the commander and vice-commanders of my nation.

Baba and the other old men aside, they were absolutely the top three knights in Brunhild. Their powers had been honed by the god of swords herself.

43

I had no patience at all for people who judged based on first glances.

"We'll help you take out those bastards." Three other Oni appeared from the forest. I could tell from their hair that they were Yae, Elze, and Hilde. Seems they'd overheard.

"They deserve to be punished… They're definitely unruly…"

"I cannot stand idly by as my allies are badmouthed, I cannot."

"Yep. They're not worthy to be knights." The three of them seemed angry. They weren't formally members of the knight order, but they still trained alongside them daily. It only made sense that they saw the knights are close comrades. I felt the same, after all.

"Alright… Then let's handle these guys together." The Oni nearby all nodded to what I said. Nobody objected, which was understandable.

"Let's see, though… Before we attack the camp, we need to make sure we single out anyone who might be alright over there."

"In that case, not these guys. They've just been chitchatting the whole time, not a cautious bone in their bodies."

"These two have been attentive and careful all night, though. Let's not target them."

"These three… Hmm, it's hard to say. Let's fight them and base it on that." We were deciding who we'd target to disqualify, and who we'd target to test. The hopeless contestants would get knocked out in one shot and that would be that. The ones that showed promise would either lose their badges or not depending on how they fared.

If they showed a certain level of skill, we'd overlook them and let them stay unconscious. If they didn't, we'd just take their badges. Everyone was gonna get beaten up, either way.

Our strategy was a simple one. Move in and rush them. We had no need to hold back, especially against those racist assholes. It was an official exam, though… so I had to take care not to torture them too much.

"Shall we?" Everyone held up their stun rods, ensured their masks were secured and stood up.

We split into three groups and flanked the bonfire. The plan was to instantly knock out the people we'd deemed as worthless, and then fight against the rest of them.

The teams were led by myself, old man Baba, and Nikola respectively. We coordinated the assault through our smartphones.

"…Three, two, one… Go!" We jumped out from the shadows, surrounding the bonfire on three sides.

"Ghah! Oni!"

"They're attacking! Let's fend them off!"

"Wait, they're behind us too!"

"Oh shit, they're coming in from the sides?!" The guardsmen all jumped into action, but the guys who were lazing around had delayed responses.

The panicked examinees attempted to draw their weapons, but it was too late. They were bashed in the bellies by our stun rods. They were way too slow! That was why preparation was vital in cases like this.

"Gwuh!"

"Hgh!"

"Hrgh!" The cowardly contestants were taken down one after one by a mere ten Oni.

There were women around them, but that didn't affect our behavior. We took them out fair and square. Well... I hit them a little softer than I hit the men. I made sure to smack the guys good, though.

"Gh!"

"Hm?"

Wow... That guy actually took one of my hits, nice... He went down on the second strike, though. I made a mental note to memorize his badge number, then left him behind without ripping it off.

As I was fighting on that side, Nikola was on the other edge of the camp, confronting the racist group. Nikola was wielding a two-meter stun rod that was shaped a bit like a staff.

"Ghuh! Haaah!"

"...Silence." One of the charging men was promptly put down with a swift strike to the gut.

"Ghaaaugh!" The man fainted on the spot, his eyes wide open in shock. Even without the stunning effect, a hit that hard would've knocked most men out.

"Hnnngh...!" The men gradually drew back as Nikola came down on them like a ton of bricks.

"...Something wrong, curs? I'm just one demi-human, am I not? Are you not going to stand against me, even when outnumbering me? Or were you all talk?" Nikola was clad in a mask and black clothing. His foxy ears were all covered up, but his bushy tail was proudly on display. There was no way the men weren't aware they were dealing with a beastman.

Nikola was the only beastman in Brunhild with fox-like traits. If they knew anything about our knight order, they'd know that. If you're wondering what the point in the Oni costume was if our members could be identified by features like that, well… Uh… aesthetics.

"S-Surround him, idiots! Swarm him!"

"Heh…" Six of them quickly surrounded Nikola. Baba, Elze, and the other Oni noticed the attack. None of them moved to interfere. There was no reason to, after all.

"HAAAAAAH!!!"

"Wastrel!" Nikola outclassed all the men in terms of speed, deftly driving his stun rod staff into the ground, he used the momentum to propel himself into the air.

He landed behind the men, outside their circle. Turning in place, he sped to strike all of them from behind, rendering them unable to fight any longer.

"Ghah!"

"Hughah!" One of the men was hit so hard that he vomited up his dinner in mid-air, then landed face-first into the splattered gastric mess. It was gross.

Each man fell after the other, and not one landed a single shot on Nikola. He was truly like a brutal oni in terms of how he handled them. A true oni indeed…

Eventually, Nikola stepped forward, facing the man who had barked orders before.

"E-Eeek!"

"Brunhild's knight order is an equal-opportunity workplace. The bigoted are not extended that privilege, however."

"Gaaaaaah!" The examinee charged forward with a sword, but it was fruitless. Nikola struck him in the neck. The man sank to the ground, a spasming mess.

I looked around and didn't see many more targets, so I headed over to see Nikola.

"Hey, good work."

"…I let my feelings get the better of me. I apologize for that. It seems I've much further to go in terms of composure and training…"

"I wouldn't worry so much. We're Oni right now, right? If it was me, I'd have stripped them naked and strung them up from tree branches." I meant to comfort Nikola with a little anecdote, but he ended up giving me somewhat of an awkward, concerned smile in return.

H-Hey, don't take me that seriously…

"I am fairly certain you did that already, Touya-dono… did you not?"

"Don't you remember back when you dealt with those thugs by stringing them up along the road without their stuff?" Elze and Yae chimed in with a story from the past.

C-C'mon… That's old news! Those guys weren't even worthy of being called people, anyway! I was just doing the natural thing.

"All finished here." I turned to Hilde and saw a bunch of fallen contestants near the fire. The stun rod didn't necessarily rob people of their consciousness, it just paralyzed them and prevented further motion. It was capable of knocking people out, though. The effectiveness of the item depended on individual magic resistance, physical fitness, and so on.

The Oni all took the badges from their fallen targets. We overlooked the skilled guys, though… Still, there were only around ten good enough people out of the hundred that had gathered.

They'd wake up in around thirty minutes. Some of the Oni retreated to the forest and kept an eye on them, making sure that none of them accidentally lost their badges.

"I'll keep an eye out, Your Highness. Please go and deal with the others."

"You sure? Alright, then."

"We'll return to the castle, as well. I don't want the staff getting worried." Hilde had a point. I opened up a **[Gate]** for her and the other girls to get back through. And after that, I parted with Nikola and left the area.

I jumped from tree to tree, branch to branch. I briefly wondered if my night vision had always been so good. I could see pretty far if I focused my sight. It was a strange ability, but I wondered if this was another awakening of my divinity…

That night, I killed a lot of magical beasts that were threatening the examinees. I also defeated the examinees that couldn't defeat the monsters, though. I helped out examinees who got caught in traps, and then promptly defeated them for getting caught in traps. After a while, morning came.

All three days had come and gone. Every badge on the contestants suddenly rang out with Commander Lain's voice.

"The examination is now over. Congratulations for making it. All of you with badges have passed the second examination phase. Please remove your badges now, and you will be teleported to the starting point." All the contestants began to remove their badges, one by one. I removed mine, too.

After teleporting back, they had to report their full name and badge number. The interview was scheduled to take place two days later.

I paid attention to the long line of applicants who had succeeded, and I saw the ninja guy, the commander guy, and the plant guy. I was surprised the plant guy survived... He looked pretty battered though, so I figured he found a place to hide and stayed there for the whole three days.

I noticed the lioness woman, the winged man, the wardog, and the arachne. They'd passed too, apparently. I was glad to see that.

I used my search magic to make sure there wasn't anyone left in the forest. Thankfully, there was not.

Tsubaki, still disguised as a contestant, approached me and covertly informed me of how many people succeeded.

"There are four-hundred-and-sixteen successful applicants. The interview portion should reduce this number to a hundred-and-fifty or so."

"Yumina's helping, so she'll be able to knock any suspicious or questionable guys out of the running... but I wonder if we'll end up having enough guys after all of that... Well, even if it leaves us understaffed, I'd rather that than have bad guys in my knight order."

The real tests began here. We'd carefully analyze every last member and make sure we knew what kind of person they were.

The doctor provided me with a polygraph test, as well. A pretty accurate one, too. Alongside Yumina's Mystic Eye, I was pretty confident we'd be fine.

When I showed the polygraph test to my fiancees, they hooked me up to the damn thing and started firing questions at me. I didn't wanna answer their cursed questions, though! It was a powerful artifact that could tell true from false, so it wouldn't react if you didn't reply! I had the right to remain silent, after all!

They asked me terrible things, like my preference on breast size, and which color underwear I preferred... That was terrifying! They couldn't ask me questions like that... Though they did make me answer whether or not I truly loved them, and they were happy with the result.

"Wasn't there a ninja amongst the successful applicants? Was he one of your guys?" I asked every high-ranking member of the knight order to tell any talented people they knew to try out for the test. If they were talented, then they'd have no trouble joining up, and we'd have reliable and powerful people swelling our ranks. The interview phase would go much more smoothly, too.

"That is possible, yes. I reached out to many shinobi from Eashen. The recent incident with Hideyooshi caused several smaller clans to collapse, leading to a lot of wandering soldiers. I called out particularly talented ones and invited them here."

"Hm? Several people? I only saw one... Are they all ninjas?"

"Yes, they are. One from the Kouga clan, one from Iga, and one from Fuma."

Kouga, Iga, and Fuma, huh...? They're pretty different ninja schools. If I remember my history right, weren't Iga and Kouga on bad terms in general?

I posed the question to Tsubaki, but she said no such thing was true in this world. They had somewhat of a rivalry and were of similar levels, but there wasn't any bad blood. They originally served the same clan and began drifting in service after it collapsed. It seemed like the clan they served was closely connected to the Hashiba clan.

"Hmm... I ended up causing that indirectly, didn't I...? I have mixed feelings..."

"The two of them left the Sanada clan and decided that Brunhild was the best option to continue their service. I don't think you need to worry, it's simply the natural course of life and war."

"I guess so, but… wait, Sanada?" *Sanada…? The Sanada Clan? Wait, the Kouga and Iga ninjas in the service of Sanada… No way…*

"Th-Those two ninja… They aren't called Sarutobi and Kirigakure, are they…?"

"Hm…? Why, yes… But how did you know?"

Oh sweet lord.

"Alright, then. Results will be posted outside the castle, the day after tomorrow. You may leave now."

"Yes ma'am!" We'd just finished an interview with five people, and they left the room at Commander Lain's order. And once they all filtered out, Yumina began talking.

"Those three on the left were no good at all. Their intentions were clear to me, at least. Two of them planned to rise through the ranks until they could push people around. The third one had far too much of a rebellious streak. It didn't seem like he'd listen to orders well. He'd be the kind of person to disobey a commander he had a personal problem with. We can't allow people like that into the knight order, as it would throw us into disarray."

"I think I understand where you're coming from, I felt similarly based on my gut instinct. Every word they spoke was laced with arrogance, as well. There were some lies, too." Lain replied to Yumina, and I gave a little shrug as I crossed out the names of those three individuals. That was it for them.

"And the other two?"

"They stammered a bit, but I didn't feel any malice and they weren't lying. I'd be fine with them. They seemed fine."

"Indeed. They had a very serious demeanor, but they passed as far as character goes in my eyes." Those guys ended up passing just fine.

We'd been interviewing people for two days at this point.

The people conducting the interview were me, Commander Lain, and Yumina. I'd changed my appearance with [Mirage], though.

We conducted interviews in groups of five. It took around ten minutes to interview a group, so that meant there were around eighty interviews to be held in total. Even after splitting it across two days, it was pretty intensive work.

I couldn't afford to be lazy about this matter, though. If we let any bad eggs through the cracks, the people of Brunhild would suffer for our negligence.

That was really the key feature I was looking for in a knight. I wanted knights who would readily be champions of the people rather than champions of the nation. I didn't need people who were fighting for me or fighting for honor. I needed true defenders.

I wanted knights who would readily fight against me if my reign became corrupt. Not that such a situation would actually come about, though…

"Alrighty then. Bring in the next five."

"Of course." Spica the dark elf was minding the door, and she called out to the next group of examinees. The lamia siblings, Mulette and Charette, were standing nearby as well.

I felt a little bad for using them, but they were important for the test, too.

The moment the next five entered, I saw three of them adopt a sour expression in the direction of the three demonkin. The other two seemed surprised, but didn't seem offended or angry. They seemed more interested than anything. Spica was a beautiful woman, while the lamias had half-snake bodies, after all.

We pretty much knew off the bat that the judgmental three were no good. We'd still ask them the standard questions, though. The questions were engineered to get a good grasp of their attitudes and personalities, and we had the polygraph in place to tell if they were lying, too.

We had liars come in, and honest people as well. I didn't really expect any candidate to be a hundred percent honest, either. A few lies now and then was something normal in life, after all. People might be hesitant in divulging certain details; they barely knew the interviewers. We'd fairly judge them based on the lies and truths they decide to mix together.

After the five left, Yumina and Lain began to talk about them. We pretty much agreed we didn't want the trio. Yumina said she could sense their overabundance of pride and their self-righteousness. Of the two others, one of them told a lot of lies, including about where he was born. I didn't really wanna employ a guy like that, since it was a little shady. And so, I crossed off four of the five and allowed the one regular guy to pass.

Spica ushered in the next fivesome. It was time to go again…

I was pleased to see that, of the next five, one was the plant guy and another was the commander guy.

They both expressed curiosity and surprise at the demonkin as they walked in, but nothing beyond that. The plant guy's demeanor got a little stiffer. He seemed nervous in their presence, which wasn't entirely unreasonable.

They sat next to each other on the left, which meant they must've had similar entry numbers.

Hmm... So the blonde in the armor is Lanz Tempest, and the plant guy is Charon...

Lanz Tempest. Born in the Knight Kingdom of Lestia. Third son of a renowned knight. His elder brothers were Lestian knights.

"Why Brunhild?"

"Ah, well. I've been hearing stories about the grand duke and his knight order for quite some time now. The stories of the grand duke and his valiant knights fighting against a horde of dragons moved me. I decided there and then that I wanted to commit my power, however meager, to such a valiant order." He wasn't aware that the grand duke was sitting right in front of him, which I found amusing. I had a follow-up question.

"You want to become a knight of Brunhild, then... But is it alright to leave your home behind and not become a Lestian knight?"

"The grand duke of Brunhild is engaged to our venerable princess, Hildegard, which means that Brunhild is as honorable to me as my homeland. I have decided that my sword will be another link in the chain that binds our two glorious nations." He wasn't lying. The guy was extremely serious, if not a little wooden. But he was from a knight family, so that was to be expected.

The next guy was Charon, the plant guy.

Charon. Born in the Kingdom of Belfast.

"...According to the Oni report, you gathered various edible plants and herbs in the forest. Where did you learn this set of skills?"

"I-I, uh... I-It's not e-exactly a set of skills, b-but, uhm... I-I come f-from a family of herbalists, s-so I've been g-g-gathering such things since I w-was little..." He was jittery. His words were a little interesting, too.

Having a pharmaceutical background was good, though. He probably knew a lot about plants and remedies. That'd be a good asset.

"So, why a knight order?"

"U-Uhm, well… I heard that Brunhild's knight order d-does farm work, too… I-I thought I'd b-be able to help in that r-regard, I-I can farm, a-and I can clear out areas. M-My combat pr-proficiency isn't t-terrible. I-I can k-kill bears and stuff…"

Huh, kind of reminds me of the matagi, the winter hunters of northern Japan. He passed the survival game, so I'm sure he'll be just fine. I get the feeling he'd do well with a nata machete.

He wasn't lying, either, so I felt he and Lanz were a good fit for the order.

After they left, I asked Yumina and Lain for their opinions on the men. They seemed to agree with me.

"We'll have Lanz assigned to the castle guard patrol. Charon should be fielded under Naito to help tame the eastern territory for farmland." Lain suggested exactly what I was thinking. The two of them were recruited right away.

Next up were the people I saw being driven away from the fire during the forest trial. The lioness beastwoman, the winged beastman, the wardog guy, and the arachne girl. The fifth member of this interview group was a leather-clad man. He looked like a generic adventurer, and I immediately lost all interest in him on account of the haughty way he was looking at his demi-human companions.

The lioness woman was named Ashley.

The winged man was named Baris.

The wardog was called Dingo.

Lastly, the arachne girl was named Lifon.

Apparently, they headed straight for Brunhild after hearing rumors that we recruited anyone for the order. They were in two groups originally, Baris with Ashley and Dingo with Lifon, but they ended up meeting on the way.

I reminded them that we didn't offer a high wage, but they didn't seem to mind. They weren't lying, either... Those wages were seriously low, so they must've been easily satisfied. I shamefully made a mental note to get the rates increased somehow.

I asked a few more questions, and I was pretty satisfied with the result. I was more than happy with them working for us.

After they left, I turned to Yumina to get her opinion. She didn't have an issue. All four of them passed. The leather-clad guy did not.

Our interviews carried on throughout the second day. The number of people was immense, way more than I expected at the beginning. We couldn't afford to slack off, so we just kept pushing onward.

After a hard day, we ended up recruiting a lot of talented people. And eventually, we came to the last three...

"Sarutobi Homura... Kirigakure Shizuku, and Fuma Nagi..." They were three girls clad in ninja gear sitting down in front of me. They were the trio that Tsubaki had recommended to me.

They were the daughters of Sarutobi Sasuke, Kirigakure Saizou, and Fuuma Kotarou, respectively.

Daughters... Honestly, I was expecting their parents. I asked them about their old men, and they said they were very elderly and retired some time ago.

The girls were all fifteen years old, around two years younger than me. They were in the same age bracket as Elze and Linze, though. Homura was bright and energetic and seemed to be in high spirits. Shizuku was a cool, calm, and collected kind of girl. Nagi, on the other hand, barely had any presence to her at all.

Homura had short hair, while Shizuku's was long. Nagi's was around shoulder length. They each had different specialties, as well. Homura was an accomplished martial artist, Nagi was an expert of ranged weapons, and Shizuku had a talent for concealing herself. They all had the basics of ninjutsu down, as well.

It was Homura who saw me standing on top of that tree, but I thought she was a guy due to her outfit…

"It may be a little difficult for you to understand, but I bear a Mystic Eye. I can see things at a long distance, and I have the ability to see through relatively small obstacles." Homura's eye was a slightly different, light brown color. It was hard to tell at a glance, though. She named this ability her "Second Sight." It was similar to my **[Long Sense],** but only used the sense of sight. It would be a useful skill, nonetheless.

I felt they'd be a good fit for Tsubaki's intel corps. I asked them if they had a problem with that, and they didn't seem to mind.

"I am proficient in concealing myself, so I believe I would do well in such a group. Private investigation or simple surveillance is nothing to me," said Shizuku.

"I'm tooootally faaast… I outran aaall the Oniii…" said Nagi. It seemed that her fast footwork helped her pass the exam.

Nagi kind of reminded me of someone… Cecile, a maid of ours. The way she spoke was kind of similar, and if I recalled correctly, Cecile was talented with throwing knives. She had been employed by Belfast's intel division, after all.

"Hey theeere. My naaame's Cecile."

"I'm Naaagiii… It's niiice to meet youuu…"

"Ufufuuu…"

"Eheheee…" I tried imagining a scenario in which they met. It was scary. Both of them had a… very particular air about them. I wondered if they were somehow long-lost sisters or something…

We finished up the rest of the questioning and ended the interview. They hadn't lied, and Yumina didn't have an issue either. Tsubaki's recommendation was the final nail in the positive coffin, so they passed.

Thus, the interview phase was complete. There were around four-hundred candidates that passed the second trial, and the interview phase narrowed that further down to a hundred-and-thirty-one. It was slightly less than we'd expected, so we had Kousaka prepare a separate interview event later on for people to fill up the civil service spots.

Now, all we had to do was assign people to the roles of spies, patrollers, and castle guardsmen. We assigned some on the spot, but the rest weren't sorted.

Either way, all the successful candidates had been selected, so we just needed to formally enroll them with a ceremony.

"Congratulations to all of you. As grand duke, it's my pleasure to induct you all into Brunhild's knight order." I stood atop the stage and greeted the crowd of successful applicants. Those that were meeting me for the first time were taken aback. After all, I was known the world over as a heroic adventurer who defeated crystal monsters, inherited the Frame Gears from an ancient civilization, killed Dragons, and solved political disputes solo.

It was natural for them to be shocked at discovering the fabled hero was a young man. They didn't seem to be taking me lightly, though. That only meant that Yumina's assessment of them was right.

"Now, you've passed the formal examination and you're in... but I want to see your skills first-hand. I would like you all to fight me." The crowd just kind of stared blankly as my request sank in. They looked around to each other and murmured in disbelief.

"So we're doing that, then..."

"Wanna bet how many of them last?"

"We shouldn't be betting..."

"Let's hope none of them come out traumatized..." We all moved to one of the practice fields outside and decided the one-versus-one-hundred-and-thirty-one battle would commence. All the new recruits wielded wooden training weapons. I would've been fine if they used their regular weapons, but they probably would've been too unnerved to fight me seriously in that case. Either way, I wasn't planning on letting them lay a finger on me.

I decided I'd use this battle to judge where to assign the candidates. All the senior members of the knight order were watching carefully, after all.

"We ready? [Accel]..." I used my acceleration spell and charged headlong toward the newbies.

It took twenty minutes for the battle to come to a close, and all of the new recruits were on the ground. Not a single one of them had been able to remain standing.

I quickly cast [Mega Heal] and [Refresh] on them, restoring them to the state they were in before the battle. I didn't want to leave them rolling around on the floor, after all.

A lot of them thanked me for healing them, but I felt a bit guilty. After all, I was the one who put them in that situation, and... it wasn't over.

"Alright, my turn... Ain't it?" Moroha walked out on to the field and swapped places with me.

That's a hell of a grin you're sporting... Make sure you don't treat them too badly...

"Listen up, new blood! I'm Mochizuki Moroha, Moroha's my given name! I'm an adviser to Brunhild's knight order and their primary swordplay instructor! Good job on joining the family, now I'm gonna whip your asses into shape!" And so it began, the grueling week-long training session we'd planned in advance. Moroha was angry at me for refusing to let her join in as an Oni in the second test, so this was the compromise I came up with for her.

"Alright, let's start by running around the castle. Fifty laps."

The newcomers grumbled and groaned. The perimeter of the castle was around two kilometers. If it was fifty laps, then they'd be running about a hundred kilometers... I felt sorry for them. Moroha was some kind of monster.

I prayed to the heavens for their safety, but it felt a little bit futile... After all, the one so harshly chasing after them was sent by the heavens themselves...

Moroha and the other gods weren't allowed to interfere with the mortal realm using their divinity, but they were still allowed to operate within the parameters of a mortal. The only issue was that they tended to be mortals at the apex of skill.

They were the kind of "humans" that reached a level of skill one could achieve after a thousand years. They weren't taking lifespan into account at all... Well, then again... elves, fairies, and other demi-humans could probably reach that level given enough time.

Either way, the hellish crucible would make our newbies stronger. They had to persevere for the sake of a brighter future.

"Haaah!"

"That's it! Stronger now!" Lanz was in the midst of a battle, facing off against another using his training weapon. It had been about thirty minutes since they started, and his footwork was getting unsteady. The battle was fierce, and his enemy showed no signs of stopping.

Commander Lain and old man Baba had left newbie supervision down to Moroha, so she had organized individual sparring.

"Guh!"

"What's wrong, hm?! Is this all the power a Lestian knight has in him?" His sparring partner, Hilde, came up from behind Lanz, armed with a sword. She was well and truly proving her status as a knight princess. The rush of battle reminded her of her days leading a squadron, and she knew she was sparring for the greater good.

Back in Lestia, she would often inspire her troops by yelling about Lestian pride, so this was her own little way of encouraging that from Lanz.

"Ghuh!" Hilde's wooden blade struck true, smacking Lanz right in the stomach. He collapsed on the spot, keeling over.

"That'll do." Moroha's voice rang out across the training field. All the knights watching the battle could barely contain themselves, they heaved heavy sighs as the battle finally came to a close.

Lanz used his weapon as a crutch and staggered to his feet, he bowed his head to Hilde.

"Th-Thank you for training me, ma'am!"

"Of course." Hilde bowed her head in turn, and Lanz sank to the ground once more.

A group of other rookies ran forward to check if he was okay, but Lanz raised his hand to say he was fine. Either way, it was clear he was at the height of exhaustion.

"Come forth, Light! Breath of Vigor: [Refresh]." I stepped forward and gave a dose of fatigue-restoration magic to Lanz and Hilde. They had definitely taken a lot out of themselves, but I was honestly amazed they'd lasted as long as they did.

"In Lestia, we're taught to hone our physical technique and eliminate any unnecessary movement. Knowing the limits of our stamina allows us to move without wasting a single step. Then, at the height of exhaustion, we're still capable of landing precise blows. Training in such extreme conditions is more valuable than a hundred sessions of restrained training!" He was pretty wild... Wasn't too surprising, though, given he was from the Knight Kingdom of Lestia.

"My my, it really did have me feeling like I was back in Lestia. It's been a while since I had so much fun training..." Hilde seemed pretty pumped up, contrary to her typical self. The Lestians really did have a bit of a warrior culture in the end, kind of like Sparta.

The newbies had been put under a grueling training session, courtesy of Moroha. But, as expected of those that passed the test, none of them were quite willing to give up. They all had renewed vigor and kept fighting.

The newbies were all assigned to different areas, so they were receiving training from their established predecessors.

I came over to see how they were doing, but it seemed like they were doing just fine without me…

The knights currently on the training field were those who had been assigned to town patrol and the castle guard. We needed them to be strong, after all. And it seemed that they were managing just that.

Nikola was here to oversee the training as well; he had tentatively taken command of the castle guardsmen. Logan was here to fight against them as well, as he was the captain of the watch. Logan was a man who'd met back in Sandora; he was helping a group of slaves at the time. He never expected that he'd end up having a decent role to play in an emerging knight order like Brunhild's, but here he was.

Norn had also taken command of the patrolmen, with Rebecca as her number two. Rebecca was an adventurer who had been working in Sandora like Logan. She was a fairly respectable female knight of our order at this point.

It seemed like my services weren't really needed. Everyone was working hard. Rebecca was training against a lot of the new female recruits, too. And so, I looked over at Hilde, who still seemed a little out of it, so I handed her a sweat towel.

"Looks like the new guys are all doing pretty good."

"Indeed. They're all new and filled with new hopes. They all wish to become strong, and you can tell they wish to become strong for a good reason. Training alone can't foster such a feeling, so I'm glad they had it from the start."

When I was interviewing them, I wanted to emphasize the hiring of people who would fight for the people. Yumina's Mystic Eye and the polygraph test ruled out those that had impure motivations for getting stronger.

Next up, I wanted to check on old man Naito's agricultural project. Hilde wanted to come along, so we trotted off to the east. These people weren't primarily fighters, so their training could be held off for a while.

Many people might not associate the image of a knight with farm work and cultivation, but it was arguably the most important thing going on right now.

This particular branch of our knight order specialized in developing experimental crops, opening up more safe land, building homes, and taking care to build and maintain roads.

The man in charge of most of the planning was Kousaka, but it was old man Naito himself who did most of the hands-on stuff.

Just as I entered the area, I found the man himself.

"Oh, Your Highness and Lady Hilde. It's good to see you." He seemed pretty laid-back in general, but Naito was quite industrious. His problem-solving skills were second to none. Without him, we wouldn't be as far along as we were now.

"So, what brings you here?"

"Just here to check up on the new recruits. How're they holding up?"

"Ah. Well, we don't need much in the way of intensive training here, so they're in the middle of basic memorization and learning our protocols." I looked over to where he pointed and saw a group of recruits using string to measure plots of earth.

Hmm... Where is he, I thought. Then, I suddenly spotted the plant guy from the survival game, the guy named Charon.

Developing the land was vital to the growth of a nation. They had many duties to attend to that would become solid ground for Brunhild in the years to come. In a sense, the knights of the agricultural sector were general-purpose knights who build up the country from the roots. That kind of didn't make them sound all that impressive, though… I decided not to say something like that to their face.

"Knights tilling the ground with hoes and measuring out plots… A rather pleasant sight, wouldn't you say? It's not something you'd see back home in Lestia, at least."

"Really? Even soldiers plow fields in Eashen, as well."

"Is that right…?" Hilde was the princess of Lestia, a major eastern power. It seemed like it was unthinkable to have commanders and soldiers do farming and manual labor. All their military thought about was polishing their skill with a blade.

Lestia's royal family was certainly above such things, but I thought that looking after the land was a good quality to have for someone who'd be defending it.

"A good few of the new recruits have Earth magic aptitude, it is proving quite the help. I gotta tell you, as someone born in Eashen, it's quite remarkable. Magic just isn't very widespread back there, and the few examples of magic I've seen are fire and wind." Old man Naito was right about that. Magic was a rarity in Eashen. Yae's family didn't have much in the way of it either.

Eashenese people devised special techniques like Ninjutsu in place of magic. Not quite the same thing, but somewhat similar either way. Speaking of which, it was time to go and visit Tsubaki's infiltration squadron.

I waved goodbye to old man Naito and headed into the western forest. It was here that you'd find the training zone for our more covert operatives.

The obstacle course was originally designed to help train dexterity for the knight order. Tsubaki recently had me install courses and runs for all three levels of difficulty, ranging from beginner to intermediate, to advanced. There were various traps and obstacles lined up along the courses, each varying in terms of danger.

The infiltration corps was being trained on the course today.

"Gwaaaugh?!" A screaming person suddenly soared through the air before landing in a small pond not far from us. She splashed into the water before rising to the surface, coughing and sputtering.

Water dripped from her short, curly hair. She was a member of the ninja trio that had recently joined our order, Sarutobi Homura.

"No good, Homura-san! Pay more attention next time. If that was an enemy's trap, you'd be dead by now. Treat this course as you would a real mission."

"Ugh…" Tsubaki shook her head as she criticized Homura's performance. At that moment, another shriek echoed through the air, and yet another girl came soaring through the air before landing in the pond.

It was another of the ninja trio, Fuma Nagi.

"G-Goodness, this is quite intensive…" Hilde seemed pretty shocked, but that wasn't too surprising given two people had just flown through the air before our eyes.

"Our mission is primarily the acquisition of intel. We need to be prepared for every possible dangerous situation, and infiltration is a must. We need to keep our eyes peeled for even the slightest out-of-place detail." Tsubaki spoke as she hopped down from a treetop.

Tsubaki's intel corps generally handled information gathering. Brunhild was recognized by other nations, sometimes for good reasons, and sometimes for bad. There certainly were countries that didn't think too highly of us. Yulong, for example, was an example of a country we had poor relations with. Yulong wasn't really a country anymore though.

But even if I was friends with a world leader, it didn't mean that members of the nobility wouldn't have it out for me. I remember hearing that a lot of Belfast and Regulus aristocrats didn't much like my engagement to Yumina and Lu. People like that could always end up trying to cause trouble in Brunhild. And that was where Tsubaki and her agents came into the equation. They would gather intel on potential threats and relay it to me. For the most part, they were Eashenese, which meant they primarily used ninjutsu. There were a few capable of Dark magic, however, which meant they were able to summon stealthy animals to assist in spy operations.

Tsubaki's people also conferred with Mr. Mittens and his cat knights, swapping information about potential threats within the castle town.

Recently there'd been some discussions about foreign dissidents trying to gather information on us. Apparently they were after the Frame Gears again... It was a hell of a headache to keep up with greedy people like that.

"Everyone seems to be trying hard."

"We are, thank you. We're doing our best."

"Would you like to train with me and Touya tomorrow? I think Yae might want to join in as well."

"Ah... I'm not sure if I can, I've got a few Grand Dukey things to take care of..." I laughed a little bit at Hilde's suggestion.

To be honest, I was pretty sure Yae and Hilde were at the point where they could beat me in a swordfight. Moroha had trained them to the point where only she was beyond them.

The two of them were incredible. Even with my magic, I'd struggle to beat them.

The daily inspection was over. I decided to split off from Hilde and head back to the castle. There I saw Sue running down the corridor toward me. Her butler, Leim, toddled on after her.

"Touya!"

"Yo. What's up, Sue? Hey there, Leim."

"Good day, Your Highness." Sue had practically tackled me, so Leim apologetically greeted me with a bowed head.

Sue could easily travel to her private room in this castle from her own room at home. There was a [Gate] tailored just for her that connected the two rooms, so she visited Brunhild often.

She was one of my fiancees, but she still lived with her parents, so this was the compromise. Only Sue could travel through the portal, so it was secure. That being said, if she consented then she could come through with other people like Leim.

"What brings you here today?"

"I came to visit Renne! It's her day off, you know? Oh, Touya. Can I use the game room? I'd like to show Renne the Overlord formation."

Overlord formation...? Oh, she must mean the Ortlinde Overlord thing her Frame Gear does... She's gonna show it in the simulator?

The Frame Gear training room had several Frame Unit simulators, and the girls could access their tailor-made machines through it as well. Regular knights wouldn't be able to use them, though.

"Sure, no problem. Be sure to show her."

"Yay! Thanks, Touya!" Sue ran off full-speed toward wherever Renne was. She was lively as ever.

"Please excuse me." Leim trotted after her. I felt a little sorry for him.

As I watched them dash off, my smartphone started to vibrate. It was a call from Rosetta.

"Yo, 'sup?"

"Master, sir?! I made a prototype, sir! I was thinking of running an experiment, yessir I was. Wanna see?"

"Oh, you finished with it? We can test it out in the northern courtyard. I'll bring Sakura."

"Yessir!" I cut off the call with Rosetta and dialed for Sakura. This was proving to be quite the busy day.

"…Grand Duke. What is this?"

"This is a special microphone with sound amplification. There's more to it, too." Sakura tilted her head in confusion as she looked at the mic stand.

I asked Sakura to help me with a special magical device experiment, and she'd brought along Spica as well.

"Preparations complete, sir!" I moved away from the mic that Rosetta had been adjusting. Monica, who was also observing, flashed a thumbs-up. That meant it was time.

"Alright, let's try… some pretty simple, light music for starters. The mic's target should be set to you, Spica, so can you move a little further away?"

"Ah, of course. Is this good?" Spica stood in the middle of the training area we'd prepared.

"Alright, Sakura. Please sing something soft into the mic. And please channel your magic into it as well, if you can."

"…I don't quite understand, but I shall…" Sakura gave an obedient nod, and then she began to sing.

Hm… This song? It was a fairly popular French song that I'd heard back in Japan, a popular, soft jazz number.

The "Cherie" mentioned in the lyrics wasn't a woman's name, but a French way of saying "darling."

"Alright, Spica. Can you try moving about, or slashing?"

"Very well— What?!" Spica moved for only a few seconds, but she covered a surprising distance. She looked down at herself in shock. She suddenly stopped on the spot and jumped into the air, finding herself propelled three meters upward.

"My body is light as a feather, no, it's like I've gotten feathers and I can fly!" Sakura, equally confused, stopped singing as she watched Spica.

"Ah." Spica's enhanced speed suddenly dropped to a standard pace.

Hmm... So the enhancements only work while she sings. And I guess the effects will change based on the style of song, too.

"Grand Duke, what is this...?"

"Let me answer that, ma'am! It's application of magic, ma'am! Doctor Babylon calls it Lyrical magic, ma'am! Your magic power passes through the microphone and your voice, and can then be applied to other people! The effects vary depending on the oscillation, and we still don't know the full potential, ma'am! But rest assured that it's support magic through-and-through, so there are no risks!" Rosetta suddenly chimed in. Apparently it was based on magic used by a species that existed during the ancient civilization's era, but I didn't know the details.

From what I understood of it, it was simply amplification through sound waves, and that's all I needed to know.

"Alright then, Sakura. Feel free to sing any kind of song."

"Okay." Sakura sang one song after another to Spica. She really didn't seem to mind what she chose as she flicked through several types of music.

There were a lot of western songs, but only stuff from the 1960s through 1980s. That was my favorite kind of music, so I'd ended up introducing her to a lot of it. My grandpa introduced me to it originally, so it was just one of those things. It seemed like Sakura was quite the fan, too. So I wasn't complaining.

There were a lot of magical effects based on the types of song she sang. Enhanced agility, increased magical resistance, a protective barrier, increased aggression, increased strength, and so on. There were clearly a ton more potential effects, but we didn't need to go through them all in one day.

The benefit of this magic was that it could affect anyone in range of the music. The effect could even be applied to the person singing, as well as anyone in the vicinity. Plus, no matter how many were being affected, it would still take up the same amount of magic as if it was only one person.

The effect ended when Sakura stopped singing, so we would have to be mindful that she didn't wear her voice out.

Doctor Babylon was currently designing some kind of aircraft that could act as mobile battle speakers. The idea would be for Sakura's voice to effectively serve as background music for the battle while empowering our troops.

That being said, we'd only be able to apply one effect at the time, so it had limited tactical use. Sakura couldn't sing different songs at the same time, and recordings didn't work either.

I pondered more as I watched Sakura's spirited performance.

After the experiment ended, I went up to Babylon with Rosetta. The Doctor was in her Research Lab, pondering over a world map on her monitor.

Her desk had a bunch of papers, books, and scattered stationery on it. I noticed a bunch of stale looking cookies, cakes, and used teacups as well.

Put your old food away... You're gonna attract bugs.

"What're you up to?"

"Hm? Ah, it's Touya. See anything strange about this?"

"Strange?" The doc motioned toward her monitor, and I took a look at the world map.

Hm? What's with that... It looks like this world's map, but the details are a little different.

"This is a map of the world as it was five-thousand years ago, during my era. It's how it was before the Phrase invaded. There was large-scale magical destruction during that time, and general resistance against their forces ended up sculpting global geography. Can you see the key differences?" She superimposed the current map of the world over the old one.

Oh, huh... There are definitely differences in coastlines and terrain... Weird... Refreese and Lihnea... were a lot larger... And the Great Gau River didn't go all the way down to Ramissh? Did the terrain change naturally, or was this all thanks to magic...? Geez...

"The Phrase couldn't be directly affected by magic, remember? There was a country that initiated a forbidden spell known as [**Grand Break**], which changed a lot of the world's terrain."

Huh... What kind of spell was that? Did it cause the ground to rupture or something? Well, there's no denying there are some serious topographical differences here, but damn...

It seemed like it was probably an Earth spell that caused a massive amount of the ground to rise up and shift, likely to try and catch the Phrase en masse.

Something so destructive would've been insane… To think humanity was driven to make such a horrible decision.

"This here is where Partheno was. It was a massive civilization that spanned all the way from where Belfast is now, covering most of Regulus, Brunhild, Ramissh, Roadmare, Felsen, Lestia, and Horn." I looked at the area she'd singled out. It was insanely huge. It must've been an incredible empire indeed. It spanned a massive amount of land from west to east. If you put it in earth terms, it'd be equal to one nation having control of all land between Europe and China.

"Back in the day, the Phrase first emerged where Xenoahs is nowadays. The nations that used to occupy the area where Yulong, Nokia, and Hannock are were the first to fall. That's why you can see so many geographical changes in this area."

That does explain all the crater-like lakes in Yulong and Xenoahs… Did they really fight that hard, though? To damage their own world in the hopes of defending it? I guess it makes sense though; they would've defended their homelands with everything they had in them. I can't even imagine how fearsome the battles must have been.

"Hm? What's that?"

"Oh, this? This is… Just north of where Elfrau is in the current era." On the map of the old world, there was an island in the sea just north of Elfrau. It was similar in size to Ramissh. The modern map didn't have that island at all, leading me to believe it had completely sunk.

"Back in the day, that island was known as The Devil's Abode. There were sea monsters like Sirens and Krakens that surrounded its waters, so going by boat was impossible. If you tried to fly, then Wyverns would kill you. The island reeked of death, and even from afar you could see its dense fog and foul air."

Sounds pretty nuts, definitely worthy of its name.

"I was a little confused as to why it wasn't here in the current era. I wondered if it sank, but I couldn't think of a reason for it to have. Thus, I used an advanced form of detection magic on the area, and this is the result." On the modern map, in the empty spot where the island should've been, a small red haze appeared vaguely matching the outline of the landmass.

…Wait, a barrier? Did someone put up a barrier around the island to make it invisible? But could something like that have seriously lasted so long? And why?

"My Babylon works on a similar principle, you know? It's been invisible in the air for the last five thousand years. I'm of the opinion that someone did this to the island back then, as well. The only questions would be who, and why?"

"…Do you think some mage escaped from the Phrase, made his way to the island, and then erected a barrier so he couldn't be found?"

"That's not impossible, but… Such powerful magic would surely be impossible… The only person other than I from that era capable of such a feat would be the Sage of Hours, but I was sure he died in a Phrase attack…" Doctor Babylon muttered as she leaned against her chair. She was in a tiny body, so she looked kind of silly.

"Sorry, Sage of Hours?"

"Yes, that's right. He was a master of Space-time magic. Foresight, teleportation, regular time-stopping, the ability to de-age or simply age his targets, and so on… He was an outrageous old man. Well, it wasn't like he could do it all on a whim. He still needed to make necessary setups and so on, but he was the only one who knew how it worked."

"He could stop time…? I didn't know Space-time magic even existed…"

"What are you talking about? You've been using [**Storage**], [**Gate**], and [**Teleport**] for how long now? What did you think that was? Still, he was far more adept; he could do all of that and more... I'm a little sad that his knowledge is lost to time entirely, if I'm honest."

Interesting... So you're saying that there was an old guy who bypassed the Null magic requirements to perform these crazy feats...? That guy definitely does sound outrageous...

But if he could so easily manipulate Space-time, then creating a barrier that blocked someone from seeing an island would be no big deal. Hell, the fact that the barrier was blocking the outside world from noticing it was practically Space-time magic in itself.

"Maybe the old guy had a disciple or something and they set it up...?"

"...Hm... It's possible he had students. But I need to warn you, if you plan on investigating it... I'd hesitate to use Gungnir because if you take a high-speed flying vehicle you might crash right into the side. It won't show a shadow, after all." That would be a pain. If I used [**Fly**] there was also the risk of it having the whole thing where it disabled magic, so I'd just end up crashing into the sea...

I wondered if I could use a vehicle that didn't need magic.

"Couldn't I go in with Kougyoku or Luli? That'd be easier."

"Yeah, I'm sure that'd work. Sending a summoned beast there would generally be the least risky thing to do. But you should still be careful; depending on the type of barrier you might end up losing contact, or even having your summoned creature get lost entirely." I wanted to head to the island right away, but the Doctor's words did kind of unnerve me.

I wasn't entirely sure what was there, so I decided to play it safe and have Kougyoku's birds scout the place out first.

If the barrier was still up, it was entirely possible that the caster was still living there.

Still, it was an island that nobody had entered even back in the ancient era. It was kind of like the Galapagos Islands back on earth, completely unaffected by the outside world... Its inhabitants might've even undergone stark evolutionary differences.

Just what could I expect in a place like that...?

A barrage of bullets rained down upon the remains of the Steel Battalion that were scattered around the wastes. These bullets were being fired at a rate of several-hundred-per-second from a Gatling gun attached to the right arm of a great, dark mecha. Leen's Frame Gear, Grimgerde, was ready to roll.

Nikola's Knight Baron had a similar Gatling gun, but Leen's was a little bit different and had a broader spread, so it was still pretty unique.

Grimgerde's chest piece distorted, causing the two Gatling guns installed around the center to blow a conflagratory hail of bullets.

Then, both of the shoulders opened up on either side, revealing missile pods. They promptly began to fire out into the air. In tandem with this motion, hinges on the legs opened up to reveal yet more missiles, and they shot out their payloads as well.

Each fingertip on the left hand was also spewing machine gun fire, and the Vulcan rotary installed on the Frame Gear's head was firing off at full pelt as well. It was truly a hail of bullets, like something out of a sci-fi movie.

"Good lord, how horrifying..." We'd been using broken units from the Steel Battalion as target practice, I'd simply pulled them out of [Storage], but the full force of Leen's Grimgerde was reducing them to scrap metal in a matter of seconds.

Grimgerde finished firing and finally came to a halt. I could see steam rising from its form, a testament to just how hot it had become in the process.

"How many bullets was that...?"

"Only around fifty-thousand, so not many, sir."

Not many... Seriously? I looked at Rosetta, positively speechless. I didn't really know what to say at all. The thing was downright unstoppable. I had doubts even Elze's Gerhilde or Yae's Schwertleite could do anything against a head-on barrage like that... Even if their phrasium armor helped defend them, they'd still sustain serious damage.

I was pretty sure that Sue's Ortlinde Overlord would be able to take it, though.

"Well, sir! It's good, but there are drawbacks! After a full-power volley like that, the Frame Gear will need to enter a few minutes of cooldown in order to restore itself to full functioning order, sir! That'll create an opening where it's vulnerable to attack, yessir it will."

"Indeed, Rosetta's right. The Frame Gear is also designed in such a way that it eats through magic at an enhanced rate. Leen should be okay, but I think only she, you, and Linze would be able to handle a Frame Gear of this type." Rosetta and the Professor raised some fair points. Magic fatigue was something we'd have to be careful of. It was, after all, pretty much the same thing as continuously invoking the [**Explosion**] spell.

"It's so hot!" The hatch on the Frame Gear's stomach opened, and Leen hopped out with Paula in tow. Paula toddled out of the opening and rolled on to the ground.

You okay there...?

"It's like a sauna in there, good grief!"

"Ah, sorry sir! Sorry, ma'am! I forgot to install a cooling unit for the cockpit!" Rosetta grumbled to herself.

Geez, you dummy. That's dangerous. If the cockpit ended up superheated, she'd bake in there like an oven-cooked chicken!

"Also, I could barely hear the radio in there, it was such a racket..."

"Hmm... So we should soundproof it too, gotcha. I'll set it so you can toggle it on and off based on the situation." The cockpit was right next to the twin chest Gatlings, so it was no wonder she hated the noise.

This Frame Gear was definitely our greatest work as far as large-scale damage went, but it had the disadvantage of catching friendly units up in its fire as well. It wouldn't really be good for group deployments, so we'd probably want to only use it for cases where it was one versus many.

"This is certainly the best Frame Gear I've ever piloted. But it's still pretty slow to handle..."

That's because it's almost as heavy as Sue's Ortlinde! It has to be, in order to withstand the shock of firing so much.

Whooooooosh...!

"Hm?" I looked up into the air and saw a blue fighter jet flying overhead.

It began to slow down and descend, transforming into a more humanoid form as it landed.

It was Linze's Frame Gear, Helmwige.

The chest hatch opened, and out popped Linze. Helmwige was a Frame Gear with sharp angles to it. This allowed it to easily shift and convert into a jet plane. The idea was inspired by a mecha anime I'd seen.

"How was it? Are you used to flying it yet?"

"I believe so, at least a little… I didn't get too fast with it, though." Linze flashed me a stiff smile. If she got used to piloting Helmwige, then she wouldn't be able to complain about me bringing her along with [Fly].

"Well, sir! Ma'am Leen and ma'am Linze are effectively equipped with their Frame Gears, sir! What about the Frame Gears still needed for ma'am Lu, ma'am Sakura, and ma'am Yumina?" Rosetta flashed me a salute as she listed off the names.

"Doc Babylon didn't decide on which one to make next?"

"I suppose Sakura would be the next one if I was to decide. I'd like to make it a support-type Frame Gear that transmits sound. Magic is ineffective against the Phrase, but using sound-based support magic on allied Frame Gears? That would be valuable. We'd be able to increase Frame Gear speed and durability that way. We'll make a Frame Gear that can project her voice to the entire battlefield."

"A support-type Frame Gear with a focus on area-of-effect, sir!"

Hmm, it's kind of like my [Multiple] spell, only broader. Well, back in the olden days they used to raise the morale of soldiers by playing war music, right? I guess it's the same principle this time, just with vocal magic.

"Alright, then get to work on Sakura's Frame Gear."

"Copy that." I sent Grimgerde and Helmwige back through to Babylon with the Doctor and Rosetta. I, on the other hand, went through a portal back to the castle with Linze and Leen.

The day's testing was over.

But I completely forgot about Paula…

After I returned to the castle, I passed by the training field and saw a bunch of exhausted newbies on the ground. They'd been training to their limit.

Moroha's intensive boot camp had ended a little while ago, but they were still dedicated to their morning and evening training.

Most of them were still being put through the wringer by Moroha herself every morning and evening. They passed the exam, though, so naturally, they were all prepared to give it their all.

"[Mega Heal], [Refresh]." I healed all their wounds and got rid of their fatigue, too.

They all noticed me as soon as their fatigue vanished, and every one of the newbies bowed in my direction.

"Good work, twerps! Morning training's over and done! Get showered, get fed, and take up your posts!"

"Yes, ma'am!" The knights all filed away from Moroha and headed toward their gender-separated shower rooms.

They had showers and an enclosed bath that I'd created by magically transporting water from a natural hot spring in one of Belfast's mountain ranges.

I was granted permission by the royal family, of course. I even installed a bath in the Belfast royal castle as thanks.

That reminded me, I wanted to talk to Kousaka about building a proper public bathhouse.

The newbies had already been assigned to their duties. Those in the castle guard would deal with entertaining visitors and would also be expected to fight or detain intruders. Those assigned to the town watch were expected to patrol the castle town and help out any citizens. The ones assigned to our intelligence corps were to train their social skills and focus on data-gathering.

Those more suited for clerical work and agricultural reclamation had already been sent over to their positions.

On top of those duties, we decided to have most of them train in the Frame Units, just in case.

We had over two-hundred knights, and the vast majority of them knew at least the fundamentals of piloting a Frame Gear. We exempted Samsa the ogre and the lamia sisters from this training, though. They couldn't reasonably fit into the cockpit. Also, the non-combatants, such as the office workers and farmers, didn't have to do Frame Gear training either.

We had no idea when the Phrase would appear next, so preparing for the future was the wisest choice. All we had to do was keep on working.

"A fishery, huh?"

"Yup, a fishery." I sat in my office, mulling over Kousaka's most recent idea.

By fishery, he meant a way to catch a bunch of fish. I don't know when he got the idea, but it was true that there wasn't much in the way of seafood in our country.

"Do you plan on catching fish from the river?" Brunhild was landlocked and had no seas bordering it. We did, however, have a big river running through our territory.

"Not the river, no. My idea was to have the fishermen collect large hauls from the sea, and then sell them for high profit."

"Huh? But we don't have any sea access…"

"Hm? Of course we do. On the other side of those dungeon portals."

"Oh!" He was right. The dungeons on the other side of the portals in Brunhild were beneath a nexus of islands. That was Brunhild territory, too.

We'd be able to harvest plenty of fish over there. There was no access to salt water in Brunhild's main living area, so it'd probably sell well. I wouldn't mind getting me some sashimi, either.

"I see, I see. Good idea, then. So you wanna build a harbor on one of the islands?"

"Quite. The islands are small, so we likely won't be able to create anything huge, though. Plus, there are magical beasts on some of the islands, which could pose an issue."

Hmph... I guess I could go chase them all down until there aren't any left, and then sell their raw materials... But I'd feel a little bad taking away opportunities for adventurers. Then again, I don't think there are any fishermen who would work under such dangerous conditions.

"What if I erect a barrier that repels magical beasts?"

"That would do nicely. We'd need to do further investigation, though. There could well be aquatic menaces to deal with as well." That was a fair point as well. We didn't want any of our fishing boats getting trashed by sea-based monsters.

In the end, I decided to summon a Kraken or a Sea Dragon, and give it the order to hunt down any potentially dangerous monsters or beasts in the area.

"What about the fishermen themselves?"

"I'll handle all of that. I can't say for sure just how rich in fish the seas around those islands are, anyway. I'll need to run preliminary checks." I decided to permit it, provisionally, at least.

I guess I'll summon a Kraken or a Sea Dragon or something tomorrow, then. I'll summon a Sea Serpent, actually. One like the Dragon who helped me out near the Kingdom of Egret. Then, he can stay around the islands and act as their protector. If it's one of Luli's subordinates, then it'll be just fine.

While I'm at it, I'll have him keep any weird looking ships at bay, too. I don't want another case of slavers coming in. It was bad enough the first time.

I checked over the various reports on my desk after Kousaka left. The voice of the people was pretty important when you were ruling over them, so they needed to be heard.

Guildmaster Relisha would also send me information on current events around the world through the smartphone I'd given her.

"Man, if this was back on Earth, then I could've just browsed the world news online..." Each national ruler had a smartphone, and often they would send me their own information as well. The emperor of Regulus sent me formal information about the engagement between his daughter and the king of Felsen, and the king of Belfast sent me information about how Prince Yamato was finally walking. He'd attached a little photo of the kid, too.

Conflicts across the continent had slowed down considerably since the founding of the alliance. Everyone was starting to find common ground. Whenever two countries had a dispute, they'd often turn to me to find the middle ground, too.

Belfast and Mismede were quickly growing their relationship, and Regulus and Roadmare had never been on better terms. Even Ramissh was ending its anti-immigration policy, and Lihnea was establishing friendly relations with Palouf to the north. Things were looking up.

I looked over these letters and noticed a distinct pattern, however. Phrase activity was on the rise in almost every nation. It was mostly just Lesser Constructs, so they were taken care of by parties of red-rank adventurers.

Hm... What rank was I when I killed my first Phrase, anyway... Huh... Wait a sec...

Something suddenly came to mind, so I opened up my smartphone and projected my photo gallery into the air. I scrolled back to a photo I'd taken long ago. Sure enough, the writing on the wall that I'd been unable to understand was still there, preserved in the shot.

It only just occurred to me that I could decipher this with [**Reading**]. I'd need to know what kind of language it was, though. It was possible that Fam would know more. I decided to hop up and head to the library for more information.

Still, if the language didn't exist five-thousand years ago, she could be in the dark about it. But it was true that the language wasn't known to any native Belfastian, and the ruins didn't have their origins in Belfast either. It was worth a shot.

But still, that only raised more questions... Who made those ruins? Why build such a place? How did the Phrase get sealed down there to begin with?

It was no good, I couldn't stop thinking about it.

I headed straight toward the library in search of Fam.

"I have never seen any language resembling this in my life." I spoke with Fam about it, but she gave me a pretty curt reply.

"They vaguely resemble the Hidden Letters of Arthema. It's certainly not Parthenese… These letters definitely didn't exist before the collapse of Doctor Babylon's civilization."

"So the language must've been invented after civilization collapsed back then?" Leen, who was reading a book, suddenly chimed in from across the room. Paula wasn't around, for some reason.

"The issue is that this language is a blind spot, an anomaly in the understanding of my library, and your world. I hypothesize that such letters were used only by a small group who died out relatively quickly." We'd found the ruins in the former capital of Belfast. But the letters weren't Belfastian at all. It was possible that this small group had created the underground ruins, but for what purpose? And what did it have to do with that sealed Phrase? "What were you saying about the Hidden Letters of Arthema?"

"It is a language I cannot read. The language was used by a small culture that didn't leave behind any written evidence. I have only come across parts of their writing in tangentially related works." That was a bother. It was possible that the culture's descendants were the ones who made the ruins, though. So it was worth a shot. I decided to try deciphering it.

"**[Reading]: Hidden Letters of Arthema.**" The letters slowly became recognizable after I cast the spell. I could understand them at least partially.

It kind of felt like vaguely understanding Chinese through knowledge of Japanese kanji because of the shared lettering.

Though it was possible that the letters used here would have different meanings to the letters used in the original Arthema language.

For example, the kanji 可憐, pronounced ka-ren, meant something akin to "lovely." It could be used to describe a pretty girl. But if you read the same lettering in Chinese, it would be interpreted as 可憐, pronounced kho-lien, and would mean something more like "pitiful." That's what my grandpa told me, at least.

The writing here felt like a similar kind of discrepancy. I could make out bits and pieces of the words, but not whole sentences.

"Our red... The glimmering monster... Sacrificed... City... Uh... Tiny? Black, and... Knight? Black Knight...? Time and space... Repaired... Returned... Er, no... Left... Repeating... Corpses...? Spilling...?"

"Red and black? What's that all about?"

Hmph. This is a bit difficult. The glimmering monster is probably the Phrase. The city is probably the former capital. But what's the Black Knight? A Frame Gear? Sounds like a Knight Baron... But what about the small part?

Given that it says our, I guess the guy was writing on behalf of all the people at the time, but that doesn't answer much. No idea what the red part after our is all about... Maybe they meant to identify the group? Like our red-haired clan, or something...?

The repaired part has my attention, though. Did they fix the world's boundary somehow?

From what I could vaguely conclude, this red tribe might have had the ability to repair the world boundary. It might've even been an artifact or something.

"I didn't really learn anything."

"You did not." The Phrase had definitely appeared a thousand years ago and destroyed the former capital. That much was certain. Someone must have defeated them back then or at least held them back enough to repair the boundary protecting the world.

I wanted to know what the deal was.

"How about you, Leen? Know anything about Belfast's situation a thousand years ago?"

"I'm afraid I've got nothing. We Fairies didn't venture out from our own home territory for quite a long time. I doubt even the current elders would know. Belfast's history isn't recorded up to that point, as far as I'm aware." It was no good. I was hoping there'd be some really ancient fairies. Sure, five-thousand years would be unreasonable, but I'd thought maybe some of them could've lived for a couple thousand years.

It seemed like species with longevity mostly kept to themselves in this world, so they were useless to learn global history from. They were the kinds who simply didn't get involved with others.

The Demon Kingdom of Xenoahs was a prime example. They didn't ask, they didn't tell.

It was just one of those things. I couldn't do anything about it.

All I could do right now was continue doing what I was doing. Doctor Babylon and the gynoids were working on the Frame Gears, while Lain and Moroha were working on whipping our knights into shape. All I could do for the time being was... Well, negotiate trade with Olba and try to increase funds. That was a little depressing, I thought I was more valuable.

As I pondered such things, my phone began to vibrate. It was Guildmaster Relisha.

"Hey, 'sup?"

"Sorry to bother you, I know you must be busy… But there's an emergency!"

"Hm? What is it?"

"A Behemoth has emerged."

A Behemoth. Also known as a mutated beast. Magical beasts that very rarely appeared, but they were always monstrously huge. I faced off against Scorpinas, a twin-tailed scorpion Behemoth a while ago. Naturally, I defeated it in a Frame Gear.

"It's in the Elfrau Kingdom, more specifically in the Snorra ice plains. The creature appears to be a mutated Snorra Wolf." Behemoths often gained special abilities alongside their massive size. I didn't know if the ability caused them to gigantify in the first place, or if it was a byproduct of gigantification.

When I fought against Scorpinas, it could shoot fierce, biting acid from its tail. Regular scorpions could only muster up a weak venom.

From what I understood, this Snorra Wolf possessed a strange power as well…

"The queen of Elfrau has called for aid against the Snorra Wolf, but the situation is dire. It's already caused massive casualties to the Elfrau military. The guild has also lost several red-rank adventurers and one silver-rank. It destroyed a village two days ago, and shows no sign of stopping."

"It beat a silver-rank? Seriously?" There were only a few people in the world on that level. I only got there after achieving the titles Dragon Slayer, Golem Buster, and Demon Killer.

I got to gold-rank after killing Scorpinas, but that was mostly thanks to my Frame Gear.

I wondered if the silver-rank guy was hoping he could kill it and become the next gold.

"This request comes directly from the queen of Elfrau. How should I respond?"

"It's a quest to me as a gold-rank adventurer, right?"

"That's right! Any gold-ranked adventurer can take it, since it's a formal guild quest. The reward is vast, a hundred royal gold coins. They also say you can have anything from the royal treasury! But at this rate, there won't be anything left in Elfrau to save."

Hrmph... It's not like I have an obligation to save them or anything. I'm not the only gold-rank in this world, either. There's that old retired perv, so he could take it...

Damn it, if I don't do it, then innocent people are gonna get hurt.

If I'm thinking practically here, I should send two or three Frame Gears to take care of it. Then I wouldn't have to go. Ah, but if I do that it won't be me acting as an adventurer, it'll be me acting as a grand duke... People will assume I ordered my knights to intrude on Elfrau and take it out.

Either would be fine since Elfrau would be saved, but I should go in person. I don't want to cause an international incident. Plus there's some stuff I wanna test out. Also, I don't wanna be known as the gold-rank guy who relies on his Frame Gears to fight all the time, so I'll just go by myself this time. I should take some time to actually fight using my body once in a while, otherwise Moroha and the others will always be physically ahead of me.

"Alright. I'll take it. Send me a message with the location, got it?"

"Got it, thank you. I'll do that now." I closed the call with Relisha and immediately called Kousaka to inform him of my trip to Elfrau. He seemed surprised, I kind of figured he'd be used to it by now.

Hearing him get like that reminded me of this old show about an older man who served a feudal lord. The man would sigh in disbelief every time his master would leave the castle without permission to do something crazy. I used to watch reruns of that show with my grandpa.

It was kind of funny that Kousaka and I had that kind of relationship the characters in the show had.

"This Behemoth Snorra Wolf... It sounds interesting, take me with you."

"You wanna come, Leen?" This was a job for a gold-rank adventurer, but Leen seemed pretty keen on coming with me, so I didn't see why not.

To be honest, Leen's magical mastery probably put her at gold-rank in terms of skill anyway.

My smartphone chimed to signal the new message from Relisha; it was the exact location of the Snorra Wolf. The Elfrau military had been tracking it, apparently. They were keeping their distance from it because it could smell them if they got too close.

The plan was to use [Gate] to move Leen and me to the little bit of Elfrau I had been to in the past during my search for the Babylon pieces. After that, we'd both use [Fly] to get to the snow plains.

"[Gate]." We left Fam behind in the library and came out in Elfrau. *Holy hell is it cold!*

"B-Brr... **C-Come forth, Fire... A Cozy Cloak Scatters Down: [Warming]!**" Leen immediately cast a spell to heat us both up to a comfortable temperature. I really thought I was gonna die for a second...

It was unreasonably cold in Elfrau. A little detail I had completely forgotten about, apparently!

"Good grief… You really are a fool, aren't you?"

"Y-You went through the portal unprotected too, Leen…!"

"…That aside, where's the Snorra Wolf?"

Hmph… Don't just brush off my comments! I grumbled a little as I opened up my map and determined my current location.

"Let's see… We should track the Elfrau soldiers first." I'd never seen a member of the Elfrau military before, but I was certain I'd be able to recognize one at a glance. I was correct. They appeared on my map after I ran the search.

I held Leen in my arms and invoked [**Fly**] to head straight for their location, I saw several of them in a forested area near the snowy plains.

We landed next to them swiftly.

"Hm?!" The Elfrau soldiers wore heavy winter coats and hats that resembled Russian ushankas. They immediately pointed their weapons at me in confusion.

"I'm Mochizuki Touya, the grand duke of Brunhild. The queen of Elfrau has requested I come here to kill the Snorra Wolf. This is Brunhild's court magician, Leen. Who's in charge here?"

"The grand duke of Brunhild?!" My feet slowly sank into the snow. I definitely wasn't dressed for the weather at all. I sighed quietly and pulled my card out of my pocket.

"A golden guild card… Goodness…"

"If you want further proof, should I produce a Frame Gear?"

"No, no… Not necessary… I have heard that the queen sent out for aid. I am the man in charge here, the name is Alexei." A man stepped forward from the group of ten, he was a full head taller than the rest of them. They seemed to accept me pretty readily, but I wasn't sure if they really believed what they were seeing.

From what I was told later, Alexei's father worked at the guild office in Elfrau and often talked about me due to my high rank. They'd been paying attention to me without me even realizing.

Either way, I passed him my guild card so he could confirm it.

"So, where's the Snorra Wolf?"

"Just north of here. It has eaten many Brudboars out on the plains, and is currently resting."

Brudboar...? Oh, I think I heard of them, those white wild pigs. Seems like this Behemoth isn't exclusively attacking humans, at least... But indiscriminately eating anything isn't really that good either. The longer it stays, the more damage it'll do. Better wrap this up.

"C-Captain! The Snorra Wolf is coming!"

"Say what?!" A soldier holding a pair of binoculars points to an area behind us. Then we saw it come into view. A massive white wolf, around twenty meters long, was kicking up snow as it charged toward us.

"Welp, alright then! Time to fight!" It wasn't quite the size of the Behemoth I'd fought last time. But it was still far bigger than a man. I didn't need to field a Frame Gear.

"Let's go!" Leen jumped forward as if to guard the Elfrau soldiers, raising her hand and charging her magic at the same time.

"Come forth, Wind! Sorcerous Stabbing Squall: [Air Impact]!"

Leen invoked an ancient Wind spell, and the enormous wolf was stopped mid-charge and blown away. She'd evidently been brushing up on her ancient spells in the library.

"This is my first time using it on a living target... It's less like a wall of wind and more like a bullet, fascinating. This has good defensive applications." The tumbling wolf fixed its balance and stood up to face us again. It stared me down with golden eyes, howling loudly as its maw gaped open.

"Grawooooooo!" A large mass of ice began to form inside its mouth. It seemed like this was the special ability it had developed when it became a Behemoth. It roared again, sending the lumpy mass our way at incredible speeds.

Oh crap. That's bad!

There was no way for me to avoid it, either. The soldiers were right behind us, after all.

"Burn forth, Wind! Gale of Flames: [Ignis Hurricane]!" A flaming vortex emerged from thin air, melting the chunk of ice into nothing. The spell I'd cast was one similar to **[Fire Storm],** but it was several times more powerful.

It was an ancient spell, known as a compound spell that fused both wind and fire affinities. Over time it's likely that usage of the spell wasn't well understood and became the basic Fire spell known as **[Fire Storm]** today.

Unless someone had both wind and fire in their affinities, they wouldn't be able to use it. That brought with it a ton of disadvantages to offset its sheer power.

"Spark forth, Ice! Frozen, Jolting Maelstrom: [Vortex Mist]!"

"Grrrgh!" A sparkling mist began to rise around the wolf. If it touched the foggy mass, it'd be electrocuted. We'd immobilized it completely. The spell Leen had cast was a compound magic designed for incapacitation.

I didn't want to use a Fire spell to finish it off, since that'd damage the value of the corpse.

There was a new spell I wanted to try out, but it required physical contact, so I had Leen disperse her spell.

The second the fog disappeared, the Snorra Wolf roared and charged straight for me. It was extremely fast, but not fast enough.

I used [Teleport] to warp to the beast's side, then I delivered a [Power Rise] infused kick to its ribs.

"Graugh, awrhhh!" I heard a snapping sound from its body, then a dull crunch. Something inside it had broken. It fell to the ground, and I dashed forward to place my palm on its neck.

"Wither, o Dark! Sap Life From My Enemy: [Energy Drain]!"

"Grawooo!" The Snorra Wolf's very life began flowing into me. It started to die, and my body started to heal. The effect on me felt much like [Recovery]. It was a little slower than a Healing spell, though. Probably because of how large the beast was.

"Grargh!"

"Hmph!" I jumped back to avoid the bite. It tried to get up, but its knees were weak. It was the end for the creature.

"Goodnight." I unholstered Brunhild from my waist and fired true into the beast's chest. A divine bullet pierced its heart.

"Awooo…" It raised a tiny howl as life slipped from its mouth. With that, the Snorra Wolf, terror of Elfrau, was dead.

I approached the wolf to ensure I'd finished the job, and sure enough, it wasn't breathing anymore.

"That [Energy Drain] is quite the frightening spell…"

"You need to keep contact to make it lethal, you know? It was probably meant to be more of an incapacitating spell, like my [Paralyze]." Leen had no aptitude for darkness, so she couldn't use the spell. Yumina and Sakura were capable, but they had no interest in learning about stuff like that.

Wh-Whoa, what's with that fur?! It's unbelievably soft! It's nicer than mink, holy shit! I mean, I've never actually touched mink, but it's softer than what I imagine mink to be! This is gonna sell for a lot!

"G-Grand Duke... Th-The Snorra Wolf..."

"It's dead. You can come out now." I offered words of reassurance to Alexei and his men, most of whom were hiding behind nearby trees. A few of them ended up slumping to the ground in relief. That wasn't unreasonable on their part.

Now all I had to do was show proof of my deed to the queen. I'd head to Elfrau castle, show off the corpse, and be on my merry way.

I stashed the dead Snorra Wolf in [Storage], and then traversed Alexei's memories with [Recall] so I could get information on Elfrau's capital, Slanien.

Then, I opened up a [Gate] that took us straight to Elfrau's royal castle.

It was seriously beautiful to see from the outside.

"We're in Slanien...?"

"So quickly...?" I asked for Alexei and his men to take me through to the castle.

Elfrau castle was pretty gothic-looking in general, and it was smaller than most of the castles I'd seen. It still had Brunhild castle beat in terms of size, though. It just exuded elegance. It felt prim and proper.

We walked to the castle courtyard, and I took the Snorra Wolf's corpse out from [Storage] as proof of my deed.

The castle guards stared in awe and disbelief at the size of the wolf.

Just as I was about to pull out my phone and call Relisha to report my success, I heard a voice call out to me.

"You are Brunhild's grand duke, are you not?" I turned to face a woman with long, blonde hair. Two soldiers stood on either side of her. She wore elegant furs in pale cream tones and wore a beautiful circlet on her head. It was adorned with green gemstones.

The thing atop her head was far too gaudy to be called a tiara, yet far too meager to be called a crown. It shone bright like a diamond.

She looked to be in her mid-twenties, and her emerald eyes were trained on me.

"...Right. I'm the grand duke of Brunhild, Mochizuki Touya. This is Leen, my court magician. You must be the queen of Elfrau, I presume?"

"Indeed. My name is Fortuna Tierra Elfrau, queen of the Elfrau Kingdom. We are indebted to you for coming to our aid." Though the queen was thanking me, my eyes were focused on another part of her body entirely. Her pointy ears. They were the same ears that Relisha had.

The queen of Elfrau was, in fact, an elf.

Aren't Elves forest-dwellers...? I know I'm not huge on fantasy, but still...

Oh, duh... The elf in Elfrau probably comes from elf. Although... Are there many elves around here? I guess it's too soon to judge.

"Shall we? I have tea prepared for you."

"Ah, right." I followed after the elven queen into Elfrau Castle.

Elfrau castle was pretty warm, which led me to believe they'd cast some kind of heating spell on the place. There weren't any fireplaces in sight, after all. Nothing I could remotely identify as a heater in the big guest room I'd been led to. Either way, they clearly had some kind of magical climate control. It was nice, like air conditioning.

I'd been to a few castles in my time. Belfast, Mismede, and Regulus to name a few, but they all paled in comparison to the beauty of Elfrau's. It felt like a masterwork, as if not a single inch of the place was wasted. It's as if it was designed to be luxurious and gaudy, but also intimate and delicate.

In a sense, it felt more like the glow of silver than the shine of gold.

I sat down on a nearby sofa with Leen, and a maid came into the room with some tea. The queen sat nearby. She also brought a small pot of jam and a little serving spoon for each of us.

That definitely reminded me of what I'd heard about Russian tea. I read about it a while ago, apparently you're supposed to enjoy the tea by taking a little spoonful of jam and then sipping the tea while it's still in your mouth. I watched the queen's movements, and she did just that.

I didn't quite know how to do it, but I gave it a shot. I took the sweet jam into my mouth, and then washed it down with the comparatively bitter tea. It was an interesting combination of flavors and wasn't half bad at all. Leen also took her tea this way and judging from her expression she liked it.

"Firstly, I would like to express my most esteemed gratitude for your slaughtering of the Snorra Wolf. Given the sudden circumstances, I truly appreciate your swift handling of the situation. Rest assured that you will be fairly compensated for your deed."

"Ah, thanks. It was nothing, really." The queen looked like she was about to go into a full-on bow, so I quickly tried to dispel that kind of atmosphere.

She seemed to notice, and she flashed me a smile.

"It was little Relisha who told you, right?"

"Hm? Are you familiar with her?"

They are both elves, I guess... Wait, is that racist? Hmm, maybe I got contacted so quickly because the queen's an elf... Hmm... Maybe.

I kept on with my jam and tea as I pondered the intricacies of elf relations.

"Well, I suppose you could say I am familiar with her. She's my niece, the daughter of my little sister to be precise." I almost spat the tea and jam out right there and then.

Niece?! Relisha's aunt is the queen of Elfrau?! The queen let out a soft chuckle; it seemed she'd caught on to my surprise.

"Relisha is my niece, yes. But she's not affiliated with this country. It's somewhat amusing, and it's a sensitive topic these days, but... Don't you find it a little strange that I, an elf, am queen of a nation?"

"Hm? Ah... W-Well, I suppose." She had me figured out, I'd been wondering.

"Elfrau was founded a little over a thousand-and-two-hundred years ago. The land was harsh and inhospitable, but we were given hope by a lone adventurer. He united with the Frau Clan, remnants of a ruined older nation, and founded Elfrau with his own hands."

"An adventurer? Who...?"

"Heheh... His name was El Carterede. He was the first king of this nation, and my husband."

"What?!"

Husband?! But that's... She's seriously that old...? That's older than Leen. No, like twice as old...! Geez, lady. You only look like you're in your twenties.

"The name of this kingdom, Elfrau, comes from his name and the clan that followed him. After he died, there was only myself. I was an adventurer, and I knew what I needed to know about governance. The elder of the Frau Clan also supported me, so I took the mantle of queen. Since then, I have reigned over this nation. All to honor my husband's legacy."

"What about succession...? Forgive me for being rude, but your children?"

"We had none. There was many a time that I have lamented that fact… If we could've only had a child before he passed."

Well, I guess succession issues weren't such a big deal for long-lived species like elves. It's the same for Xenoahs, I guess… Though the overlord does have a tentative heir, so it's a bit different.

…What about my kingdom, though…? I turned to Leen, pondering the future of my nation.

If I end up becoming a god properly, then I probably won't die of old age… I might end up reigning forever… Frankly, it might be better if I pass on the mantle to my son and retire forever to Babylon or something.

Though, I don't know which one of my wives will give birth to a son… I guess if he, or his son, or his son's son, does a bad job, I'll descend from the sky and kick his butt.

"It must be a harsh duty, reigning for so long."

"It isn't as tough as you might expect. The Frau Clan are a gentle and peace-loving people. They speak their mind, but not in a cruel or impolite manner. Everyone here has a fairly open policy and a broad mind. We're typically free of major disputes, and the land is so barren here that we're not at risk of other nations coming to attack us. There might be little arguments here and there, but I've been queen long enough that solving them is a trivial matter. I also have a team of capable advisers." She had been there since the founding of the nation, so it wouldn't surprise me if she was somewhat of a necessary symbol for the country at this point.

Elfrau was around the same size as Ramissh, but most of the land was uninhabitable. The uninhabitable land was the dominion of an Ice spirit, but it was through keen negotiation and proof of skill that the spirit allowed land to be granted to the people who would go on to found Elfrau.

Apparently, the queen herself was the one who negotiated with the spirit. Leen informed me that Elves had an innate affinity for nature, and thus could appeal more to the supernatural.

It seemed that if anything happened to the queen, then the contract would be broken and the kingdom would regress to a land of inhospitable ice and snow. A permanent frosted wasteland.

Still, it was interesting to hear more about spirits. This was the third time I'd heard or seen about them, the first being the incarnation of darkness in Ramissh, and the second being the tree spirit back during the Pruning.

I wanted to meet with this one sometime, too.

"Ah, yes. About that Snorra Wolf... Would you mind selling its remains to us?"

"To you?"

"Yes. Snorra Wolf pelts are extremely high-quality, and they're an uncommon item. If you could, we'd ask you to part with it in exchange for compensation. I think you'll find our offer more than generous."

"Sure, no problem. I can imagine it'd be needed more here than elsewhere anyway." I wondered if she actually just wanted a nice fur coat, but I didn't think too hard about it. The Snorra Wolf's meat was apparently tough and gross, so it was no big loss to me.

"Thank you, then. If you could give us a little time to prepare your reward, I'd appreciate it. In the meantime, I believe you were promised a treasury grant."

"Ah, yes."

Oh, right... Part of the reward was to take an item from the royal treasury.

The queen guided Leen and I down to the basement, and we finally came to the treasury. There were a lot of items arranged orderly on shelves and in fancy cabinets. There were items that could immediately be recognized as treasures, but other items that simply made you blink in confusion.

I asked about various things, but there wasn't really much that caught my eye. I was fairly sure that most of the stuff collecting dust in Babylon's storehouse was more valuable than the things in here, after all.

Leen seemed a lot more engrossed than I, she was asking about all kinds of things.

She looked down at one particular item and beckoned me over.

"Take a look at this."

"Hm…? What's… Oh!" What Leen had shown me was some kind of ax. It was a little special, though. It was a heavy battleax with a red tint covering it entirely.

But that wasn't what had caught her eye about it. It was the writing inscribed on the handle.

It was the exact same lettering I'd seen back in Belfast. It absolutely resembled the Arthema lettering, but was slightly different, just like the words in the ruins. There was no mistaking it, this ax must have had some relation.

"Your Highness, what is this?"

"Ah, this was a gift given to us by another clan when Elfrau was founded."

"What clan was that?"

"If memory serves, they were the Arcana Clan. They referred to themselves as the Red Folk. In their culture, the color red was regarded as sacred."

The Red Folk... That must be it, then. This matches up perfectly with what I could piece together earlier.

Leen prodded me with her elbow as if to tell me to connect the dots already. But I already did in my head!

"[Reading]: Hidden Letters of Arcana." I quietly invoked my linguistic spell.

What does this say... Dusk... Judgment...? I don't get it.

There wasn't much writing here, so I thought I'd be able to get it. But it seemed like this language was slightly different as well. That was kind of a problem. Arthema... then Arcana... Somewhere along the line, the tribe and their language must have slightly changed, and it might have changed again before they wrote the stuff in Belfast.

"Does this weapon have a name?"

"Ah yes, I believe this one is called the Twilight Condemner. It amplifies the strength of the wielder at least tenfold."

Twilight Condemner... So my reading wasn't too far off, but it wasn't fully accurate to the meaning. Damn, translation sure must be a difficult job. It looks like a handy ax, but I don't really need it.

"Do you know if any of the Arcana Clan's descendants exist nowadays?"

"I'm not sure... They were a nomadic tribe, you see. I wouldn't be surprised if there were living remnants or descendants of the tribe, if they successfully found a good place to settle." Apparently, the queen hadn't met the Arcana representatives in person, it was only her husband who had. I tried asking about Belfast, but she had no knowledge of the country's state a thousand years ago, either. Elfrau was pretty far from Belfast and Regulus, after all.

Hmph... Well, even if this isn't a perfect lead, I should count myself lucky to have this much info on the Red Folk already.

"Would you perhaps like the ax?"

"Ah, no... I was just curious about its origins... Hey, what's this thing?" I pointed toward a nearby pendant. It was a small oval, around three centimeters in diameter. It resembled a pearl more than a diamond or gem.

"Ah, this is an artifact known as the Lifeblesser. If a woman wears it during intercourse with her partner, then it massively increases the likelihood of her conceiving a child. For some reason, no matter how I wore it when my husband was... with me, it never bore any fruit. We did lend it to our household retainers, and they easily produced heirs, however... It's possible there are certain criteria you need for it to take effect."

Hm... Sounds like the guy might've been shooting blanks or something... Obviously, I didn't say that out loud.

Still, this is kind of a perfect item in a way, isn't it? If a couple wants a kid but hasn't been able to have one, this would really save them. Then again, it's not like it guarantees pregnancy, just makes it more likely. I feel like if this kind of thing was sold on the market, people would look at it suspiciously. Well, it's clearly an artifact since it's full of magic power at least, but I can't tell its effectiveness at a glance.

"You know, Grand Duke... You do have many fiancees, don't you? Perhaps you ought to think about producing an heir soon enough." The queen offered me some advice, probably from her personal experience.

One of those fiancees is right next to me, you know... Leen sort of leaned in a bit, desperately trying to act calm, collected and indifferent. She was clearly interested.

Hmm... Don't tell me that the reason I have a bunch of kids in the future is because of this thing... Well, no... I'll have nine wives, so if you think about it like that then at least nine kids is kind of a given.

I glared down at the pendant in front of me. I didn't really want my kids not to be born, and I was comfortable with having a child with each of the women in my life.

"Would you like it, then?"

Hmmm......

"And that's how I got this thing, Duke Ortlinde."

"Ohoho!" I was at the Ortlinde estate, sliding the Lifeblesser across the table toward the good duke.

In the end, I chose the pendant, said my goodbyes to Elfrau, split with Leen, and headed straight for his estate.

Leen went back to the castle, and I was fairly certain all my wives-to-be would know about the Lifeblesser before the day was up.

Well, I had no plans on using it yet at any rate.

"So you want to give this to me, lad?"

"Tentatively, yes. The queen gave me it, so it's mine to do with as I see fit. Before I even think about using it, I'd like you and your wife to test it out."

"Ahaha... Then we're your experimental subjects, hm?" He wasn't exactly wrong, honestly. Though apparently, it had worked for dozens of people in the past without any negative effects, I was still curious to see it with my own eyes.

When Sue joined Brunhild as my bride-to-be, Ortlinde was left with no heirs. In a way, I felt like I owed him, so I thought I'd help him make another one.

"You have those uh… vigor pills I gave you the other day, right?"

"Ohoho, yes I do. I gave a few out to some gentlemen I know, and they were quite shocked by the results."

Well duh, anyone would be. They could make even the most wrinkly old fogy sexually active and virile again. And it's even worse if you give it to a young guy, since apparently they can go to town on a girl for three days and three nights non-stop with them.

"Would you perhaps be interested in selling those pills to the general public?"

"Not right now, no." I didn't really want Brunhild being associated with big dick energy. We were just a fledgling nation, so it'd be bad for our image. I didn't want people calling me Pervy Duke, either.

"Anyway, I'm lending this to you for now. It'll work if your wife wears it during the, uh… act. There shouldn't be any weird side-effects either, so I'll let you have it for a year and see what happens."

"Is it fine for us to borrow one of Brunhild's national treasures? If it's just testing, then we needn't keep it for the whole year, right?"

"Mm… Honestly, I still have my personal doubts about its effectiveness, so I wanna see. It's not really a proper treasure of Brunhild, either. We haven't used it. I'll register it as a national treasure once Sue's little brother or sister gets born, right? Plus, it'll help out the Ortlinde household, so it's the least I can do." To be honest, it would be impossible to prove whether or not any pregnancy was caused by the item. I had my reservations about it, or maybe I just wanted it to be fake… Hmph.

It's gonna be a serious hassle proving whether or not this thing actually works. Is it even worth it? I sighed slightly, mulling over such thoughts as I looked over at the smiling duke.

I headed back to the castle, only to be greeted by Kougyoku flapping her wings around the corner. I extended my left arm and let her perch there. She was in her small parrot-like form, so the weight wasn't that bad.

"A message has come from one of my subordinates I sent to the island. But there's something you need to know…"

"Hm? What is it?"

"Well, to be blunt. The island is swarming with Behemoths."

"I'm sorry, what?!"

Behemoths? S-Swarming? What? I expected some evolutionary differences, but an island full of giant beasts is a little much…

"Are there any people there?"

"Yes. There are several locations on the island with erected barriers not even the Behemoths can breach. Within these barriers are towns with living people inside. There are four in total, one in each cardinal direction. In the center of the island, there's a large structure that resembles a temple, connecting them all."

Whoa, there are really people there? I bet the Sage of Hours is behind this, given that it must have taken serious magic to put up barriers like that.

"What does the barrier do? Negate magic?"

"Not quite. It disperses magic. And there's an effect applied to the sea that causes vehicles and people to lose their routes."

I see… So the barrier cuts off magic at the source, interferes with artifacts, and even leads ships astray? Guess that explains why stuff would crash or lose their way in the area.

It meant that [Gate] was probably possible for me, since having my magic disrupted a little wasn't too big of a problem for my deep reserves.

I had a better understanding of the mysterious island thanks to that intel. I was amazed people were living there, but now I had to figure out what to actually do.

Kougyoku said it was swarming with Behemoths, so it was totally this world's Galapagos.

I was super interested, as the mystery of the place wasn't lost on me. But on the other hand, I was conflicted about actually interfering with them.

They might not have known anything about the outside world, after all. I didn't want to create an incident by intruding on their territory.

"Hm… What to do." If I were a tyrant, I'd simply invade it under the banner of expanding my territory. Or I could go in with attempts to open up trade, like Commodore Perry and his black ships.

Come to think of it, 1853 was the year that all went down, right? There was a mnemonic way to remember it, but I can't quite recall…

Even if I go in there and tell them I'm a ruler from a foreign land, they might not entertain me. If I don't handle the situation right, they might even try to kill me. Unless I leave an impact that has them thinking I'm someone amazing or someone worth talking to, they probably won't give me the time of day.

There was always the option of going in with about a hundred Frame Gears…

But I wasn't so fond of that, since I'd just be doing what Commodore Perry did. I didn't want to threaten them, but I almost felt like I might not have a choice.

Then, there was the matter of whether or not it was right for me to take this action alone. From a trade perspective, Hannock, Elfrau, and Palouf probably wouldn't be interested in trading with them. Xenoahs was a no, as well.

Honestly, I wasn't even sure if there'd be merit in opening up trade with them to begin with. Well… ultimately, I decided it was too soon to tell.

"Nothing we can do right now. Just keep up the scouting through your subordinates for the time being. Collect info on their culture, and what kind of society they have. Remember to be safe, though."

"As you wish."

It would be nice if the Sage of Hours left behind something of magical importance…

He could've left a secret behind on that island.

I still didn't know what to do with the island, but if there was any possibility of something like that, then I'd have to confront them someday. Even if there was nothing there, I'd have to investigate.

When it came to saving the world, there was no such thing as a wasted venture.

I affirmed my resolve there and walked down the hall.

"Alright, this is the newest product."

"Ohoho… Just what is this thing…? There's something inside?"

I was talking to Olba Strand in his company's Brunhild branch building.

The upper part of the device I was showcasing was clear, filled with goods. Below there was a slot for money and a handle you could rotate. Below that, there was a hole where something could come out.

In short, I had invented the capsule toy dispenser. Though the capsules inside weren't exactly spherical.

"I guess you could call it an automated lottery machine. How about you give it a try?" Olba put a small bronze coin into the gap and turned the handle. A small noise came from the machine as it moved around. In response, the machine released a small, cylindrical capsule through the prize hole.

"What's this?"

"Open it up and see." Olba unraveled the string tied around the leather-wrapped capsule, and out popped a miniature Frame Gear. The figurine he'd gotten was a tiny Chevalier. I'd crafted it from a rubber-like substance created by breaking down animal horns. I made sure to include all the details of the real thing.

"Oho! This is certainly well-made… But can't we just sell these the regular way? Why the machine?"

"The little capsules don't just have Chevaliers inside, it's down to random chance which one you get. Here's the full list." Olba looked over the list I'd written, and he went wide-eyed upon realizing just how many varieties there were. He still didn't seem to quite understand, though.

"Ah, well... I'm still a little confused about the little boxes... Can't we just sell the items in stores? Why the extra fanfare?"

"Well, let's say you want a Knight Baron figurine, right? You'd be able to just buy it from a store for one bronze penny if we sold it regularly. But if we put it in one of these machines, then..."

"Oh! Ohhh! I see now! You aren't likely to get it in one try! You'd need to keep on trying until you get the ones you want! Maximum profit potential, you're a genius!" In short, we were playing on the impulses of the masses. It was still cheap enough not to ruin anyone, and it'd ensure we saw a steady stream of cash. What's more, we'd encourage people to trade in ten of them for a copper coin. That'd allow us to refill the machines more regularly.

I took out another of the capsule dispensers from [**Storage**].

"This one has higher quality goods than the older one. One try costs one copper. It costs ten times more than the previous machine. But the prizes in this one are made out of metal." It was like comparing a child's machine with an adult's machine. Though it wasn't like it'd be an issue if a child used the copper one, or if an adult used the bronze one.

Olba turned the handle on the more expensive one. The prize he got this time was a Blue Moon Frame Gear, the Blue Knight. That was the specially modified Knight Baron that Vice-Commander Norn used.

This one was slightly bigger than the rubber one, and despite its weight, it would look good as a decorative or collector's piece.

The full list of potential prizes was:

Gerhilde (Elze's Frame Gear)
Schwertleite (Yae's Frame Gear)
Siegrune (Hilde's Frame Gear)
Ortlinde (Sue's Frame Gear)
Helmwige (Linze's Frame Gear)
Grimgerde (Leen's Frame Gear)
The Shining Count (Commander's Frame Gear)
The Knight Baron (Vice-Commander's Frame Gear)
The Blue Moon (Vice-Commander's Frame Gear)
The Chevalier (Standard Frame Gear)
Dragoon (Ende's Frame Gear)
Various Miniature Weapons

On top of that, there were prizes that weren't based on Frame Gears, too.

Black Dragon
Wyvern
Snorra Wolf
Mithril Golem
Scorpinas
Demon Lord
Bloody Crab
Wood Golem
King Ape
Various Tiny Magical Beasts

So we had a monster collection and a mecha collection.

I added in the monster collection because I wanted there to be some decent variety to start with. I didn't want people being like "Aw man, it's just a Chevalier again…"

Either way, there was still a chance that someone out there might constantly get Chevaliers… That was simply a matter of chance.

For the third time, I took a capsule machine out of my [**Storage**]. It was the real deal, this time. The main piece. Bigger than the last two, and much fancier.

"This one doesn't require money to turn the handle. I was thinking that when someone spends enough money in your store, they get one turn of this as a freebie. The items inside this one are a far higher quality than the last two; they're crafted out of dragon bone. They're also properly colored and their limbs are fully articulated." They were action figures, fully articulated to the point where certain models, like Linze's Frame Gear, could even do a full transformation sequence.

"Spends enough money… Like one silver coin?"

"Mm, well I'm not sure honestly. You're the financial expert here, so I'll leave determining that to you." A silver coin was around ten-thousand yen, so I wasn't entirely sure. But at the end of the day, it was a free gift, so it was his choice.

Making them wasn't all that difficult, either. The articulated ones would take a little more effort, but Olba had a dedicated dwarven craftsman working for his company, so I was sure it'd be fine.

We installed the bronze penny machine inside Olba's store, if we installed it outside there was always the risk of theft, after all. A group of kids immediately came over to see what it was all about, and they began turning the handle.

Oh, a Dragoon. That's pretty rare.

"This is interesting indeed… If we alternate the contents, I'm sure we'll save on cost…" Olba muttered to himself as he watched people turn the handle. He was probably making a bunch of business choices internally already.

I passed on the various molds for the figures to Olba, then left the store. I was confident he could handle the rest.

I walked down the main street when some commotion up ahead suddenly caught my attention. There was a small crowd gathered, so I peered through the gaps and saw someone making an arrest.

"Pin him! He's under arrest!" Four of our knights were restraining two rowdy men. They were quickly bound with rope, and then three of the knights carted them off.

"Sorry for the trouble, everyone. It's quite alright now!" The last knight stayed behind to calm down the panicking people. I recognized him.

"Yo! Good job just now."

"Hm? Ah… Y-Your Highness!" The blond-haired knight immediately attempted to genuflect. It was Lanz Tempest. He was one of our newer recruits who came from Lestia.

"Hey now, don't worry about that. You can stand. It's a little troublesome if you decide to do that every time you see me, so please don't worry."

"V-Very well…" He sounded a little confused, but he stood up. His behavior made sense, he was from a kingdom of chivalry, after all.

"So, what happened?"

"Ah, well. A waitress in a nearby restaurant was being harassed. Her son ran over to inform us, and we immediately apprehended the perpetrators."

I see… So they were getting a little handsy with a waitress, huh. That's despicable. I'll make sure they pay for their crimes.

Once I saw they were restraining criminals with rope, I was a little puzzled. It looked like something out of a historical drama. I was sure there had to be something more convenient than that in this world… Did they have no shackles or iron clasps?

"Tsk… Guess I'll have to make some."

"Hm?"

I reached into [**Storage**] and produced a steel ingot, which I promptly transformed into a pair of handcuffs.

Oh right, gotta make the keys too… It took a few minutes, but I created a fine set of cuffs.

"Your Highness, what is this?"

"Handcuffs! They're light and easier to carry around than ropes or shackles. Here, give me your hands." He stuck out his arms and I clasped the cuffs on to his wrists.

"I-Incredible… They're surprisingly tough, too…" Lanz tried to resist the cuffs, but they refused to budge. I used the key on them and they easily snapped open.

"You can keep them. Use these instead of tying people up, alright? I figure we'll make this standard for the patrol. You won't be able to unlock them without the key, though… Hold on, I'll make a spare."

"V-Very well!"

Man, you're so wooden... If I recalled correctly, Logan was in charge of the patrol. I made a mental note to go check the details over with him later.

"So, how's life in Brunhild?"

"Quite fine, sir. Everything I see here is so lively and interesting. It's a truly wonderful, kind country." I was happy Lanz felt that way. It made me happy to know that people from afar thought so highly of Brunhild.

"Oh? It's you, Touya? Hm, Lanz as well?" I suddenly heard the voice of Micah, proprietor of the Brunhild branch of the Silver Moon Inn. She was carrying a lot of stuff with her. She must've been out shopping.

"It's been a while since you dropped by the inn. How're you doing? Staying healthy, I hope."

"I'm doing well, thanks. I'm keeping healthy, promise." I smiled towards Micah; she hadn't changed a bit. It reminded me that I hadn't had lunch in the Silver Moon in a long time.

"M-Miss Micah... Wh-Why are you speaking so casually to our leader...?!"

"Ahaha, don't worry about her. She's an old friend of mine. I've known her longer than any of my fiancees, even. She's fine." Lanz looked like he was about to fly into a panic. She was basically the first friend I made in this world, other than Fashion King Zanac. I only met her a few hours after him.

"So you know Lanz, do you?"

"Sure do! He's been visiting a lot lately, you know? He's a repeat customer!"

"A-Ah, uhm... that... That's only because your cooking is so lovely, Miss Micah! I-It's just that the flavor is like no other, it reminds me of home, almost!" Lanz suddenly stood rigid and began stammering. His face was beet red, too...

Hmm... I wonder what that's all about...

"She's got you under her spell, has she, Lanz?"

"Wh-?! Y-Your Highness, I... Wh-What?!"

"...The spell of her cooking, of course. Did you think I meant something else?"

"Ngh... N-No! Not at all, sir!"

Ahahaha... This guy's head over heels... Micah simply tilted her head, unable to read the atmosphere.

"Micah, those bags look heavy... You should help her back to the Silver Moon with them, Lanz."

"Oh, yes! That'd be a big help."

"V-Very well! I'll do my best!" Lanz, still red in the face, took Micah's bags and began walking to the inn. I waved the two of them off.

Micah was around twenty years old, while Lanz was twenty-two. They certainly seemed to be in a good enough age bracket, but... Micah's father was a muscular, bearded giant. He'd need a lot of luck to face that mountain of a man.

"Their relationship's becoming pretty interesting, y'know?"

"Whuh?! Where'd you come from?!" Karen was suddenly by my side. I hadn't sensed her presence at all. Just where the hell did she come from.

"Ufufufu... In the presence of budding affection, you'll find me! In the presence of blossoming love, you'll find me! It is I, god of love, Mochizuki Karen, y'know?!" She struck an elaborate pose and made a peace sign, but I just stared at her flatly.

"...I was just keeping an eye."

"Sure you were...!"

Man, you'll get in trouble one of these days. Still, her reputation as the love goddess was spreading, she gave out a lot of advice to people, and those people often ended up getting together.

Still, there were those who broke up after getting together, and she would often persuade those with hopeless affections to give up on the people they cared about. Karen said that giving up on unhealthy things was also a valid part of love, and she encouraged it.

"Don't meddle too much, alright?"

"You shouldn't be rude, y'know? I don't interfere with anyone's love life unless they ask me directly! Love is a natural feeling in the end, y'know? You can't hurry love." She sounded pretty reasonable, but I still had my doubts. After all, she wasn't the kind of person who held back often.

"So, what brings you here? Did you get them together?"

"Mm… Oh, that's right! There was something bothering me a little, y'know? I can sense some divinity in the south-east!"

"Wait, what?!"

Is it the servile god again? I can't sense any right now, but Karen and Moroha are much, much better at it, I guess…

"Is it the servile god or something…?"

"Nope! Smells different, y'know? Definitely belongs to a lesser god like me and Moroha. I didn't think that was possible, though…"

Wait, what? I had a bad feeling in my gut…

"Yep, looks like a third one's come down to join us, y'know?"

Wait, what?! Gimme a break! I sighed quietly and pinched the bridge of my nose. Just what kind of god could've landed?

"So, where are we looking?"

"Around here, you know? I didn't get a solid read because the divinity vanished in a matter of moments." Once we got back to the castle I opened up a map and asked Karen to pinpoint where she felt the spike of divinity. She pointed at an area to the southeast, past Ramissh and near the Kingdom of Ryle. It was just a bit into the Sea of Trees.

The region she guessed at was pretty big... I honestly had my doubts we'd be able to find the god. Moroha was in the Sea of Trees when we met her, too. That led me to believe that there must've been some kind of landmark or special aspect of the area that made it more convenient for gods to descend.

"So, let me get this straight... This person, or, uh, god, I guess... can freely use their powers?"

"In a sense, yes and no. We're not allowed to interfere with the lower realms using our godly powers, but we can use those powers to make ourselves appear more human, you know? Interfering down here is fine so long as we don't use any divinity in the process, too. Loopholes are pretty handy, y'know?" *Guess that makes sense... Kinda. Neither of my sisters have been able to use their divinity except for dealing with that servile god, after all... Even if Moroha's super-powerful, I guess she just counts as apex human instead of god... Though I can't help but suspect she must be cheating a little.*

"Even in your case, Touya. You probably shouldn't use your true divinity too much, you know?"

I was at a loss. I couldn't tell where the other god was, so there was nothing to be done for it.

Well whatever, I guess it's fine. Still, I kind of hope no other gods show up. Karen's bad enough as it i— My thoughts were cut off by my intense pain.

"You were thinking of something impolite just now, right?!"

"Ow, ow! I'm sorry! Let go!" Karen was squeezing my cheeks. That chick had a supernatural talent for knowing what I was thinking! Though, she was supernatural herself…

"And just what's all this commotion…?"

"Ah! Moroha!" The other sister appeared as if from nowhere, to save me from my suffering. It kind of made sense that she'd be here too, she probably sensed the divinity like Karen did.

"You felt it too, huh?"

"Sure did, you know? We were thinking about whether or not we should go meet the new visitor."

"Hmm… I wouldn't mind giving them a little visit myself. Mostly I just wanna know who up and rolled down here. It won't be a big deal unless it's the god of apocalypses or something."

What?! If it's that guy then send him back right away!

"People can only come down here if they have the permission from the World God, so I doubt it's anyone hostile. Could be the god of the forge, the god of agriculture, or the god of commerce."

"Aww… Forge and agriculture are fine, but… I'd rather not have it be commerce, you know?"

"You two really don't get along, huh?" I listened to the two talk and learned that certain gods just had bad affinities with each other.

"I'd personally be pretty pleased if it was the god of katanas, god of spears, or god of war. Touya over here hasn't been giving me much fun lately."

Oh, gimme a break. Training with you even wears me out, sheesh… Hell, last time I sparred with you I had to rest up for a full day! Of course I ain't gonna play around with you if you come at me with killing intent, you lunatic! Not to mention the fact that I haven't won a single match against you. Fifty-two losses! Can you blame me? I knew nothing of the god of spears or the god of katanas, but I had the sinking feeling they'd be similar to Moroha. Though… If it was one of them that came down and they agreed to be Moroha's sparring partner, that would actually be a major relief.

"Well, that aside… Let's go look around. There'll probably be a reaction or something if I let loose some of my divinity in the area."

"Gotcha. They'll know about you as well, Touya. So I don't think there'll be an issue meeting up, you know?" I opened up a **[Gate]** to the Kingdom of Ryle's border. More specifically, it was the large expanse where I had fought the Scorpinas Behemoth. After that, we walked toward the Sea of Trees.

"Hm… Can't you two fly?"

"I mean, we could, but we shouldn't really be using our divinity." Moroha had a point. Still, going through the Sea of Trees was a problem, so I decided to finally use something interesting I'd found in the storehouse.

I opened up **[Storage]** to reveal the matter of interest. I spread it on to the ground. It was a little bit big, more than wide enough for the three of us to sit on.

"What's this?"

"It's a magic carpet, apparently. Let's sit down and see how it goes." I told my two confused sisters to sit down on it, and they obliged. Then, I sat down in front of them. In almost an instant, the carpet began floating a full meter into the air.

"Alright, let's go." The carpet slowly began to move forward. There was a barrier that automatically deployed around it in order to prevent wind resistance or accidental falling. It was a pretty handy feature. I also applied **[Invisible]** so nobody saw me gallivanting around like I just leaped out of a Disney movie.

"Oh gosh… This is really nice, you know?"

"The only issue is that it takes a ton of magical power to operate, so it's useless for most people." The two of them gradually got used to it, so I took the speed up a notch. I didn't get to do any cool loops or acrobatic tricks, though.

Eventually, we arrived above the Sea of Trees. I stopped the carpet, and we hovered in the air looking down at it.

"I'll release some of my divinity, then." I triggered my Apotheosis very, very carefully, and almost immediately afterward a flash of divinity came from the forest in response. It seemed like they had sensed mine, then flashed theirs back as a signal.

"Hngh?!"

"Hmph?!" Karen and Moroha briefly had goofy expressions on their faces, like they'd been electrocuted for a few seconds.

"Something wrong?"

"Ah, well… That divinity we felt just now…"

"It came from multiple sources, you know?"

Multiple sources?! What the hell is that supposed to mean…? There are multiple literal gods over there? What are they doing, having a goddamn party?!

"What does this mean?"

"I don't know… But there's only one way to find out, you know? Let's go, Touya!" I didn't know what to say, so I had to go and see in order to believe. I made the magic carpet head toward the source.

Gradually, I could make out someone in a small forest clearing. Not just someone, but several someones.

As we got closer, we could hear some lovely music. On top of that, there was the sound of laughter and a delicious smell.

"…What the…?"

"Goodness…"

"That's amazing, you know...?"

They were actually doing it. They were actually having a goddamn party.

A young man was playing the mandolin as a little red-faced girl sat chugging booze. If that wasn't odd enough, there was a middle-aged man nearby shoveling berries and nuts into his mouth while a young woman merrily grilled meat nearby.

What the hell is this? I jumped off the carpet as it landed before turning to Karen.

"It's the god of music, the god of alcohol, the god of the hunt, and the god of agriculture, you know?"

What the hell?! There's four of them?! I stared on in abject confusion as the little girl noticed us and waved us over.

"Heee~! It's the blade goddess and the love goddess, hic! Come and have a drink, hic!" She was a little girl with long, blue hair, and looked to be about seven years old. She was clearly younger than Sue as far as appearances went, too. Though, oddest of all, she was clumsily waving a bottle of booze around.

What the hell, this kid is the god of alcohol?! The one playing the mandolin was clearly the god of music. He looked to be in his twenties, he seemed like a pretty-boy as well. He smiled gently in my direction, his blond hair swaying in the breeze, but he didn't stop playing for a single second.

It kind of felt like he was expressing his feelings through his notes. The tune he was playing had subtly shifted once he noticed us, in fact.

The older-looking man stuffing his face with berries looked to be in the prime of his life. He was laughing merrily. His eyes were slightly narrow, and he looked pretty relaxed in general. His hair was a plain brown and he had a fairly simple air about him. I assumed him to be the god of agriculture, which only left the green-haired girl with the ponytail to be the god of the hunt. She had some improvised arrows by her side, along with a bow.

She was grilling some meat, presumably sourced from some game she'd hunted down herself. I wondered just what the hell she was cooking though, as the meat looked almost identical to those on-the-bone hunks you'd see in manga. It looked really good!

"Well then… Why are you guys here, you know? There are way too many of you to have been sent against the servile god, you know…?"

"Nope, ain't that. Mhhh… We ain't… **Chomp**… Here for no servile gods." The god of the hunt muttered as she tore her way through hunks of meat. She sure was a wild person… er, god. But I wondered what she meant by her statement.

"We're here fer you, laddie. Assigned to ya, in fact."

"Huh?!"

The narrow-eyed older man… er, god… pointed toward me. I absentmindedly pointed my own finger toward myself as well.

"Touya? What do you mean you're assigned to him?" Moroha spoke up before I even had a chance to voice my confusion.

"It is how it is, lass. World God gave 'im divinity, aye? An' he's gonna reach godhood with the old feller's blessin', too. It's our duty an' honor as senior gods to make sure the little whelp kin follow on in our footsteps as a proud an' powerful god, won'tcha agree…?"

"Yeah, yeah! Hic… We thought of a cool story to justify it so, hic, we're gonna play down in the mortal world for a bit, woohoo!"

…Please don't be so frank about it! Did you guys seriously use my budding divinity as a convenient excuse to goof off down in the mortal realm?!

The god of the hunt let out a boisterous laugh all of a sudden.

"Naaaw, it's fine! Been a long time since we mortalized ourselves, yeah? We just gotta get used to our bodies for a bit, bwahaha... I tried fighting two of those magic beasties and doing it as a mortal was pretty damn refreshing!"

"Yahoo, hic! Been forever since I drank anything other than sacramental nectar! I'm getting all boozed up, hic! Hell yeah!"

"Aye, been a good while since I came an' ate some've the soil's bounty myself. S'delicious an' pure."

"......" The god of music simply remained silent as his strumming seemed to transmit the sound of contentment. Was he seriously not going to talk?

"That's great, you know? Good job on getting his permission!"

"Yeah, it was no biggie! We said to him that we wanted to go, and he said he didn't have a problem. He asked us to keep an eye on the little guy over here, so that's what we'll do...!"

"...Little guy?" *Gimme a break... I feel like the old man was trying to do something nice, but he sent down a bunch of weird eccentrics to get the job done...*

"Pshaaaw... It's no problem! C'mon, drink up!" The god of the hunt shoved a wooden cup full of booze in my general direction.

I guess I can legally drink, sure... but don't be so pushy about it!

"...Where'd you guys even get the alcohol from?"

"Hmhmm~? Hic, we beat up a bunch of nasties for a tribe in the area, and we got aaall these lovely drinkies as a reward. I'm the god of alcohol, hic, but drinking in the higher realm does nothing for me, hic! That's why I'm happy down here, you feel me? I get all buzzed and shit! Eeheheh!" The god of alcohol's face was almost entirely red, and she was laughing like an idiot.

A-Are you drunk already? Is that okay? The fact that you look so young is kinda throwing me off... Your eyes are spinning, are you seriously alright?!

She unsteadily stumbled toward me and started pulling at my pants leg. I had no idea what she wanted.

"Hey, Big Brooo, hic... Gimme some snacks, some snacks! Squid... Edamame... Yakitoriii, hic! I know you're holding out!"

H-How... How did you know that?! I have all of those things in my [Storage] *right now... Is that divinity at work?*

"Oho, sounds yummy. Let's have some, yeah? We don't have much to eat here, and we gotta celebrate! We're super-duper celestial beings, but for now, let's forget about that and party!"

"Aye, yer right! I wanna try havin' a bite of what the ground world has ta offer, too!"

"........." The god of agriculture nodded along with the god of the hunt's words, and the god of music simply intensified his strumming. Karen and Moroha simply looked at each other, then me. Their expressions were one of defeat.

"Geez Louise... Guess it's just one of those moments."

"It'll be fine, you know? Bring out the food, Touya."

I shrugged my shoulders and listened to my sister, opening [Storage] to pull out a table, several chairs, and a lot of food and drink.

The god of the hunt started wolfing down the food as the god of agriculture slowly savored his food. The god of alcohol, on the other hand, was alternating sips of booze with handfuls of snacks. The god of music played slow, somber tunes and didn't eat a single bite. After a while, the god of alcohol shoved a yakitori into his mouth and the tunes became merry. It seemed like he expressed his feelings through the notes he strummed, but frankly, I wished he'd just put the damn thing down.

Even my sisters began to get drunk and merry, and they joined in on the festivities. I was effectively participating in a divine banquet.

Frankly, it was weird as hell…

I wandered away from the main group and picked up my phone.

"Just what's the big idea here?"

"Ah, well… They have been working very hard for very long, you see. I thought perhaps some time off would do them some good."

I was on the phone with the old man, the big G himself. Frankly, I wasn't too keen on my world becoming a pleasure cruise destination for any gods who were needing some downtime. I wondered if it was really alright for gods to be doing that, before remembering that a lot of early earth legends had gods coming down and doing reckless things as well.

"Come now, boy. I'm sure they will not be a bother. Treat them well, and they will surely behave… I think."

You think?! You totally know they're gonna be a pain!

"And remember, someday your own divinity will exceed even theirs. It is important to get used to them sooner rather than later."

The situation was a little messy for me to internalize, but it kind of felt like a company president telling his son to mingle with the staff in order to get a good feel for work and employees before taking over despite being completely unqualified.

I sighed slightly, then said my goodbyes to the old man. I had no idea what to do.

"Big Brooo! Come, hic, dwink! Dwinkies, gotta dwink up and everywon will be happy! Fowget about the transient nature of mortal depwession! Chug, chug, chug!" The god of alcohol laughed obnoxiously as she somehow twined around my leg like a snake.

131

You're trouble, damn it! And how the hell are you dragging me like that?! Don't tell me you're some kind of master of the drunken fist... After being forcefully dragged to the table by an overpowered little girl, Karen forced a wooden cup upon me. *What the... Your face is all...*

"Hey, Touuuuuuya. How about you tell your big sis just how far you've gone with those little girlies, you know? I'm just dying to hear about what you did to them, you know?!" Karen, completely drunk out of her mind, began yammering on and grinning like an idiot.

"...You're drunk."

"Am not, you know? Am not, am not, am not! Can't prove it, you know?"

I can smell it on your breath! You're acting like a total drunkard. Plus, you're breathing really heavily too...

I turned to Moroha for help but she was already unconscious.

How the hell is the god of swords such a lightweight?! I figured it was better than her suddenly brandishing knives and forks after getting drunk, but I was kind of relying on her to save my ass.

The god of alcohol kept on chugging, the god of the hunt kept on laughing, the god of agriculture kept on eating, and the god of music kept on strumming. I had nobody to help me.

Good lord... Are these lunatics really our gods?

We decided that the new arrivals would take on the roles of my uncle and his kids. I didn't want to add any more siblings, after all.

I definitely didn't want the god of agriculture, who looked about forty, to be my brother anyway. Making him my dad would be troublesome from a political perspective.

Either way, he became my uncle, and the other three became my cousins.

My uncle was Mochizuki Kousuke. (God of Agriculture).

His eldest son was Mochizuki Sousuke. (God of Music).

His eldest daughter was Mochizuki Karina. (God of the Hunt).

And last but not least, the youngest daughter was Mochizuki Suika. (God of Alcohol).

Only the god of alcohol looked younger than me, so it gave me an excuse not to be as formal with her.

When I introduced them to the others, everyone was less surprised by my new relatives and more surprised by the fact that Suika was absolutely blackout drunk. I quickly improvised an excuse on the spot, claiming that if she didn't drink a shitton of booze, then she'd suffer debilitating spasms due to her mysterious illness. I was pretty sure they bought it.

According to Leen, dwarven children started drinking around the age Suika resembled. So, though I couldn't write her off as a dwarf, I just so conveniently happened to remember that her mother was, in fact, a dwarf. What a weird coincidence.

"Hm... More of your family, then?"

"Yeah, sorry... It just kind of happened." I was walking east toward the farmland with Yumina when she suddenly spoke up.

She and the others knew I came from another world, which meant they also knew my sisters weren't blood-related. And so, it went without saying that they understood my relation to my uncle and cousins was also not a blood-related arrangement, either. I couldn't exactly tell them the truth, though.

"So then... these new relatives are the same as your sisters, yes...?"

"Ah... Well... I mean, skill-wise, sure. They all have individual talents, but not all of them are combat-related. Karina is a serious huntress though, she's almost unmatched with a bow." That was to be expected of the god of the hunt, though. She'd never let her prey escape. She also seemed to be talented with machetes, guns, axes, and snare traps. I briefly wondered if that actually made her better than Moroha, but it likely didn't. Moroha was specialized in sword combat, while Karina was simply more versatile.

The four of them quickly got used to life in Brunhild and began to work in their own ways. That was why I was heading over to the farmland. I wanted to see how they were getting on.

"Oh... I-Isn't that your uncle now?" Yumina pointed toward a man in the distance, and she was right. He was tilling a field with his hoe. Uncle Kousuke was wiping his brow, the straw hat on his head protecting him from the sun. He looked like he'd worked up quite a sweat, though. His farm clothes were all sweaty. The guy certainly suited the look. But that really went without saying, he was the god of agriculture after all.

"Mornin' Touya, Yumina. How're you two holdin' up?" He greeted us with a little smile. The man really came off as... unremarkably plain.

"You're tilling the field all by yourself? You know you can hire people for that, right...?"

"Ain't how I do it, lad. If a man ain't willin' to till the soil... then he ain't worthy've tastin' nature's bounty... Well, iffin' I'm bein' honest that's a mighty hardline approach ta take... Really, it's just what I wanna do, aye? I'm happy that we kin reclaim some've the wildlands an' set down the seeds fer harvest." If he used his divine powers he'd probably be able to get all this done at once, but there wouldn't be any love or fun in that. Also, he wasn't allowed, which was a good point too.

Still, he was definitely living up to his title. I could see he was making the most of his specialized knowledge. He started scattering some stuff along the fields, and I asked him what it was. Apparently, it was bone meal made from the ground bones of magical beasts. He said that the magical qualities of the creatures' bodies did uh… something to promote… something or other. I didn't quite get it. Lakshy the Alraune, on the other hand, seemed to take great attention to this detail.

He wasn't just willing to till or sow, either. He also said he'd tend to the rice paddies. He was such a plain and simple man it was almost hard to imagine he was actually a member of the divine pantheon.

We returned from the farmlands only to notice an unusual sound coming from the central plaza in town.

"Is something going on…?" As we got closer, we determined the sound to be music. I had an inkling as to who it was.

I pushed through the crowd and saw the face of the god of music, my cousin Sousuke. He was skillfully playing a guitar in front of a water fountain.

The guitar was one of the instruments I'd made on Sakura's request. He must have taken it and brought it out here to play. I first made a piano, but quickly moved on to flutes, trumpets, castanets, and all kinds of other things. I kind of went a little overboard and might have quietly challenged myself to make every instrument imaginable. I didn't know how to play them though, so they ended up piling up and going unused. I left them in the knight order barracks since a couple of the recruits ended up having more than a passing interest.

Sousuke's performance ended, punctuated by a rapturous applause. Some of the people were even moved to the point of tears. I was surprised his performance was that amazing…

"What a wonderful display…!"

"Yeah, I don't think there's anyone that can outdo him…" We left Sousuke as he started up his encore, and walked through the streets past the guild. I happened to turn my head and look towards the bar, only to see…

"What the…?" There were a bunch of guys at the entrance to the bar, all steaming drunk.

They were all on the floor too, so I stepped over them and checked inside. Just as I expected, Suika was there chugging booze like no tomorrow.

There was a man sitting opposite her, clutching his glass. He was wasted.

"Oh, Big Brooo! Wanna have a dwinking contest? When I win, set the money down there, gahahaha!"

"…Why would I do that?" Suika was merrily swaying her glass around, but I was just plain annoyed.

The other patrons were either unconscious or unsteadily heading for the door. They must've all tried to challenge Suika, only to be drunk under the table in no time. I wondered just how long this had been going on for.

"You're laaate, so we're gonna start you with three cupsh, hic…"

"I'm not here to drink, get it? Enough of this."

"Aww…"

I took Suika's drink out of her hand. She was absolutely the worst out of the four who had arrived. After that, I took her with me and apologized to the barkeep. He actually seemed fine, though. Apparently, he'd made a tidy profit from all the drinking that had gone on.

"Geez… Please don't drink this much."

"It's beehn awhile since, hic, sincesh I had a drink, you dummy! Lemme jush cut loose a little… How about Yoomina and I get close over shome whishkey, hic!"

"I-I'm quite fine, thank you…" Yumina smiled very politely and gave a dismissive handwave.

I wondered what the bar was thinking by letting someone so little drink so much, or even at all, but apparently, she had just flashed the royal name of Mochizuki and no questions were asked.

Seemed they weren't sure whether or not to believe her, so they had to call some knights over to verify the situation. I made a mental note to apologize to those guys later on…

"Oh, Touya and the others, huh?" Karina walked out of the guild as we walked out of the neighboring tavern.

She registered with the guild pretty quickly and immediately set to work doing hunting-based quests. She didn't see the need to delve into dungeons or seek out treasure. For her, the thrill was in the hunt… and in eating the products of said hunts.

It seemed like she'd just got done hunting, as well. There was a very large bird in her hands.

"Caught you guys at a good time. This is dinner for tonight, tasty stuff. Give it over to Crea for me, wouldja?"

"Roger."

Karina kept bringing in all kinds of wild game recently, so our diet was gradually growing a little more varied. I opened up [Storage] and stashed the bird in there.

"If I'm honest, I wanna hunt bigger beasties than these. There's nothing so spooky in Brunhild though, so you better take me out into the world later!"

"Sure, why not. I'll do a little investigating into Mismede's hunting grounds for you." Brunhild didn't have much in the way of large monsters, but I was certain that Mismede would have them in abundance. The Sea of Trees was also filled with stuff that'd make any big game hunter squeal with glee.

It seemed like the four Gods had settled into Brunhild perfectly... *Man, I'm really happy they're all helping in their own ways. Except for Suika. Suika is the worst.*

"Hmph, hic! You thinking of something ruuude, Big Bro?!"

...Damn. She can read my thoughts as well as Karen. I guess I really can't treat these guys lightly...

"So... what did you learn about the island?"

"A few bits and pieces. Culturally, they're not too far from us. But there aren't many people there, and they don't have much in the way of living space. I'm gonna go out on a limb and say that's due to all the Behemoths, though. They can't really do anything to expand beyond their protective barrier, but they do have a couple of unshielded outposts."

I answered Leen's question as I munched down some ramen that Crea had prepared. I'd looked up the recipe online and she replicated it perfectly. I was glad. The soup was a little bit watery, but it tasted damn great. She even managed to replicate the narutomaki, so I felt blessed.

I should make her do gyoza next time... Probably won't taste quite the same as the stuff you can get in convenience stores, though.

Leen and myself aside, I shared this room with Elze, Linze, and Yae. Yumina was spending time with her little brother Yamato, Hilde was off in Lestia seeing her older brother, and Sue was at home with her parents.

Lu was learning how to cook almond-based treats with Crea, and Sakura was helping out Fiana with school-related activities.

"So the barrier's still intact... Since people are living there and surviving..." Linze muttered as she ate her ramen, taking a moment to blow on it. She wasn't very good at using chopsticks, so she used a fork instead.

"The barrier itself is covering the exterior island, the four main cities in each cardinal direction, and the temple in the middle. I'm going to assume that the temple is probably the source, and probably something the Sage of Hours left behind."

That would make it an artifact. It would also mean they couldn't change the areas that were being protected. Their safe zones were inherently limited, which meant they couldn't expand. In other words, the people would be attacked by Behemoths as soon as they wandered from the safe zone. Still, the Behemoths were too big to get much out of eating people...

It was more likely that they'd be focused on hunting each other, or magical beasts. Though, if people decided to build outside the barriers, then the Behemoths would trash anything built out there. They couldn't get much more than an outpost created, for fear of destruction.

"Can't they kill the Behemoths? They'll win if it's a life-or-death situation, right? There are enough of them."

"I'm not so sure about that. They do have enormous catapults that they use to ward off any that come too close, but they're playing it safe and fighting defensive for the most part." Besides, if they hadn't been playing it safe, I doubt they'd have lasted all these years. I wondered if they'd figured out their own ways to deal with Behemoths due to the isolation. Either that or they were counting on the barrier to save them.

"It is only humans on that island, is it not?" Yae spoke up as she skillfully slurped her ramen. Soba and udon existed on Eashen, so her proficiency didn't catch me off-guard. She was already on to her third bowl, too.

She didn't gain weight at all, despite the fact that she kept shoveling away food. Then again, she worked out a lot, so it wasn't like she had some innate fat-blocking talent. It was a simple case of calories in vs calories burned.

"Actually, no. There are mostly humans there, but there are a few beastmen and demonkin mixed in there as well. There isn't any discrimination in their society, either. They all live equally." I felt like our society could learn a lot from that approach. That being said, the prejudice might have just been put by the wayside in favor of survival. They needed to work together in order to stay alive in such a hostile land.

"There aren't that many people living there though, even with the limited territory, but that's probably because they can't fish or do proper agriculture."

Even if they managed to fend off monsters to claim farmland, a Behemoth could just walk in and trash it the moment anything was ready to harvest. Having such hard work go to waste would make it hard to consider even attempting in the first place... It'd be too demoralizing to even try.

It'd be wiser to build their farms inside the barrier. Have something like the houses built around the perimeter of the barrier, and the crops on the inner area.

If something attacked, the houses might be trashed, sure... but the food would be okay. It'd increase their chances of surviving that much more.

"Still... an island of Behemoths, eh? It really makes me curious... I mean, why would magical beasts have evolved in such a way in one place?"

"Doctor Babylon proposed the theory that Behemoths are spawned based on magic element density."

"Element density?" Elze and Yae raised a brow in confusion at my words.

The theory that the doctor had was that magical beasts evolved from regular animals that absorbed residual magic elements from the air. For example, a bear species that gradually built up elements of Wind magic in the air might have mutated into the Thunder Bear species.

The theory expanded into the idea that Behemoths came about when a dense amount of magical elements were infused into a creature.

Typically, the residual levels of magic in the air were too thin to have an effect. However, there were a few places in the world where the density was greater than others. Places rich in nature, holy mountains, the sea floor, and the depths of huge forests were all regarded as these so-called Mana Wells.

According to the doctor, those Mana Wells created Behemoths frequently.

I asked her why Behemoths didn't just appear all the time in these places, and she said that the number of creatures that could actually absorb elements from the air was surprisingly low. Apparently, humans were capable of it as well, though.

Anyway, the issue with the mysterious island was the very barrier that protected it. The magic in the air couldn't disperse, so all of it was trapped inside. In other words, it was constantly cycling around the animals and probably being absorbed by any compatible ones. Just because it was being spread around to them didn't mean it'd disappear, either.

That was why the island itself had basically become an artificial Mana Well, and also probably why there were so many Behemoths as a result.

"So wait, does this Mana Well thing affect people?"

"Humans can't absorb more magic than their maximum capacity, Elze. That being said, mana sickness is a thing, and can also be caused by overexposure as well as underexposure." Leen quickly responded to Elze's query.

In the case of the Behemoths on the island, it wasn't likely that these creatures were born as regular animals. It was probably that after several generations of being in such a magically dense place, the Behemoths simply became the evolutionary norm.

That being said, Behemoths typically weren't capable of successful mating due to their genetic irregularities... Though, it was also possible that the Behemoths on the island could just be very old. They had extended lifespans after all.

I guess the real issue was whether or not the Behemoths were now being born naturally or not...

It would be fine to have them pop up now and then, since they were just freak mutations, but we could be dealing with an entirely new species here, and I wasn't sure how to proceed in that regard.

Still, the place definitely gave me a Monster Island kind of vibe. It would've been pretty convenient if a silver warrior from space came down and sorted it out for me. I wasn't quite sure if he'd be able to clear out the island before the Three Minute Rule was up, though.

"Then will the possibility of Behemoths being born go down after removing the barrier, will it?"

"Most likely, yeah. But I can't say for sure… and I don't know if the people maintaining the barrier know that either… or even if anyone is maintaining it…"

Either way, the barrier had to come down at some point. If not, the people in there would be trapped indefinitely.

"At any rate, I've been thinking I want to contact the people on the island. I need to tell the neighboring countries about it. Elfrau and Hannock agreed to meet, but I haven't got a reply from Palouf yet. I'm hoping Lihnea's king can persuade them to come, but I'm also unsure about how much I should tell them…"

In the worst-case scenario, we'd proceed without Palouf's consent. Opening up trade with the island would give the rest of the world access to relatively cheap monster materials. However, the island seemed to have a strange half-barter based currency, so I wasn't sure how it'd go. They definitely had gold, silver, and copper coins, so they at least recognized how the system worked.

"It'll take a while before we open up channels with them, so I guess it's not urgent… But I think we should—"

I was cut off by the familiar buzzing of my smartphone. It was a mail from Relisha. Odd.

"What is it?"

"A message from Relisha. Seems like some Phrase have been detected. They'll come through any time starting tomorrow and ending a week from now..." I answered Linze's question as I scanned over the mail.

"Did she mention how many? Or their power?"

"Not yet." Phrase appeared regularly around the world, but typically it was just Lesser Constructs, the kind of thing a coordinated party could take out. A few people were even good enough to take on the Intermediates.

Still, the Advanced Constructs and, god forbid, the Dominant Constructs, were way too much for regular people to contend with. Brunhild was typically only asked to help if it was a major issue. When we were called out it was typically a given that something big was going to come out.

"Where is the emergence point, Touya-dono?"

"Regulus. I'll have to tell Lu."

"Tell me what?"

I turned to find an apron-clad girl standing in the doorway. She had almond tofu on a tray. Lu placed it on the table, and man did it look good...

I decided to talk about the Phrase situation after trying out the treat. Couldn't pass the stuff up.

Mm, that's good... I scooped up the white stuff in my spoon and shoveled it into my mouth. It was tasty and had the texture of gooey snow.

"They aren't here yet..."

"No, they aren't," Lu sat on a nearby rock, muttering a little.

We were in the Islum Plains in the middle of Regulus territory, just a little bit north-east of their capital city, Gallaria. The place resembled the plains of Mongolia, vast fields and rocky mountains in the distance. There wasn't a cloud in the sky, either.

It had been four days since we brought out the Frame Gears and deployed a forward base. The Regulus guild had sensed that the Phrase were incoming, but we had up to a week until they actually showed up. There was nothing to do but wait.

It wasn't like I wanted them to appear, I just hated the waiting game. We couldn't go back to Brunhild since they could emerge at any moment.

The girls took turns going back to the castle through a [Gate].

Lu, Sue, Linze, and Leen were currently deployed. Yumina and Sakura were back at the castle having some downtime, while Yae, Elze, and Hilde were sleeping back home after finishing their patrols.

We couldn't really afford to drop our guard because we knew that an Upper Construct was coming... but constantly keeping tense was pretty rough, too.

"Touya, it's lunchtime. Would you like to eat?"

"Already? Sure. Sounds good to me." Lu took out two boxed lunches and two flasks from her bag. One was larger than the other.

She poured us a bowl of soup each from the large flask, and a cup of tea each from the little one. Then she handed over a boxed lunch to me. I opened it up and saw a tasty display of rice and side dishes.

"Wow, it looks amazing. Did you make this, Lu?"

"I did. I made it this morning. Crea made everyone else's, but I wanted to make yours..." Lu formed a bashful smile as she spoke. The little princess had quite a talent for cooking, and she'd further refined it after coming to Brunhild. Crea had taken Lu under her wing and used many recipes from my world that I'd provided in order to make the girl into an excellent chef.

I looked down at the meal, smiled, and started eating the fried prawns. It was delicious. Better than the ones made by Crea, even.

"I love it. You've really improved, Lu."

"Thank you so much... I'm happy to hear you say that." The karaage and tamagoyaki were really good, too. Truly the way to a man's heart was through his stomach. Just when I thought it couldn't get any better, I tried the stew.

"Man, this is seriously good... I wanna eat this every day."

"I-I think when we get married I'll be able to do that! Hehe...!" Lu started munching down on her food with a red face. I was grateful for my current life. I really had a lot to thank god for. Suddenly, I remembered something.

"Lu, currently we're working on Sakura's Frame Gear... but what about yours? I imagine you'll want a high-mobility type with twin blades?"

"Uhm, let me think... I quite like that style, yes... but I'd like to prioritize adaptability. Elze, Hilde, and Yae work as vanguard units right now, while Sue, Sakura, and Leen are rearguards. I believe that I should be a commando unit that can alternate between those, much like Linze."

"A commando?"

"I think versatile weaponry would be useful. The ability for me to alternate between long and short-range combat."

Hm… I guess that's doable. It'll need to transform from a high-mobility mode to an armored or more powerful mode, I guess. We'd need it to be able to transform on the go, too. Don't want any time wasted or cooldown on the battlefield. I can see a transforming Frame Gear being useful for unconventional tactics…

"Alright. Let's try and do that, then. Right now we only have the Dragoon as far as high-mobility types go, anyway." I looked over toward the green-painted Dragon Knight nearby. It was the same model as Ende's, but it was an old model nonetheless.

Lu currently piloted the Green Dragoon while she waited for her personal Frame Gear to get produced. Still, Lu was plenty capable of handling it so it wasn't that bad as a temporary measure.

"Thanks for the food, Lu."

"No problem, I'm glad you liked it." I wrapped up my lunchbox and smiled. After that, we took a rest and sipped our tea.

"Grand Duke, Princess, is now a good time?"

"No worries, Gaspar. What's up?" I looked over to the source of the voice and found Regulus' Knight Commander, Gaspar. The attack was in Regulus territory, so a lot of their knights were on hand to help.

"I'm glad to see the two of you are close as ever. Brunhild and Regulus will truly prosper at this rate…" Gaspar laughed heartily as he spoke.

"Something going on?"

"Well, nothing in particular, no… I was simply wondering if we might have more units from the Regulus military."

"Hm? Even more?" I was surprised by the request since I'd already given Regulus more Frame Gears than usual. Twenty-seven Chevaliers and three Knight Barons.

"In truth, much like Brunhild, Regulus has done a recruitment drive for its knight order. We'd like to allow our newer men to get some battlefield experience. That being said, I am aware there's a strong one amongst the Phrase, and I won't endanger us by having the newbies in the vanguard. That's why I'd like you to authorize one other group of Frame Gears who would focus on the Lesser Constructs." That made sense enough to me. Brunhild was also deploying a squad of newbies to give them hands-on experience with the Phrase, so the request wasn't unreasonable. I didn't want them fighting an Upper Construct, though. Basically, their job was to follow instructions and just get a general feel for the atmosphere of a combat situation.

"Have they used the Frame Units to train?"

"They've finished their training, yes. I wouldn't have made the proposal otherwise. So long as they don't get rushed, I feel as though they'll be able to handle the weaker ones without a problem." I wasn't too concerned since the emergency escape magic would save anyone that got defeated... But I imagined it wouldn't be necessary if they were given proper instruction.

"Alright, then. I'll give you one more Knight Baron and nine more Chevaliers. How about that? If they get damaged, Regulus will have to pay for the repairs."

"Very well, thank you." I contacted Monica and told her to send ten Frame Gears down from the hangar.

Even though an Upper Construct was coming, the readings didn't suggest a massive amount. There weren't even ten-thousand coming through. We were using the new Frame Gear models, too. I didn't see the fight posing much of a challenge.

After Gaspar left, I asked Lu for another cup of tea.

"Hm… Regulus has more people in its army, eh?"

"It seems so. After the coup, Regulus lost a lot of military power after all…"

"That general really went too far…" General Bazoar had tried to kill the emperor of Regulus using the power of the Blockbracer and the Drainbracer. He ended up summoning various demonic creatures and even caused a full-on coup.

After the coup, he and his sympathizers were all put to death. A great number of people in the military were given hefty sentences as well. The knight order of Regulus was separate from the Regulus military back then. But after that, the military became a subdivision of the knight order. They were guilty of dishonoring the nation, so they needed to have a close eye kept on them until they were reformed.

Luckily my connection to them had resulted in their foreign relations becoming much, much better. Thanks to that they didn't need to worry about defense from foreign nations as much. They were fine with Belfast, but thanks to my intervention they'd also bridged peace with Roadmare and Ramissh.

"It was a tragic incident for the empire, but I'm still glad it happened. It's how I met you, Touya. Is it wrong for me to think that way?"

"Not at all. Without that incident, I'd have never met you either. If you put it that way, I might even owe that general a little for his wicked plans. Even if it's selfish, I'm glad we met." The two of us smiled at one another. I was truly thankful to have her by my side.

Lu was a hard worker. She was also focused to the point where she didn't give up on her goals. But despite that, she was gentle and kind.

We gazed off into the distance and sat close together. Gradually, both of us closed our eyes. And then…

"Ohoho… How bold…"

"Shhh, Sue. Keep your voice down."

"Hmph… I'd be lying if I said I wasn't a little jealous." The sudden appearance of hushed voices made us open our eyes up.

Sue, Linze, Paula, and Leen were all sneaking a glance at us from behind a rock in the distance.

"G-G-Girls?! Wh-When did you girls start peeking on us?!" Lu suddenly went red in the face, stammering toward the three people and one animal.

"Since Gaspar was here, I guess?"

"W-Well, we were just curious about lunch… s-so we came to ask about you guys, and we didn't want to ruin the mood…"

"I told them not to interfere, good grief…" The three of them replied in their own ways as Paula stood proudly at Leen's feet. She puffed out her chest with pride. It was a little bit annoying and out of place, but that was Paula for you.

Lu crouched down and put her hands over her face, the poor girl was completely beet red.

"Uwaaah… H-How embarrassing…"

"You shouldn't be embarrassed, silly. Touya's our husband-to-be! There's no shame in getting a little lovey-dovey as a couple!" Sue very plainly spoke up, tilting her head as if she didn't understand the problem.

"I-I'm not quite ready for the next level…" Lu averted her gaze at Sue's provocation. She was right. It wasn't like we were at that stage, yet. Still, I felt like a lot of personal barriers had been broken over time.

"Our precious little darling doesn't do things like this with us very often. I'd like to get a little bit more up close and personal with him, myself…"

"That's right! Touya needs to flirt with us a little more, if I'm being honest!"

"Wh-What?!"

Gimme a break, I'm Japanese! My culture is socially modest, so most of the guys from my generation don't even get girlfriends! You're asking me to climb a mountain here… If I did something like publicly flirt in my old world, I'd invoke the ire of keyboard warriors. Seeing that kind of thing makes you wanna scream "Die, normie! Get the hell outta here!"

"That's right! I want you to gimme a big squeeeeeeze, Touya."

"Me too. I want to walk hand-in-hand with you, and feed you food in restaurants…"

"That sounds nice. Can't we do that much, at least?"

Hngh… It's just a big hurdle to climb for me… I don't wanna piss anyone off by doing that publicly.

"It's fine, right? How about if we do it without people around. Let's cuddle in private." Sue suddenly charged headlong into me and started cuddling me from the front.

H-Hey! Just because nobody's around doesn't make it less embarrassing!

"A-Ah… M-Me too!"

"Hm… I want in on this."

"Gh— What?!" Linze and Leen suddenly attacked me from the left and right.

Ugh! G-Gimme a break! Even Paula joined in on the attack and hugged my leg.

"D-Don't hog all of him! Me too!"

"Whoa!" Lu suddenly spoke up and grabbed me from behind. I was surrounded with nowhere to escape. Four enemies, or uh… cute girls, surrounded me from all angles.

It's not like this isn't nice, but it's still embarrassing! This is worse than I feared! Someone save me!

"Attention! Crack in the sky located! The Phrase will be mobilizing soon! All units, prepare for battle!" An alarm suddenly sounded, and the surrounding area woke up with noise. Linze and the others suddenly detached from me and headed to their Frame Gears.

I was saved by the bell… Though, I did have mixed feelings about the Phrase rescuing me from my situation.

It wasn't like I didn't wanna get flirty with them… All nine of them were engaged to me, after all… I knew I had to be a little social with them, but still…

Well, I decided to take it slow. I didn't need to be flirty in public… I just didn't want anyone to get mad or jealous about it, after all. In this world, someone could literally make me "get the hell out" with a well-placed spell!

I heaved a sigh and headed toward our base of operations.

The Phrasium bullets that came out of Leen's Gatling gun reduced an entire crowd of Lesser Constructs to shreds.

"Hoho, they're more fragile than I thought." Leen grinned as her Grimgerde tore down an entire squadron of airborne Manta Phrase with a hail of bullets.

The chest hatch opened up and yet more Gatling guns emerged to obliterate yet more enemies. After the barrage, Grimgerde began its cooldown period to prevent overheating.

Several Chevaliers moved in during this period to shatter any Phrase cores that her barrage had failed to destroy.

Leen's Frame Gear had several drawbacks. The first was that her allies couldn't go in and attack during her barrage. Friendly fire was a massive risk due to the imprecision of her assault.

Secondly, her attacks weren't precise enough to hit the cores all the time. Even if the enemies were smashed to pieces, if the core was intact they'd just regenerate. That being said, she was capable of concentrating her volleys.

The third and final issue was that she couldn't keep a sustained fire going on for a while. The body of the Frame Gear slowly heated up as it continued its attack. Grimgerde was partially constructed out of Phrasium, so there was an element of self-repair in its make-up, but it wasn't enough to mitigate the damage of a constant barrage. That was why the cooldown period became necessary.

That was also why we needed to pair her up with people who could cover for those weaknesses. Grimgerde was defenseless when it stopped firing, so the airborne Phrase began focusing their attacks on the inactive machine. But suddenly, bullets appeared as if from nowhere and destroyed the lot.

"Thanks for the assist, Linze."

"No problem!" Helmwige flew by like a jet plane and destroyed a ton of the ones still in the air. Good job, Linze!

Linze's Frame Gear soared around the battlefield and supported various areas with raid-styled attacks. Much like what we wanted Lu's Frame Gear to be, it took the position of commando.

On the ground, Lu rushed around in her Green Dragoon, slicing through the enemies with her twin blades.

Leen and the others had already begun another fight to the rear.

"Stardust Shell!" Sue raised her voice as the Ortlinde Overlord raised its left arm, producing a wall of star-shaped shields of light. The shields lined up and defended her allies in the area.

The Stardust Shell was a powerful shield that completely bounced back the beams that had been fired by a bunch of airborne Koi Carp Phrase. At that exact moment, the golden mecha raised its right arm and fired off the entire forearm at the elbow.

"Cannon Knuckle Spiraaaaaal!!!" The fired hand flew into the air, crushing the Koi Carp Phrase one after the other in quick succession. The rocket punch flew in an arc before returning to the main robot body.

Wow... They added in a motion that makes it do that... Well, I guess that's pretty handy.

I told Sue to use Ortlinde to focus on defending the HQ. Her mech was suited for that, given its high defensive capabilities. Plus, I didn't want Sue out on the front lines. She was still too young for that. I didn't want her to think I was being unfair, though.

I used [Fly] to soar across the battlefield and check up on a group that looked like they were having a rougher time.

"Fifth Squadron! Just because they're Lesser Constructs doesn't mean you need to face them one-on-one! Support one another and pay attention to your allies."

"Yes sir!" I instructed them all through my smartphone. The Fifth Squadron was composed of the new recruits. They weren't quite used to battles that weren't just one-on-one. They needed to pay more attention to their circumstances, really. Their power was a double-edged sword.

"Entwine thus, Ice! Frozen Curse: [Icebind]!"

I invoked a restraint spell and cast it on the Phrase attacking the Fifth Squadron. Their legs were snared in ice, restricting their motion. They could easily escape by snapping off their limbs, but even stopping them for a short while would be a great advantage.

The Chevaliers of the Fifth Squadron began to shatter cores one after the other. I felt they'd be fine at that point.

As I looked around, I saw three Frame Gears come in from the HQ. A red one, a purple one, and an orange one.

"Kept you waiting, huh?"

"Please forgive our lateness, Touya-dono!"

"A-Apologies for being late!" It was Elze in her Gerhilde, Yae in her Schwertleite, and Hilde in her Siegrune.

The three of them had been sleeping in the castle, so their late arrival was to be expected.

Yae took the lead, dancing through the battlefield with her Phrasium blade. She sliced the Phrase cleanly in two, not missing a single core.

Thus, the three maidens of death began their rampage.

"My liege. There's a large spatial distortion about one kilometer from the HQ. The Upper Construct is coming soon."

"So it's nearly here, huh…? All squads, distance yourself from the projected emergence point."

"Roger."

Tsubaki confirmed that the big one was coming, so I used my [Storage] to pull out some hunks of Phrasium to use for my Meteor Rain attack.

The plan was to pelt it the moment it came out. Using a strike like that probably wouldn't be enough to take its core out, but wearing it out with the surprise attack would be enough to weaken it and then finish it with an all-out attack.

I invoked [Long Sense] to check the perforated area in space. It was cracking wider, meaning the creature was about to emerge.

The sound of splintering glass rang out into the air. In a matter of moments, the Upper Construct came screaming through the tear in reality.

"GRAUUURGH!" It screamed into the heavens, its body shimmering and sparkling in the sunlight. The creature's mountainous form caused the very earth to tremble underfoot.

Its back was large, curved, and smooth. Its six legs were stubby and chunky. It had a long, snake-like tail with several spiked, thorn-like protrusions running along it. Its short head jutted outward.

It was a giant turtle. Or perhaps it was more similar to a tortoise. Still, no tortoise I ever saw had six legs and sawblade-like lining on its shell.

As far as cores went… It had only one. I could see the dull orange light come out from deep in its shell.

"It's huge! Although… maybe it's about average for an Upper. If anything, that just makes it an easy target… Let's get this over with… Meteor Rain!" I invoked [Gate], opening several above the beast. The crystalline "meteors" started raining down upon it, their weight enhanced by [**Gravity**]. Just as I was certain of my success, the tortoise withdrew its head, tail, and legs into the central shell. I could only look on in shock as my barrage pinged off the shell, doing absolutely no damage at all.

"Gh… Its defenses are that good?" It seemed like it was a defense-oriented Phrase. I sighed slightly as the massive creature protruded its thorny tail from its shell. All of a sudden, spines fired outwards in multiple directions, like a missile barrage.

"Tsk, no good! All units, evasive measures!" The spines splintered as they flew through the air, creating more fragments. It was like a cluster bomb attack.

Goddammit! Fortunately, the damage was negligible. Everyone had already vacated the area preemptively due to my Meteor Rain attack. That being said, several Frame Gears were impacted. They stopped moving, and their colors grayed out, signifying that their pilots had been warped away.

"Gaaah! Shatter!" Elze's Gerhilde charged toward the lumbering giant, smashing against one of its massive legs with a pile bunker. She got two hits in, the first causing a short crack, and the follow-up shattering the leg entirely.

Still, the tortoise had three pairs of legs. It wasn't going down so easily. I considered using [**Slip**] to get it on its back, but Elze was in the way. I didn't want it falling on her.

Elze suddenly retreated, allowing Hilde and Yae to close in with a two-pronged attack that crushed the remaining two legs on the same side.

The creature immediately lost its balance, falling to the left. Yae and Hilde withdrew in seconds, skillfully avoiding its falling form.

We couldn't rest easy, though. It might have been immobilized, but it still opened up its mouth to gather particles of light.

Crap! It's gonna fire a beam?! Leen's Grimgerde launched a devastating salvo, but each shot simply pinged off its shell like it was nothing. The shell wasn't just hard in terms of structure, it also had some kind of naturally reflective property. In a sense, it was similar to Spica's defensive fighting style.

"Cannon Knuckle Spiraaaaaal!!!" Sue's Ortlinde Overlord smashed a rocked-charge fist straight into the tortoise's head, shattering it into tiny pieces. The gathering light faded away as its neck dangled limply.

Good job, Sue! Unfortunately, I celebrated too soon. Its legs and head began their regeneration cycle. We needed to break the core, but the only issue was figuring out how.

As I wondered what to do, my smartphone started vibrating.

"Touya... Don't you want to try using... **that**...?" It was Doctor Babylon.

"Wait... you mean **that**...?! The thing Rosetta made...? Didn't you say **that** thing takes up a ton of magic, though?"

"Well, it does... Even combining Linze and Leen's magic, you'd only be able to get one use out of the thing... Still, it's better than nothing, right? I have their consent, too. It's all up to you."

Hrmph... I kinda wanted to get a chance to test it first, but the situation's a little dire...

Helmwige and Grimgerde got into formation, bracing themselves against the heavy cannon that materialized before them. A huge anchor came out of the cannon and rooted it deeply to the ground, preventing any major recoil damage.

This was effectively a giant magic-powered cannon. I called it Brionac. Its barrel was three times the length of a standard Frame Gear and fired a massive, specialized bullet imbued with [**Explosion**].

It was also imbued with the [**Spiral Lance**] spell, causing a fragment of the bullet to rotate after impact for maximum velocity and damage potential.

It took time to charge up the gun with magical power, and it couldn't exactly fire in rapid succession. Even so, it was capable of devastating damage output. It was a kind of one shot, one kill blast.

"You two ready?"

"Yes, we are!"

"As we'll ever be." Linze channeled her Fire magic into Brionac as Leen channeled her Wind magic into it. The gauge on the side of the barrel gradually began to climb.

"Seventy-five percent... Eighty... Eighty-five... Ninety...!" The doctor kept us updated on the situation as I looked back to the tortoise. We were aiming for its throat. A shot there would be able to penetrate through to the core and explode inside the shell. It wouldn't be able to defend.

Its head and legs were almost completely restored, so we needed to take the shot immediately.

"Ready to fire!"

"Got it! Take the shot!" The Brionac let out a thunderous bellow as it spewed flames. The barrel of the gun itself splintered and cracked as a result of the recoil.

The massive bullet came flying out of the end, and smashed into the tortoise's neck. *Alright! Show them what you're made of, Brionac!*

After the initial explosion, the bullet, now somewhat more pointed and grooved, began to violently rotate against the tortoise's body. It was drilling. The Upper Construct was completely powerless to prevent it from breaching its crystal body, so it could only roar as it was violently penetrated.

The trajectory of the bullet led it straight to the core, pulverizing the orange sphere in a matter of seconds before making a swift exit right out the back of the beast.

The Upper Construct stood still, and then its entire body began to shatter.

The cracks connected and the entire structure collapsed, creating a glittering mountain. In a matter of moments, it was nothing but debris littering the beautiful plains of the Regulus Empire.

"We did it…" Steam rushed right out of Brionac as its cooling mechanism set in. Helmwige and Grimgerde also stopped moving entirely, falling to one knee and going completely silent.

"You two alright?"

"S-Somehow, yes…"

"That… That was terrible, darling… All of my magic is practically gone… Agh… A second shot would be impossible." It really did take a lot out of them. I figured we could maybe squeeze a second shot out if we used Yumina and Sakura, though. I couldn't do it myself, since the recoil was strong enough to wreck a Frame Gear, and Brionac itself was damaged in the process… It was honestly pretty dangerous.

Either way, I felt like we'd be able to improve it for future use. The doctor had her ways, after all.

"Alright, people. The Upper Construct is done. Commence cleanup operation."

"Roger!" The Frame Gears began mopping up the remaining weaker Phrase, one by one. I didn't actually end up doing anything important in this fight, either…

There were several new Frame Gears being used, and the girls all worked great in tandem, but it seemed like I didn't need to do anything special.

Still, I sighed in relief and was about to commend myself for a job well done... When I noticed all the Phrase in the vicinity had stopped moving.

What's with them...?

"T-Touya, look!" Linze used Helmwige to point up at the sky, showing a new rip in space. The sound of tearing and cracking spread through the air. Far more intensely than it did when the Upper Construct came through.

Oh shit, don't tell me...! Something came through. Something small. Something humanoid. It leaped through the hole in space and began surveying the area.

A body of crystal, a human form, unbelievable power... A Dominant Construct.

This was the fourth one I'd ever seen. I remembered Ney, the female-looking one that sought to hurt Ende. I remembered Gila, the battle-crazed guy. And I also remembered Lycee, the female-looking observer who sided with Ende.

This one, I didn't recall. It was someone new. He had a handsome face and looked distinctly male. I didn't know if sex or gender was important to the Phrase, though. His 'hair' was long and elegant, but his eyes were chilling like ice.

I descended to the ground in order to confront him. He looked at me, but the expression on his face didn't budge an inch.

He slowly pointed toward me, extending his finger in a skewering motion.

"Wh—?!" The finger extended toward me, and I deflected it using Divine Brunhild.

That came outta nowhere! If I was a normal human, I'd be dead for sure! His finger shattered, and I noticed a subtle change in his expression when he noticed that. He seemed a little shocked, but only for a moment. His finger restored itself in a matter of seconds.

"…Hmph. Then that must make you Endymion's accomplice."

"You can talk?"

"Gila shared the language of this world with me. You must be the Touya."

"…Uh, sure."

Who the hell is this guy, and how does he know about me? Has that Gila bastard been spreading rumors about me over there? Damn it… I sighed, quietly cursing Gila's name.

"I am not like Gila, I have no interest in a wretch like you. I have something I must take care of before the recoil kicks in. Stay out of my way."

The recoil…? The thing that sends Dominant Constructs back past the boundary? Ende had explained to me that this recoil would draw creatures of a certain strength back to the other side, but it would gradually get less effective on them as they came through more. Eventually, they'd be able to freely travel across the world with no limitations.

The Dominant Constructs couldn't stay in the world for long. Even Gila could only remain for a total of thirty minutes. Even so, that's enough time for them to wreak havoc, so I had to take care of this guy quick.

"I don't know what you aim to do, but there's no way I can stand by and watch while you do it."

I used [**Teleport**] to warp behind him. Then, I brought my weapon down above his head with the aim of cleaving him in half down the middle, but he dodged and I only caught his arm.

He turned to me from his new position, glaring at me in shock.

"…I see, now. Gila truly had a reason to rave about you as much as he did." His right arm began to regenerate itself before my eyes. The speed at which his body could recover was far faster than the other Phrase.

"I am unlike Gila. I find no pleasure in war. I have no interest in you, either."

"…So you're just here for the Sovereign?"

"I was, once."

"Huh?" Before I could ask him what he meant by that, I noticed a flying hairtail fish Phrase heading in our direction.

I got distracted, so I didn't notice the Dominant Construct run up to me and attempt a palm-strike.

"Guh!" I instinctively raised my left arm, but I was knocked back by the incredible force.

Holy hell…! I shifted my position to prepare for a follow-up attack, but the Dominant Construct had already made his move. He jumped over me, landing on the back of the hairtail Phrase.

"The recoil is coming, soon. I have no time to entertain your petty battles this day. You may call me Yula. We shall meet again, Touya." Yula started soaring away on the flying fish.

Like hell I'd let you escape! I invoked [**Fly**] and gave pursuit. Just as I was about to catch up to him, his body suddenly let out a blinding flash of light.

"Hngh?!" My field of vision was reduced to a pure white. When I could finally see again, Yula had vanished.

Was that a smokescreen tactic...?!

"Search! Airborne Phrase!"

"Search complete. Four results." My smartphone displayed the results, and I saw that three of them were still on the battlefield. That meant the other one had to be the one Yula was aboard. It was heading west, tremendously fast.

I made a beeline to intercept. I flew for about five minutes before finally catching up with it. It was facing me, and ready to fire a beam of light. However, Yula was nowhere to be seen.

"Goddammit!" I angrily pulled out Divine Brunhild and shot a bullet straight through its core. It was just a measly Intermediate Construct, in the end.

It fell down, pieces of it glittering as they smashed into the ground.

"Search. Dominant Construct."

"...Search Complete. No Results Found."

Wait... nothing? What the hell? Did that recoil thing send him back already? Or can he block my magic somehow...? Just what was he going after, anyway?!

Suddenly I felt a stabbing pain in my arm. I looked down and saw it was just about broken. I was so absorbed in the chase that I didn't even notice. And so, I cast a recovery spell to relieve the pain.

The Dominant Constructs were unable to stay in this world for long, not for as long as the backlash was active. They'd always get pulled back to the space between worlds, so the only question I had was just what that Phrase was trying to accomplish in so little time.

I didn't have an answer... but an ominous and foreboding feeling settled in my gut that day.

"Hrmph… Seems I'm back." A victim of the recoil, Yula found himself back in the space between worlds. There was a small bump in the road, but he didn't mind. He'd done what he set out to do, after all.

"Yo! How was the other side? Anything interesting?" Gila's voice echoed out from the dark. Yula looked at him, seemingly dissatisfied, then heaved a sigh.

"I met with the Touya that you had so loudly spoken of. He's a powerful creature. One of my arms was lost in a scuffle with him."

"Pfftahaha… See? Told you my most magnificent appraisal abilities were dead-on. Lemme just make this clear though, alright? Both that little punk and the Sovereign Core are my trophies to claim. Touch either and I'll break you just as bad. Got it?"

"If you say so. I have no interest in either the core or the Touya."

"Tsk. You're as hard to read as ever, y'know? I ain't got any idea what your plan's all about, but I don't give a shit so long as you keep outta my business." Gila once again sank into the black. Gila was a person who thought simply, and only considered two things. Enemies to fight, and foes to subdue.

Yula, however, was cut of a different cloth.

Yula sought power, it was true. But it wasn't the raw physical strength that Gila desired. Yula sought absolute domination, the ability to make any other cede to his will.

Yula once sought absolute power over the Phrase, the power of the Sovereign Core. It was an ability that would give him control over the entire race. An ability that would even let him dominate other Dominant Constructs. That was why he worked so hard to discover the method to forcibly travel worlds. That was why he shared it with his species.

But the more he traveled, the more he fought, and the more worlds he razed, he began to feel a growing emptiness inside him.

If he were to take the Sovereign Core... If he were to take that power into him, he would have dominion over the Phrase. That much was true, and yet... It wasn't enough. He would *only* rule over one world. Slowly, he realized the diversity of life. The vastness of the cosmos. Simply ruling the Phrase was no longer an option. He wished to rule all life, in every form.

But how could he manage such a feat? The conclusion was simple. He would need to become an existence beyond the Sovereign.

In his travels through the various worlds, Yula had become aware of vague existences. Something he couldn't quite comprehend, but could undeniably sense. What he was sensing was divinity, something that belonged to creatures called gods.

He couldn't see them. He couldn't really feel them. He'd never met one, and he had no way of proving they even existed. But he had seen glimpses of their divinity here and there, across the myriad worlds he had traversed. The evidence he had found wasn't really all that much. Sacred treasures, holy blades, items of mysterious rumor and strength. But as small as his evidence was, he still sensed the faint divinity hidden within.

Yula had sensed something before the rip opened up and he descended upon this new world. It was a pulse, similar to the wavelengths emitted by the Phrase, but also quite different. The pulse carried with it the scent of Divinity. There was surely a god in this world, Yula could feel it. It was calling out to him.

The moment he felt it, he raced toward the boundary. An Upper Construct had broken through not long ago, giving him the perfect opening. After he had broken through and dealt with the Touya, he headed toward the source... and obtained it. Despite the obstacles, he had managed to acquire it just as the recoil brought him back into the space between worlds.

The nature of the item he had acquired was simple enough. It was a tiny egg that shone a brilliant gold.

"Hm…? What…?" The egg began vibrating and shivering, before dissolving into a muddy substance and slipping through Yula's fingers.

Slowly, the amoeba-like blob solidified and changed color, until it took the form of an old, human male.

It took the form of a skinny older man with white hair. The old man stared around the area, and then at Yula himself.

"This is… the space between worlds, hm? Oh, lovely. They won't find me here…"

"…Identify yourself."

"Me…? Er, well… I'm a god, of course."

Yula felt the muddy divinity emanating from the old man, and he believed his words immediately. A crooked grin began spreading across the crystal creature's face as his plan swung into motion…

"This is bad, sir…!" Rosetta grumbled slightly as she looked over the Helmwige and Grimgerde chassis in the hangar.

"The damage to both Frame Gears is serious, sir! The Brionac really does pack a punch!"

"Should we, like… swap out the parts and stuff? And need I remind you that it was your idea to create that thing, Rosetta…"

"Aw, c'mon, Monica! That giant cannon was the centerpiece of the battlefield, yessir it was! Even if it was overpowered, even if it was messy, and even if it was dangerous, it had passion and style!" Rosetta and Monica were about to start bickering, so I snuck away.

Frankly, I was happy to have had the Brionac on our side. The tortoise Phrase would've been a huge hassle without it.

We needed to think of more strategies for the Upper Constructs, though… Just using Brionac every time would be a little much. The fact was that it would damage itself and the bracing Frame Gears after each shot… Repairing that stuff wasn't cheap, so I figured we'd be better leaving it as a last-resort option.

The major issue was standard weapons couldn't hit an Upper Construct's core. Realistically, we'd need something like a spear, or a long and powerful weapon… The only issue then would be that only something like Sue's Ortlinde Overlord could wield it.

And honestly, I wanted Sue to remain on the defensive as far as battles went. It really did seem like we could only use something long-ranged like the Brionac.

I had to think about stuff too. My Meteor Rain clearly wasn't ideal... I didn't want a repeat of what happened today, after all.

Sue was all like "Get me a hammer! A hammer! A giant hammer!" or whatever, because apparently she saw a really cool one that obliterated enemies in an anime. But that was fiction, and completely unfeasible for us...

I tried thinking it over for a little while. I fired up my smartphone, surfing sites focused on mecha anime.

"Hm... Some kind of photonic disturbing gravity wave...?"

I wonder if I can fashion something like that using [Gravity]... I'll ask the Doctor about it, but still... she'll probably end up making something horrific.

I decided to save talking about that until later. In the end, we needed more versatility on the battlefield. It was the key to victory, after all.

I also needed to get better at alternating attacks.

I returned to the ground and found myself face-to-face with the three kunoichi recruits in my castle hall. If I recalled correctly, they were Sarutobi Homura, Kirigakure Shizuku, and Fuma Nagi.

"Uhm, milord! We have a request!" Homura and the others suddenly knelt down and bowed toward me.

What's the big idea...?

"Please grant us the same communications device that Lady Tsubaki has!"

"We beg of you, milord!" Shizuku and Nagi began speaking after Homura.

What were they asking for? I wondered. Then, I realized they must've meant her smartphone.

"…I'll ask to be sure, but why do you need one exactly?"

"Ah, well. We will need to travel far and wide for the sake of our missions, and we will need to perform many infiltrations. That tool allows communication with allies regardless of distance, which is why we thought we could make use of it…"

Hmm… I see. Well, it makes sense enough. Plus, it'd be handy for infiltrating. They could take photos and video evidence of stuff, come to think of it.

"Where exactly are you headed this time?"

"The Burning Kingdom, Sandora. We heard unusual rumors from that region, you see. The three of us will be headed there tomorrow."

Sandora… Now that Yulong was gone, Sandora was the only nation left that still employed slavery.

They had a strict caste system, and it was a case where if someone was of a higher social order than you, then you couldn't ignore their commands. They had an isolationist culture and didn't generally interact with other nations.

The country made widespread use of the magical artifacts known as the Submission Collars. That was how they created a labor force of slaves that couldn't rebel against their masters.

Sandora didn't have a huge population compared to its landmass, and about a third of those people were enslaved.

More interestingly, a lot of these slaves were people from all over the world. There was a saying in this world that went something along the lines of "If you can't find your daughter, check Sandora first." Elves and dwarves were sold there for a hefty profit, too.

Sadly, slaves were seen as simple tools and were often worked until they broke. After that, another slave would be purchased to replace them. It was a trivial matter for the people of that nation, as they considered it the same as changing out a worn pair of shoes for some new ones.

In all honesty, it was a country I didn't want to deal with at all. Their Submission Collars also caused problems in other nations, though. Those guys who were trying to enslave people on my dungeon islands used them, too.

"Hm... Well, I guess so. They'd be useful for intelligence officers... Please give me a little while." I didn't want those girls getting enslaved due to them slipping up or anything... And so, I contacted Tsubaki and had her come to the courtyard.

I arrived there with the three girls, and Tsubaki was already there. Her speed was impressive, even by ninja standards...

"Anyway, I'll be giving smartphones to these three." Tsubaki heard my explanation and shot a glare toward the trio behind me. She was probably mad they went over her head and asked me about it directly. They shrank back in absolute fear.

"Hey, now. I was planning on giving phones to everyone in the knight order eventually. Plus, given the nature of their jobs, it makes sense the intel corps would get them first, right?"

"...If you wish it, my liege. Thank you very much for your generosity." I cast an enchantment on the smartphones that allowed them to return back to their owner's hands if they ever dropped or lost them. In a worst-case scenario, if a knight ever tried to steal one, I could use the enchantment to bring the phone into my own hands as well. Nobody was stealing from me again.

Each smartphone had its own serial number, too, so I knew which belonged to who.

I opened up [Storage] and took out about ten smartphones. They were more rudimentary models than the ones Tsubaki and the world leaders had, and they were colored lime-green.

"Alrighty. You can check your own numbers if you look in the phonebook." I handed over smartphones to the girls. They were gazing at their smartphones with stars in their eyes, glee overcoming their faces. Tsubaki still ended up shooting them another death glare.

"In addition to that, I'll give you guys something to help with mobility."

I took out three magic carpets from [Storage]. I thought the intel corps could benefit from it, due to the fact that it rendered people invisible during flight.

Hell, they could do a stereotypical ninja thing and back it up really close to a wall and hide behind it! Though they'd get found out if anyone walked too close to the wall.

I'd send them to the outskirts of Sandora with [Gate], and they'd be able to make their own way back with the carpets.

"Thank you so much. We owe you a great debt."

"No, I just want to be more prepared than I was when we dealt with Yulong. I've heard really bad rumors about Sandora. I think if anything happened, it'd be too late by the time I found out."

That Submission Collar they made use of just didn't sit right with me. It was ultimately part of how their country fundamentally worked, though.

The fact remained that I was capable of safely removing them from people, but I didn't want that becoming public knowledge. That would've caused some serious trouble.

Rumors could start spreading, stuff like "go to Brunhild to be freed from bondage." That'd be troublesome. I could see Sandora sending assassins in response, much like Yulong did.

That being said, if an attempt was made on my life, I'd respond without mercy.

"If you had to sum it up… what kind of place is Sandora?"

"Well, I can only give you my opinion, but… The king of Sandora stands at the top, and everyone else is just different levels of less valuable than him. The rich become richer, and the poor have no opportunities to rise up. Their place in life is determined the moment they are born. No matter how talented, one born to a slave will always be a slave. No matter how lazy or miserable, the child of a citizen will be a citizen. But if your social rank lowers, then there is no way back."

In the allied nations, it was true that nobles were often separated from commoners… Still, it was still possible for someone to reach their potential through hard work, natural talent, or simple perseverance.

A person with nothing could become an adventurer, gain a reputation, and even end up becoming a knight or something beyond that. My own story was like that, even.

"It might be possible for citizens to abandon their homeland and leave for other lands, but slaves cannot. They often die working, barely fed enough to keep going."

"That sounds horrid…" They seemed to be treated as completely disposable.

"So what about the king of Sandora?"

"There is very little to say about him. Few people speak openly or honestly about him, after all. The people of Sandora simply say stock sentences such as 'He is wonderful,' 'We are thankful for his protection,' or 'He is the very sun in our sky.' There is no honesty when it comes to him."

"Why, though?"

"Who knows... It could be that the upper class of Sandora actually feel this way, but it's likely that most citizens just don't want to get socially penalized for speaking ill of him to the wrong person." It seemed like the people of the upper class in Sandora were immune to criticism, too... Subordinates couldn't speak out against their leaders, either... Sounded like a pretty sweet deal, when I considered how much I was bossed around.

"We cannot forget to underestimate their military might, either. Their Magic Beast Knights are extremely dangerous."

"Oh, right! Those Submission Collars were originally made to tame magic beasts, right?"

The Magic Beast Knights... It was the name given to a group of knights in Sandora that used Submission Collars to tame and mount magic beasts. Sandora didn't border any other nation, so they didn't ostensibly need a big defensive force... However, they were surrounded by dangerous territory, filled with monsters. The desert and the Sea of Trees all had their fair share of powerful creatures, and they often wandered close to Sandora.

The Magic Beast Knights were charged with wiping out those threats. The only thing was, they were a knight order in name only. In truth, a great many of the riders were just as collared as the monsters they rode into battle. They were slaves. False knights forced to battle.

Ultimately, Sandora left any dangerous legwork to slaves. National defense was no different.

"I feel a little bad sending you girls over..."

"Please do not worry. We will report in every day, and flee if things look bad. The purpose of intelligence operatives is to provide information, after all!" Homura puffed out her chest with pride. I couldn't quite place it, but a wave of concern and anxiety washed over me when I wondered if they'd actually be alright...

"Ah, Touya lad. You've been investigating Sandora lately, right?"

"Oh, I heard the same!"

"You two sure have keen ears…" I grumbled quietly as the king of Belfast and the emperor of Regulus spoke up.

We'd had our regular alliance meeting, and now all the world leaders were chilling out in the playroom.

The king of Belfast, the beastking of Mismede, the emperor of Regulus, and I were all playing mahjong. The knight king of Lestia and the king of Lihnea were both playing billiards.

The doge of Roadmare and the emperor of Refreese were being serenaded by Kousuke and treated to various confections by Crea. In the other half of the room, Karen, Moroha, Sousuke, and Karina were quietly discussing matters of the gods with the pope of Ramissh. Suika was completely unconscious on the couch. She had a bottle of sake still clutched in hand.

"Well, you aren't the only one with an interest in Sandora. The beastking has been looking into them as well."

"There's a lot about Sandora that worries all of us, frankly…"

"Such as?" I picked up a tile as I spoke.

Useless… I discarded it.

"After Yulong was dissolved, more slavers have been making a home in Sandora. I've also been informed of Regulus citizens being taken into the slave trade."

"Same here! A buncha bandits have been attacking our village, making off with men, women, and children alike. It must be slavers, you know? Beastmen like us are prized as fighting slaves due to our sturdiness! And the only one that deals with slaves these days is Sandora, so it's gotta be them…"

In Mismede's case, it was a fairly easy country to attack due to its proximity to the Sea of Trees. The unique qualities of beastmen made them valuable items, too.

"It sure would be nice if someone took care of that troublesome country, you know? Ahaha…"

"Haha, I know, right? I bet someone like Touya could do it in under a day… Maybe we could help him, haha…"

"Hahaha… I bet if we used Frame Gears we could totally gain control of their capital city in less than a day, hahaha… Haha… Imagine that."

"…You guys are so easy to see through right now that you may as well be windows. You're trying to joke about it, but you actually want me to take down an entire country for your own convenience, don't you?!"

All three men went silent, and they turned away from me.

Look at me, you bastards!

"As far as destroying Sandora goes, we weren't serious. Though, we do want something done about the rampant slavery."

I could understand that at least. It seemed more like the slavers intruding on foreign territory was more of an issue than the actual country. That being said, the slavers might have just been obeying what higher-ups in Sandora's government told them.

Sandora had no diplomatic relations with any country, Yulong aside. There certainly wouldn't be any country troubled if we destroyed the place, but… No, that'd cause a problem. Refugees would start flooding into the Kingdom of Ryle, and nobody wanted that.

"In the end, the trouble boils down to the collars…" I wondered where they were even producing those Submission Collars. Perhaps they had some kind of enchanter working for the government.

Null Magic wasn't hereditary, though... Assuming the collars had been around for more than one generation, how could Sandora have kept producing them?

Then again, the collars still existed even if their wearers died, so it might have just been a matter of smart recycling. But who was the mastermind behind the slavery to begin with? The king, or someone else?

"Ohohoho... Too bad, Touya. That's my win."

"Gah!" The beastking slapped down his tiles, revealing a winning hand.

Damn it! How could I have lost so easily...? I sighed slightly as we started a new game. My starting hand was terrible...

"...Wait, wasn't Sandora originally founded by someone known as the Slave King?"

"Yes, that's right. Back in the old days, Sandora was a fragmented land of squabbling tribes. It was said that a man appeared one day, and led one of the tribes, the Flari Tribe, to unify the others. It was through his efforts that Sandora was created."

The story was similar to the founding of Elfrau... A lone man founding a kingdom with people important to him... It reminded me of my own experience, in a way.

"They say the man was a gladiator slave from a distant land, and that he always walked with the shackles that once imprisoned him on his legs."

So that's why he's called the Slave King... Did he desert his home country and head to the sands? I shouldn't have been so surprised that there were slaves back then too.

"That's only one side to it. Other stories say he enslaved the tribes that served him."

"Mhm... They say he created the Submission Collars himself, even if the mass-produced version was created by another later on." The beastking and the emperor's words made me raise my brow. That was another angle, I supposed. I wondered if he actually used the collars to force the tribes to follow and fight for him. Still, I felt like there had to be another side to all of this. I wondered if he found an artifact somewhere that made him strong enough to dominate them, though the truth didn't really matter.

Rescuing the current slaves in Sandora from captivity wouldn't be a big deal... but I wondered what they'd do afterward. Would they run, or would they rise up?

They probably wouldn't forgive the people who had shackled them. Even the nobles were products of their circumstances, as they'd have just been brought up to see slaves as less than human. But there was no way the slaves would care about that.

Hmmmph...

There was always the possibility of going up to the king and demanding he free the slaves taken from other nations. Though, there was no guarantee he'd actually listen to a demand like that. He had no reason to, after all.

We could've put on some economic pressure, but that was also a no-go situation. They had no diplomatic ties to speak of.

Slaves weren't fed well, slaves weren't treated well, and they didn't need to rely on outside aid for crops. Two-thirds of Sandora was desert, and the remaining farmland was just used to feed the small elite.

They didn't interact with other nations at all. Sandora was completely isolated. I wondered if I should just pull a Commodore Perry, and build a bunch of black ships...

Hmph... This sucks.

Destroying Sandora on a whole was a bad idea, but it was beginning to sound a lot easier than just nixing the slave trade.

"Oh, Touya. That's my win, now. Read them and weep, ahaha!"

"Wha—?!"

Goddammit, I can't keep getting lost in thought! I'm gonna keep losing if I keep on thinking about Sandora... Er, I mean... it's just not good for me to get so anxious about Sandora! Obviously, politics is more important than a silly a game...

I decided that the best course of action for the time being was to wait to hear back from the three kunoichi.

The next day, rain began to fall in Brunhild. The knights decided to take a break from training, instead taking time to study, read, or maintain their weapons.

I was sitting on a chair and reading a book atop my balcony. It was shielded by a little outcrop of a roof. Suddenly, I heard music coming from the distance. It must have been Sousuke.

He was playing quite the appropriate melody for a rainy day, but I had the feeling nobody would start singing in it or dancing with his umbrella.

The rain was pretty strong, though... I wondered how long it'd last. I didn't want the river to end up overflowing...

It'd be summer before long, either way. There wasn't a beach at Brunhild, but we'd be able to enjoy the sea along the dungeon islands.

People would probably be happy if I hurried along with opening a fishery and public access beach over there. It'd be fairly easy to keep dangerous sea creatures away if I summoned a Leviathan to keep them at bay. That wouldn't be enough to chase the jellyfish away, though.

It could be fun if I set it all up with beach houses and food stalls. It'd be like a summer festival... That reminded me, Brunhild didn't really have any festivals or holidays. Then again, it hadn't even been a year since the country was founded, so we hadn't needed an anniversary celebration or anything. New Year's had come and gone, though.

There weren't any Shinto shrines, either... Still, it wasn't like the festival had to be Japanese-style. I'd kind of need a god to focus on if I was gonna make a shrine, too... Well, not that there's much to worry about on that front. There was only one god that I truly revered. And I didn't want to launch a religion about him.

He probably wouldn't get mad if I made a little shrine to him, but I felt like I should probably ask permission.

Hell, there were a lot of gods hanging around the area. Although really they were just lazing around, like that good-for-nothing god of alcohol! I grumbled as I remembered Suika's nonsense, but then my smartphone started ringing.

The screen said Sarutobi Homura. That was one of the ninjas. It must've meant she'd already made it to Sandora.

"'Sup!"

"A-Ah! Y-Your Highness, is that you?! I-Is it?! P-Please... h-help! The p-people in town, they're... Th-They're...!"

"Calm down. I don't know what you're saying." She sounded like she was panicked. That had me concerned immediately.

"Th-The people! They... They sparkle, a-and then die! Th-Their b-bodies... Ah... Forgive me, Your Highness. This is Shizuku, I've taken the phone."

Shizuku's voice was much more composed than Homura's. That was a good thing. Homura was so mortified that she was clearly in no position to talk.

Tsubaki had turned off her smartphone, so that explained why they called me directly. It wasn't her fault, since she had a meeting.

"Where are you? What's going on?"

"We are in the city of Astal, east of Sandora's royal capital. We stopped here to stay overnight in an inn before moving on to the capital, but... something unusual has happened."

"What's that?"

Astal was the second largest city in Sandora, so it would've been a huge deal if something bad happened there.

"The citizens of this city are all dead. Every last one."

"What?!" I stood up from my chair in shock.

All dead? But that's a massive city! How can they all be dead?!

"Crystals started sprouting from the bodies of the citizens. It was as though all the moisture in their bodies was sucked up... They dropped dead not long after the crystals appeared on their bodies. The condition has affected everyone in this city..."

Crystals...? Like... the Phrase? But I've never heard of this happening before...

It had to be some kind of virus. That meant the girls were in danger.

"Are you guys okay?! Any abnormalities?"

"We are fine. For now, at least... Nagi has reported feeling unwell..."

"Get out of the city! Go anywhere but there! Just leave immediately, do you understand? I'll come to you in an hour or less."

"U-Understood!"

I closed the call. After that, I opened up a map of Astal, projected it into the air, and ran a search for living people. Three dots appeared, heading toward the city's outskirts. That must've been the three girls.

But it was true... Then there wasn't a single living soul in that city other than them.

How... How could they all be dead? Just what the hell happened?

"No point freaking out about it now, I guess... I better go meet them."

I called up Flora in the alchemy lab and had her prepare quarantine procedures. No need to take any chances. I also asked the good-for-nothing child-lover, Tica, to head there on standby as well.

After all that, I headed through a [Gate] into the sunny sands of Sandora. I was in the part of Sandora I'd traveled to when looking for Babylon.

The skies were far clearer in the desert than they were in Brunhild. And it was damn hot, too...

I opened up my map and then invoked [Fly], heading toward the girls.

Eventually, I passed over the city, and everyone below me was clearly dead. I couldn't believe my eyes. They were all shriveled and dry, their skin cracked.

After taking in the sickening sight, I flew faster and faster, attempting to clear the horrific image of malnourished corpses from my mind.

I located the kunoichi trio a little bit out of Astal.

Right away I made sure to cast [Recovery] on them, then I opened a [Gate] and sent them to the quarantine zone. I asked Flora and Tica to take care of it from there.

If it turned out to be a viral contagion, then the situation would become far worse. I felt like they'd be alright.

Moroha and Karina were passing by, so I asked them to come along with me. If it was a virus, it wouldn't matter to people like us with divinity in our souls.

I didn't want to waste any more time, so the three of us set off to Astal on the magic carpet immediately.

En route, we passed a roving caravan of traders heading in the opposite direction.

Magic had rendered us invisible, so we didn't have to worry. They seemed like roving merchants. The map had signified no survivors in the vicinity, so it was likely that these had made a pit stop in Astal before seeing the atrocity and fleeing.

We carried on until we saw a walled fortress of a city. We'd finally reached Astal, the second largest city of Sandora.

It had a large wall surrounding it, made out of red mud-brick. But it wouldn't serve in any defensive measure, as the gates to the city had been left wide open.

The people in front of the gates were dead. From the look of their armor, they must have been the guardsmen.

"Good lord…" Their faces were warped in nightmarish anguish and also dried up as if mummified. I could see small protrusions in their skin, bizarre crystalline outcroppings that jutted out from the inside of their bodies.

I used Brunhild to poke at the crystals, and they dropped off the corpse along with their roots. Then, I picked up one of the crystals to take a look at it and immediately concluded that it was far too fragile for it to be Phrasium. It crumbled away under the slightest bit of pressure.

"Just what the hell happened here?"

I muttered to myself as my sisters looked over the corpses with worried expressions on their faces.

"There's no way…"

"This is terrible…"

The two of them glanced at one another and exchanged a silent affirmation.

"Do you know something about this?"

"Yes, we do. I don't know how it happened, but the souls of these people have been consumed."

"Their souls?" Just what was that supposed to mean? I'd heard of souls exiting the body during comatose states, but I had no idea what they meant.

"To put it simply, when someone dies their soul will leave their body and come up to our realm. The soul will be cleansed up in the heavenly realm and sent back down to a lower realm where it'll be housed in a new body. That's how the cycle of transmigration and rebirth has always gone."

"The souls of those that were wicked and cruel require extra purification, and typically their souls are only fit for the bodies of beasts by the time the work is done, but…"

"The souls of the people here will never rise up to heaven at all. Touya, try to focus your God's Eye. Invoke your divinity and spread it across your eyes." I followed Karina's instructions, focusing my divinity upon my eyes and staring down at the bodies.

I could see something inside each of the corpses, a tiny little shining orb. I could recognize at a glance that it must've been their souls. But as I looked closer, I noticed that these little orbs had holes in them here and there. The light inside was slowly leaking out through the damaged, bitten exterior.

"Can you see it? They're just soul food now. Their souls will leak out and disappear forever. They'll never be born again, they'll never go anywhere else again. They'll simply be lost to the cycle of reincarnation. They've been completely obliterated on the base level."

Completely obliterated...? Gone from this world, and all others... forever? Just thinking about the notion made my heart ache.

"Couldn't we find a way to save the souls...?"

"We could. But it'd take a miracle even for us. We couldn't do something so leisurely while we're in this realm. And you can't either, understand? The burden on your body would be far too great at this point." My hopes were crushed in an instant. But it wasn't like I had any to begin with, I had no idea how to bring them back.

"We need to raze the city. Burn it all to ash. If a soul doesn't ascend to heaven, it'll simply leak out in the body and infuse with it. They'll rise again as the undead, suffering forever. If that happens then they'll just be shambling Zombies, seeking out the living." According to Moroha, undead creatures were created when the souls of creatures didn't move on and instead rooted themselves inside a dead body. Some undead were created by deep-seated feelings of lingering grudge or attachment, but undead with damaged souls had no purpose at all.

After being killed or purified, an undead creature's soul would be released up to heaven... But those with damaged souls would simply cease to exist. They had nowhere to go but the void of death.

It was sad to think about, but they'd be entirely removed from the reincarnation cycle.

I entered the city and glanced around, and found that it wasn't only people who had died. I saw horses, dogs, and even little birds with crystals jutting from their disheveled corpses. Their souls were devoured, too. *...No, this has to be the work of the Phrase.*

I took various factors into consideration before concluding that the entire place needed to be burned down.

There would still be money and commodities inside the stores and houses, but I didn't think it would be morally right to pilfer what was essentially a mass grave.

If I left the city as it was, I was sure that bad people would end up coming by and looting the place, anyway. It was better to allow the stuff to burn to ash along with their former owners.

I considered passing on the stuff left behind to the Sandora authorities, but it was still possible that there was a virus causing all of this. Plus I didn't want them using any proceeds from the salvage to create more Submission Collars.

I searched the map to confirm that there was no longer anything alive in the area, and then I prepared to purge the city in purifying flame.

The buildings, the people, their souls, and the city itself. All would be gone.

"Rage forth, Fire. Purgatorial Flame: [Prominence]." The magical flames I called forth wrapped the entire settlement in a blaze. Blazing hellfire screamed and danced, burning the very heavens above as it clashed against the dark night. The city fell to ruin in its all-encompassing scorch.

Houses began to collapse, roofs began to cave in, everything melded into the savage lick of flame.

I gazed at the city as it simply faded from existence, and felt nothing but utter helplessness.

"...Do souls get eaten like this often?"

"Sometimes, but not frequently. Wraiths, Phantoms, and Specters are all monsters that we'd classify as Soul Eaters. They're attracted by negative thoughts. They like to feast on people who are mired in despair."

"They specifically target fearful people. Those with anxieties, concerns, or depression plaguing them... They corner their targets, intensifying the dread. It's like seasoning their meal. In the end, fear of the unknown is one of the most unsettling things to experience." I remembered hearing that the fear of the dark was inherent to all humans. It's easy to imagine that something exists in the dark, and that serves to intensify the feelings of fear. The fear of the unknown, ultimately, is born from the power of the human imagination.

I was aware of the evil spirit kinds of monsters that could eat souls, but I didn't believe this was their work at all.

Those crystals were far too suspicious and didn't feel like the work of a natural creature from this world. It was possible that thousands of Wraiths came down to the city, but it'd be an unprecedented incident and wouldn't account for the crystal formations.

I looked out in the dark, certain that *something* horrible was making its move out there.

"There is one thing, though..." Moroha muttered quietly as she watched the city burn.

"Something that eats souls and grows from them... It could be that a wicked god is attempting to rise."

"Ah, I see... That could be it, then... There's no sacred treasure in this world, aside from Touya's smoffo... Uh... smarphone...? Smartphone. So this could be the work of that servile god." I wondered if that was true. Traditionally such spirits were born from the divinity of sacred objects after they accumulated dark thoughts and grudges. Something like that would be weaker than a servile god, but it'd still be a major threat to humanity.

Even if it was called a god, a wicked god or evil god wasn't actually one. Gods typically didn't interfere either since they were a product of the lower realms. Though it was certainly true that they were only able to be born because of divinity, so the gods would often give a hero or someone important something special to deal with it on his own time.

I wondered if the servile god was trying to create a sacred treasure and a wicked god alongside it. "Well, even if there is one it'll be fine. This world has Touya looking after it."

"It's not a real god in the end, anyway. Plus, this'll just be a creation of a lowly servile god. It won't even be a fair fight if it faces off against you, Touya. You're favored by God Almighty, after all."

"...Then I guess it's fine..." I didn't really like that they were already counting on me to take care of it. But if it was lower than that NEET god, then I was sure I'd be fine.

I was more worried about the crystals, though. If the servile god had joined forces with the Phrase, that'd be a nightmare scenario. The idea sounded stupid, but I couldn't shake the feeling...

If the Phrase were experimenting with divinity, that could actually be a threat. I only had intuition to go off, however."

"...What? Something's not right... There's something moving in the fire." I looked over to Moroha, who was muttering something at the blaze. I wondered what she meant. Then, I saw it. Shadowy figures swaying in the hellfire. It was impossible. Those flames were enough to melt steel. Before I could even think any further, a Crystal Skeleton burst out of the ravaged city and attempted to charge me.

"Augh!" Karina shot a Phrasium arrow at its head.

The head splintered to pieces and the Skeleton fell to the ground, but it immediately stood up and regenerated the lost material.

What?! Th-That's just like the Phrase! The Crystal Skeleton began shambling toward me once more. Inside its ribcage was a small, golf ball-sized sphere. It was glowing red.

"That…!" I took out Brunhild and pulled the trigger, aiming for the sphere. It burst on impact, and the Skeleton shattered into pieces right away. It didn't get back up.

It was the same regeneration ability. The core was maintaining the function, just like the Phrase Constructs. That meant magic was ineffective as well, which explained how they managed to resist the flames.

Is this because of those crystals growing out of their bodies?!

"They're coming… All the human bodies in the city have been turned into Phrase lifeforms."

"Fall back to the desert! They'll follow!" The others retreated on my order. The Crystal Skeletons all began to shamble out through the gates of the ruined city. As they came toward us, Karina and I took shots at their cores, one after the other.

There were Skeletons of all shapes and sizes, including little ones… and tiny ones crawling on all fours. Children and toddlers, reduced to soulless, mindless drones. It was a fate worse than death.

I swallowed down the misery the sight inspired in me, and I kept on taking my shots. Their souls were done for. The best thing I could do for them was let them die and never come back to this hell.

Moroha moved forward and cut out several cores with her blade. They weren't unified, but there was a massive amount of them. If there were less I could've just used [**Apport**] to pluck out their cores.

Still, Moroha's swordplay showed me that they were fragile enough to take out with blades. Which meant I could call in backup…

"**Come forth, Dark! I Seek an Armored Warrior of Bone: [Skeleton Warrior]!**" Ivory white Skeletons rose from the ground one after another. They each wielded a sword and shield.

Eye for an eye, tooth for a tooth… Skeleton for a Skeleton.

"Kill the Crystal Skeletons that are coming out of the city! Aim for the cores in their chests!" The Skeletons were different from the other Phrase in that they had their cores fully exposed. You could easily hit them through the gaps in the ribs.

I called out more Skeleton Warriors in quick succession. Thousands of them. I really owed this feat to my vast magical reservoir.

A battle then erupted between the Crystal Skeletons and the regular Skeletons, amidst a sea of flames. It seemed like the Skeleton Phrase were drawn to humans out of instinct like the rest of them. There were other exits to the city, but they'd all converged on the one closest to us.

My Skeleton army swiftly and efficiently blocked the blows from their crystalline foes, while biting back without mercy. They were truly good at following orders.

One thing I found interesting was that only the human bodies had become Phrase Constructs. There was probably some method to it, but I had no idea.

"Skeletons tearing apart Skeletons… It's like a vision straight out of hell." The burning city behind them just made the imagery worse. This was one of the most disturbing things I'd seen in recent memory.

Two hours passed, and finally the last of the Crystal Skeletons fell to my army. The flames also began to die down, finally. I looked on my smartphone map to see if there were any stragglers, but found none.

Thus, Astal, the second largest city in the Kingdom of Sandora… was wiped from the annals of history.

The next day, I called an emergency meeting with the representatives of the alliance. I informed them all about the situation in Astal. It was a little awkward to explain that I had to obliterate the entire city, but the more troubling aspect was the cause.

Flora couldn't detect any pathogens or unusual qualities within the three kunoichi, so it was hard to tell what had actually triggered the reaction that turned the townspeople into Skeleton Phrase.

The other world leaders responded to the news with pale faces and fearful glances. That was only natural, of course. They were clearly afraid it could happen in their own territories.

This world was familiar with humans becoming undead, so they didn't particularly take that news badly, but... Well, the problem came with just how big of an incident this was, and the fact that we couldn't be certain if this was some scheme by the Phrase or some coincidental attack from ghostly monsters.

I was of the resolute opinion that the Phrase had to be behind this. After all, how else could the Skeletons be explained?

The only good news out of all of this, if you could call anything that had happened good, was that the Skeletons were so weak they could be killed by even the most novice of adventurers.

Still, I felt like the Skeletons themselves were a simple byproduct, and the actual goal of the attack was the consumption of human souls.

I was fairly convinced that the servile god had a part to play in all of this, as well.

I couldn't exactly tell the other kings about that, though. Even if Her Holiness the Pope would understand, it'd be too complicated to explain to the others.

There was nothing we could do but wait and see, but we had to keep a vigilant eye out for anything suspicious.

That was why I compiled several key points of information and decided to pass them on to Relisha and the other guildmasters.

Point One: There is a creature, or creatures, designated as a Soul Eater.

Point Two: The humans that it consumes will transform into the Skeleton Phrase.

Point Three: This is just unconfirmed speculation on my part, but they are likely to appear in places with a high density of negative emotions.

Creatures like Wraiths and Specters often fell into the Soul Eater category, and they consumed souls just like the wicked god did. There was a common feature between the two, and couldn't be overlooked.

Astal was known as the Slaving City due to its high concentration of slave trade activity.

If any city was going to be mired in negative emotion, it'd be that one. The wanton desires of the slave traders, the overwhelming despair of the slaves, the anguish of the oppressed workers, and the arrogance of the oppressors.

It was ultimately just a theory, but I didn't think I was far off from the truth.

I wondered if the fragmented parts of Yulong would get affected like Astal did, but those places were way too spread out to create a concentrated source of misery. I still couldn't be certain, however, so I decided to remain vigilant.

As I said, it was just a hypothesis. I didn't even know who had started this mess. It could've just been a single strike against the city for all I knew.

I decided to put the Sandora recon mission on hold for a little bit while I got my bearings. It was possible that Sandora, as full of negativity as it was, would end up being a buffet for whoever was orchestrating this. I might have managed to save the three girls this time, but they just got incredibly lucky, so I didn't want to run the risk again.

That being said, I really didn't want a wicked god to be born from all of this... It wasn't a complete god, but my sisters wouldn't be able to interfere at all with their full power. Which, basically, meant that in the end... I'd be the one who'd have to fight it.

Man... This is a pain in the ass... Can't a legendary hero pop outta nowhere and save me?

"...I never expected them to appear in Lestia of all places..." Ten days after the attack on Sandora, the Skeleton Phrase emerged in Lestia, out of a small town named 'Merica.

The local lord in charge of the town had been imposing severe taxes on the citizens, relying on his distance from the capital to keep people from finding out. As a result, the elite of the town were getting fat from the spoils and suffering of the poor. The misery wasn't as great as it was in Astal, but it was certainly enough to manifest negative emotions en masse.

The souls of everyone in 'Merica were devoured, and its inhabitants became Skeleton Phrase. Or rather, they became crystal-boned Zombies. As it turned out, the fire I'd set had simply burned away the flesh in Astal.

The Zombies were quickly dispatched by a team of adventurers who were in the area, along with a small unit of Lestian knights.

The Skeleton Phrase weren't threats individually, but it was important to remember that if an entire town became a Zombie horde, they could be a big danger. If they weren't killed quickly, they surely would've filed into the wilderness and attacked innocent people.

I managed to successfully conclude that the transformations weren't caused by anything viral. The knights and adventurers were completely fine.

That meant there was something directly consuming the souls of the living. It was probably the wicked god's premature form, which I'd taken to calling the Seed of Evil.

It probably came through the dimensional tear and then swiftly exited back through, just like the Phrase. It was possible that the recoil affected it like the Dominant Constructs, but frankly, I found this creature to be a lot more troublesome to deal with.

To make matters worse, our technology could only detect Lesser, Intermediate, and Upper Phrase Constructs. It was likely traveling alone, as we had no readings in the regions that were attacked.

Honestly, it was a real pain in the ass. I resolved to beat the crap out of that thing the moment I set eyes on it.

"Touya... Your eye's twitching, are you quite alright?"

"Ah, sorry, Hilde. I was just a little bit annoyed." Hilde was sitting with me in the castle drawing room, smiling across at me as she usually did.

I was too annoyed by my thoughts, so I quickly downed the lukewarm tea in front of me.

"Oh my, oh my... It seems like the king is getting pretty riled up. Perhaps you could... Relieve his tension by... mumblemumble... Ohoho."

"Wh-What? What are you talking about...?!"

"Shut it, you dumb pervy maid. Don't whisper nonsense into people's ears." Hilde's face turned a shade of red as Cesca indiscriminately muttered in her direction. I pretty much understood the nature of what she said, so I chastised her immediately.

Hilde was gullible and easy to get to listen to you, so she was pretty ignorant of the way the world worked. She was plain simple to deceive. Even if her swordplay was exemplary, she was the kind of person who would fall for lies that even a child wouldn't buy.

She was a sheltered princess, trained in the way of the sword, and was completely unaware of the world around her. She was completely pure of heart, unlike her perverted grandfather...

She was quite similar to Elze and Yae in that regard. The three of them, despite being rough and tumble fighters, were quite delicate in matters of the heart. Still, that was a boon to me, as they weren't pushy and always trying to kiss me.

I wondered if it had something to do with the fact that they excelled in physical disciplines. A healthy body led to a healthy mind, after all. Plus, Leen, Linze, and Yumina, our magic specialists, were often surprisingly bold in their approaches now and then.

I turned my face toward Hilde and gave her a small smile.

"Don't worry, I was just thinking about the general situation in Lestia."

"Ah… My elder brother was disappointed as well. He thought that perhaps if he had noticed the corruption in 'Merica, this disaster could've been averted…"

"He shouldn't think like that. No matter how great a king he may be, he could never see everything that goes on in his land. It was simply inevitable." Even though I said that to comfort her, I was kind of hoping larger nations like Lestia would take a leaf out of Brunhild's book and keep a closer eye on the smaller areas they governed.

A country exists to protect its citizens, not the other way around. That's why in Brunhild, I had spies, knights on patrol, and even Mr. Mittens' cat knights report any unusual activity directly to me.

"So, what will happen to 'Merica?"

"I called my elder brother and asked him about it, but… they're going to focus on rebuilding for the time being. They're inviting people to come and repopulate it… The only issue is that not many people are interested in living there, due to the Zombie outbreak that destroyed it and all…" That made sense enough to me. People would naturally be reluctant to live in a town that had been infested with Zombies. It would likely rouse superstition and fear about the land itself.

Hallowed grounds, graveyards, and toxic bogs… All these places were associated with Zombies. It was just part of the aesthetic.

Apparently, souls that died in places like that found it harder to reach heaven, which meant they were likely to infest corpses and become Zombies.

Zombies and Skeletons belonged to the same general undead category. The only difference was whether or not flesh remained on the bones. Skeletons also tended to move faster than Zombies. I wondered if that was because there was no meat to weigh them down.

"I guess I can get why they'd be scared to live there."

"It's entirely possible that if the people living here become afraid, the negativity could rise again and attract whatever's eating them up."

Hmph... That's true enough. Cesca raised a fair enough point.

Fear was one of the most basic negative emotions a human could possess. If repeated incidents occurred, they would pile up and intensify a person's anxiety. That anxiety would ultimately invite more fear, creating a vicious cycle that traps people. That accumulated fear would then summon whatever was feeding on it, which would, in turn, leave a wake of more fear.

I needed to destroy the root of the issue before a cycle of anxiety and fear took over the people in this place. Ultimately, I needed to catch the Seed of Evil and crush it before it could germinate.

"Touya, your eyes are twitching again..."

"Ah, sorry." I'd been getting more irritable lately for some reason. It was frustrating that we kept on showing up late to these disasters and that so many innocent lives were lost. I felt like I was being bullied by the universe.

"Geez... I could really do with a change of pace around here..."

"Heheh... So you've finally decided to do naughty things with us, hm?"

"H-He has?!"

"If she speaks, there's a ninety percent chance she's speaking nonsense. Ignore her."

Goddammit... I'm gonna go bald due to stress one of these days...

"Terrible news!" The dining room door flung open loudly, and Tsubaki charged into the room.

Gah! Knock next time! Linze almost choked on her tea. Tsubaki's cheeks flushed red with embarrassment as she realized her rudeness.

"Calm down, calm down. What's the problem, here?"

"We received a message through the Gate Mirror! It's from Pam in the Sea of Trees. The tribes of the region are under attack by Sandora, they've sent in their Magic Beast Knights!"

"What did you say?!" *Why the hell would Sandora be invading the Sea of Trees? Didn't they have an unspoken peace arrangement going on...?*

"The invading army has been capturing tribespeople alive and dragging them back to the capital city one by one. They intend to enslave the general population and have them serve Sandora. Pam and her tribe are currently preventing the other tribes from angrily charging into Sandora territory, but the situation is dire..." I was disgusted by what I was hearing.

This isn't just a goddamn slaver run, this is an organized assault on a group of people with the express purpose of enslaving them... What the hell is this?! If Sandora kept this up, it'd be an all-out war between the regions.

"Then I guess those rumors of Sandora producing more Submission Collars was true..."

"It seems so..." I tried sending the three kunoichi there with the intent of discovering credibility, but this was clear proof enough.

It would be meaningless to have more collars without necks to put them on. They needed a good source of fresh slaves to subjugate. It seemed like Sandora was aiming to get as much out of the Sea of Trees as they could. The more warriors they enslaved, the bigger their army could grow. No matter how talented the tribesmen were, they'd have a major problem facing off against tamed magical beasts.

I wondered if they intended to bolster their numbers, and then take over the whole region. "It wouldn't be good if Sandora and the Sea of Trees get into a scuffle. It could erupt into all-out war."

"So, what are you gonna do?" Elze muttered in my general direction.

"Fortunately for us, Brunhild has a good relationship with the Rauli tribe, the tribe in charge of the Sea of Trees. We will negotiate between the two sides, and demand that Sandora return the captured people."

"Do you think they'll return the slaves?"

"They better... And then we'll make them pay reparations for their damages, too. It will definitely have negative political repercussions, but it might be the only way we can avoid war. We don't want the tribesmen launching their own guerrilla attacks, either." Their goal was to obtain slaves, so I doubted there'd be mass murder... But if they'd already killed any of the captives Pam told us about, then war could be inevitable.

The tribespeople in that region put their familial pride above anything else. It was doubtful they'd forgive Sandora for so brutally wounding it.

"This might be a good chance for us to learn more about Sandora... Send a message to Pam, and send a message to Sandora, too. We'll have their king and his men talk to us directly."

"We can send a messenger, but... Who? We cannot send Commander Lain... Nikola, perhaps? Or me...?"

"Nope." I shook my head toward Tsubaki's words, and then grinned broadly.

"I'll be going."

"Eh?!"

"Won't be a problem, right? I'll change my appearance and go in as Brunhild's messenger." I didn't want to send the important people of Brunhild to such a dangerous and horrid place. It was a country with nothing redeeming about it, as far as I understood. Hell, a lot of people started calling it 'kidnap country' because of how many visitors ended up going missing.

I could've sent my sisters or cousins… They definitely wouldn't die or anything… But they weren't exactly fit for negotiations. Kousuke could probably do it, but he didn't exactly look the part.

Mostly, I just wanted to find out just what the hell was going on in Sandora.

Plus, the new secret weapon that had been developed in collaboration with the research laboratory and the library was finally complete, so I had that as a backup.

If Sandora ended up speaking cruelly to my demands, then I'd ensure that the kingdom never collared anyone ever again.

I had a personal problem after Sandora infiltrated our dungeons and tried to pick away at newbie adventurers.

Sure they were independent, but Sandora was the buyer. It meant that they had information about my country, too. They probably thought they could take people covertly without dirtying their name directly.

I talked to the other world leaders and discovered that slavers in their respective territories all reported to a higher authority, one linked to Sandora on the administrative level.

The slavers were effectively employees of the state. They were government workers. They, working for Sandora, kidnapped people from other places. In my eyes, that made the country accountable.

I couldn't tell whether Sandora's king was actively in charge of all this slavery nonsense, or if he was just being manipulated by the people around him. Regardless of the situation, I felt only negative things about the nation.

I wanted to get to the bottom of it all. Depending on what I found, I was prepared to come down on them with a vengeance.

The carriage rattled through the streets of Kyuray, the Sandy Capital of Sandora. The roads weren't exactly of the best design. Luckily for us, Rosetta had designed a shock-absorbent carriage, so it wasn't as bad.

I looked out at the old, worn streets from outside the window. There were various collapsed walls around the place and sunken roofs. There were wooden huts mixed in amongst ruined houses of red mud-brick.

This was a place where the lower-classes lived. The second-class citizens.

"The people here aren't exactly cheery…"

"Are you surprised? They don't exactly lead the happiest lives." Lanz, the newbie knight who sat next to me, muttered quietly as he looked out the window.

I told Kousaka that I intended to go to Sandora and talk to the king, so he had Lanz come with me as an escort. He didn't believe I was just trying to talk it out… I found that a little unpleasant given that I typically had a non-violent policy so long as they didn't attack me first.

He actually wanted Vice-Commander Nikola to come along with me, but I didn't want someone with such a high status coming along on a mission like this, so Lanz was a good fit.

There were four other soldiers with us aside from him, but they were in another carriage following behind us.

I wanted to immediately shoot off to Sandora by using [Fly] or something like that, but right now I wasn't being Mochizuki Touya, I was being an envoy from Brunhild on behalf of the united tribes of The Sea of Trees. I did end up using a [Gate] to get to the outskirts, though.

When Pam handed over the written list of demands, she had a fierce expression on her face. She didn't even have to say it, but I knew she wanted me to smack the king hard in the face if I actually got to meet him.

Her tribe and the other tribes of The Sea of Trees would go to war with the Kingdom of Sandora if we weren't careful, so it remained to be seen if I'd actually do any punching. She wanted to come with us, but couldn't due to her status in keeping the tribes tentatively at peace.

"There are about as many slaves as I expected. Many of them look malnourished, too... It seems you were right, Your Highness. They're not being fed well at all. That being said... the fighting slaves do look like they've been eating well."

"That's because they're fighters, Lanz. You can't have someone fight on an empty stomach, or they'll just be meat shields." I saw slaves dotted around as we passed by, which meant that even second-class citizens could own them. There were strong-looking slaves standing by the entrances of stores, likely keeping guard for their shopkeep masters.

There were beastmen and other demi-humans amongst the slaves, too. They'd likely been brought to Sandora from other parts of the world. The ones I saw wore crude, ragged clothing, and their arms and legs were fully exposed.

"Oh, that's another thing. You can't address me as if I'm the grand duke, Lanz. I don't want anyone overhearing you, or you could blow our cover."

"A-Ah... Please forgive me. What... What should I call you instead?" Lanz looked at me with a mortified expression, and I realized I hadn't given much thought to my fake name. *Hmm...*

"How about Dolan? That's Micah's dad's name, right? You should have met him by now."

"Wh— Ah! Y-Your Highness...! M-Miss Micah and I a-aren't like that, I assure you!"

Lanz squirmed in place as his cheeks reddened. *You fool... You fool! I know all about your visits to the Silver Moon! You can't stop my all-seeing gaze! Or er... Karen's all-seeing gaze!*

I decided to stop teasing him, though. I'd thought of a name idea.

"Robin Hood... Or, er, no. Robin Loxley. That'll do."

"Robin... Loxley? Then I should call you Ambassador Loxley, sir?"

"Yep. I'm not really good at using bows, though."

"Hm?" I was wearing light green clothes, so the name just sprang to mind.

I hadn't changed my whole body using [**Mirage**] this time. All I'd done was change my hairstyle, my eye color, and my hair color. That was enough to trick anyone who'd only seen me at a glance. I didn't really expect there to be anyone in Sandora that knew me well enough anyway.

The coach went on through the second-class district, and finally reached the gates to the first.

A couple of armor-clad soldiers suddenly walked over and blocked our path with crossed blades.

"Identify yourselves! This area of the city is for authorized individuals only!"

"Goodness me… We're an envoy from the Duchy of Brunhild. Did you not receive a notice about our arrival in advance?"

"Brunhild…? Tsk… Wait there and shut up. We'll ask our superiors." The soldier peeked through the window, sneered at us, and grumbled off into the gates.

"To act so rudely to a foreign envoy… Just what kind of training did they have? If this were Lestia, he'd have been stripped of his rank immediately."

"Sandora doesn't really do foreign relations, so these crappy manners are probably just a result of inexperience." I still got a little annoyed, though. Sometimes you have to do a little extra work as part of the job, no reason to get upset about it.

They kept us waiting for a while, but we were finally allowed inside.

"Go on. But don't you dare cause a fuss." He was still being rude despite confirming who I was. I got the feeling he didn't think too highly of us. Sandora was geographically isolated, which meant it had pretty much been free of outside invasions in the past… It was possible that he was simply smug and satisfied knowing that outsiders could do nothing in his nation, but it could also just be the fault of his upbringing. He didn't know any other way, after all.

The coach started to move again, and I was immediately surprised by how smooth the roads were compared to the ones we'd been on before. The second-class road was bumpy, coarse, and uneven. This one was smooth, flat, and perfectly maintained. The houses around were all pristine and white, too. Everyone in this district looked extremely gaudy and well fed, as they walked around with their slaves.

The slaves in this area looked extremely well-dressed as well, but their faces were just as miserable as the faces I'd seen in the second-class district.

"I'd heard living conditions between the classes of Sandora were stark in contrast, but this... this is extreme..." Lanz shook his head in disbelief as he looked outside. There was an absolute world of difference in terms of quality of life.

The end of the road took us to a magnificent castle, constructed of smoothed-out stone. It was largely an angular, square castle, with four cylindrical towers that rose up out of the ramparts; it certainly inspired awe and majesty.

However, I also knew that this castle was also the product of slavery.

We arrived at the gates and were let through with little issue at all. Seemed like the news had already gotten this far in, but we were still met by the same disdainful scowl from the gatekeepers.

We were let out of our carriage before meeting up with a grumpy-looking robed man who came out of the castle. He was clearly not happy to see us. We followed after him into the gaudy halls of the castle.

Lanz and I had all our weapons stripped after a thorough search. They were exercising caution, but that wasn't unreasonable. We were meeting with their king, after all.

We were brought into the meeting hall and forced to kneel down. There were other men in the vicinity, generals and retainers. Naturally, they were accompanied by their warrior slaves. There were a lot of them, too. They wouldn't go down with just a couple of weapons, so I wondered why they even bothered stripping us. Then again, it was better to be safe than sorry.

"So... this is the envoy sent by Brunhild? I've heard it said that he carries with him a request from the tribes in the Sea of Trees. My, my... What an interesting situation." A bald man wearing a red-and-black robe spoke up in a sardonic tone. He seemed to be the country's prime minister.

In the middle of the room sat a plump little man, smoking a long pipe. He looked like he was dozing off on his glimmering throne, half-lidded eyes surveying me lazily. At a glance, he honestly resembled a pigman orc, the kind of fat monster you'd see in certain anime.

Next to the throne sat a girl wearing a Submission Collar. She wore clothing so thin she might as well have been completely nude. She was kneeling by his side, her body completely still. I realized she was holding up an ashtray.

The pigman was wearing a golden crown, which meant that he was the king, Abdul Djerba Sandora III. He certainly didn't look like a good guy. Though I was trying not to judge people at a glance. It was entirely possible that this disgusting, crude-looking man was completely fine, and not at all like the several disgusting, crude-looking villains I'd taken out in the past.

His throne was accentuated by a beautiful golden armor on one side, and a gaudy golden blade on the other. The sword had way too many gemstones encrusted into it, but I got the feeling that it might actually be usable. As for the armor... I didn't think the pigman would be able to use it at all... He was the wrong size entirely.

I looked directly at the King of Sandora, careful not to say any of the rude things I was thinking.

"My name is Robin Loxley, my liege. I am here today on behalf of the Sea of Trees, to request that you release the tribespeople captured from—"

"Denied." He completely cut me off mid-sentence, using his chubby fingers to flick ash from his long pipe. Then, he made his slave girl refill the leaves and light his pipe back up. Then he began smoking again without a care in the world.

He ran his fat, greasy palm over the slave girl's cheek, licking his lips in a disgusting manner as a grin crept over his face. He continued this motion, but then began to speak, tracing her skin inappropriately without even looking at us.

"We don't have enough slaves yet. Why would we return the few we caught?"

"...Then you expressly launched an assault on The Sea of Tress with the intention of capturing the people there as slaves?"

"Is that a problem? You have no authority over us, little man. Brunhild is a little country, it is barely even worth a second thought. You would do well to mind your own manners." The king of Sandora turned his face in my direction, grinning madly as he spat out vitriol.

That was all the proof I needed. The country itself was responsible for the cruelty of the slavers.

"...Then you wish to wage war in the Sea of Trees?"

"War? What part of this is war? This is fun. It is sport. They're just a small gathering of tribal savages. Do you think my Magic Beast Knights would fall to creatures like them?"

"The reigning tribe of the region has a friendly relationship with Brunhild. Do you wish to wage war on us as well?" The king's brow twitched slightly, he stopped caressing the slave and leaned forward in his chair.

211

"Don't speak so confidently, boy. Your little grand duke seems to have a big head, but we won't buckle so easily. Those giant warriors of yours mean nothing to us, you hear? You had best not rouse the sleeping serpent, understand? Sandora is no country that will lay back, chest heaving as you violate it. There are many superb assassins in our service, understand? Should I wish it, the grand duke's head will roll around on the ground, and I will kick it like a ball." Everyone in the vicinity laughed heartily at his words. These guys were really hopeless…

Everyone in this court was rotten to the core. They clearly never had any benign intentions to begin with. I honestly envied their ignorant self-confidence. They clearly had no idea what was going on in the outside world.

The king of Sandora snapped his fingers, and all the slaves in the vicinity drew their weapons.

Lanz and I stood up, and the guardsmen that brought us in also drew their weapons.

"Just what is the meaning of this?"

"Hm? As far as I know, no envoy ever came to Sandora. We don't have enough slaves after Astal was destroyed, understand? We can get uninitiated slaves from other nations, and train them hard for about a month. We'll take you, and simply claim you never arrived. We have the best trainers available, after all. We'll break everyone under us." I stared, dumbfounded, at the obnoxious laughing king. I couldn't believe what I was seeing here, or how readily he was admitting it.

So they really had been kidnapping people from other nations. It was exactly as the other world leaders had told me. This country was messed up, and it was my mistake to even expect anything from them…

I hadn't lost my temper or anything, but no way in hell was I going to keep treating someone like this with respect. I decided that their behavior meant I really had no reason to hold back.

I was a bit annoyed, since I just came to Sandora for information and didn't really expect this kind of treatment.

"...You really are a dumbass."

"Huh?!" I used [Storage] to produce a finely-crafted armchair that matched the king of Sandora's throne in terms of quality. Then, I parked my ass on it and crossed one of my legs over the other, then I rested both arms on the rests.

"I said, you really are a dumbass. You know? What a joke. Alright, everyone. Guess it's a war, huh? Let's wrap it up, then. If they want a fight, we can give them a fight."

"You bastard... Don't you understand your situation?" The king stood up and glared down at me.

Heheh... Getting angry, lardass? Your face is all red.

"I have a full grasp of the situation, buddy. I have a full grasp of you, and your country. I can see a dumbass king and his dumbass advisers. The fish in the sea know not the land, get it? There's a whole world that you bubble-living idiots are clearly unaware of."

"Kill them!"

"Not even gonna listen to me talk? Wow." The warrior slaves charged toward us, but were hastily stopped by an invisible barrier. Obviously, I'd erected a [Shield] in advance. Idiots.

"Wh—?! You wretch, Robin! Just who are you?!"

"That's just an alias, friendo. You can call me Mochizuki Touya, grand duke of Brunhild. Nice to meet you, lard— Uh... Lord Abdul of Sandora. Now, what was that you were saying about taking my head?" I dispelled my [Mirage], reverting my hairstyle, hair color, and eye color. There was no need to hide it after they tried to kill us.

"Wh— Th— What?! Grand Duke?! Impossible, why would... Why would a world leader venture this far...?!"

"I started out as an adventurer, you know? I'm the type of guy who likes to roam around. You could take a leaf out of my book, fatty." The pigman king started grinding his teeth together as his brow furrowed. The pipe in his mouth almost snapped. The warrior slaves looked at him, then me, then slowly started backing off.

"Idiots! If he's really the grand duke, then this is a prime chance! Bring me his head!" The warrior slaves and his soldiers came at me again, only to be repelled by my defensive spell.

"Tsk... Then how about this?!" A mage in the backline attempted to channel a **[Fire Arrow]** spell at me, after wisely noting that physical attacks were ineffective.

"[Reflection]." I nonchalantly bounced it back at him. The Fire spell hit both the mage and two retainers at his side, taking them out for the count.

"You'd attack me even after knowing who I am? Then, this really is a declaration of war, eh?"

"Idiot. Once we kill you here, we'll cover it up and do what we want!" The king of Sandora started jeering at me. He was a complete moron. All I had to do was summon a **[Gate]** and I could be gone before another roll of belly fat jiggled on his wobbly gut. I wasn't going to, though.

"I'll ask you once more. Is this a declaration of war?"

"My magnificent country has both war slaves and the magical beast knights! They are my magnificent soldiers, who will fight to their last breath! With Sandora as your enemy, you'll never recover! Never!"

Christ... This guy really is a moron.

"Sorry, but Brunhild has no need to make Sandora its enemy. I'll just take care of you, instead."

"Excuse me?" He glared at me in confusion.

I leaned back in my chair and waved my hand in his general direction.

"**[Apport].**" A Submission Collar appeared in my hand all of a sudden. The slave girl, who was now hiding behind the throne, suddenly brought her hands up to her neck in disbelief. I was holding the collar she was just wearing. The king looked as if he couldn't believe his eyes.

"What?!"

"These Submission Collars... I've done my research. I see that they read the magic wavelength of a high authority and respond to it. In other words, all the Submission Collars are tuned to your magical wavelength, right?" I calmly explained the situation as the warrior slaves tried to break the barrier again. I was staring the king down directly as I spoke.

It was pretty obvious, in the end. The slaves obeyed their masters, but if someone gathered a large number of slaves, they could've always tried to stage a coup or a revolution.

That was why the king of Sandora had the contingency plan in place. His magical wavelength was in all of the Submission Collars, allowing him to control anyone wearing them.

He probably did this through use of a magical artifact that was handed down the Sandora royal family, or something.

After all, if the power couldn't be inherited, then the new ruler of the country couldn't rule over the slaves when the old king died. It couldn't just be blood-related, either, or else anyone with royal lineage would have control.

What it amounted to was an ability composed of two parts. An artifact that allowed someone to exercise control, and a biorhythmic wavelength that belonged to the royal family.

"In other words, you're the slave master that rules over this country. Right?"

"...Correct. What of it? On my command, all the lowly slaves in this nation will bare their fangs and rip you to shreds. Surrender now, and I may yet let you live." The ability was definitely terrifying. It was a good thing that the mass production of the Submission Collars was only a recent development, or it could've ended with him having control of many people all over the world.

People would enslave other people for profit, without realizing that they were simply adding more numbers to the king of Sandora's army. A new world order, composed entirely of slaves... That was likely his lazy plan the entire time.

But I wasn't going to allow it.

"So what happens when your control gets overridden, hm?"

"Excuse me?" I'd been fiddling with my smartphone for a bit, targeting every collared person in Sandora with the **[Multiple]** spell. There were so many that it took a long time to sort out, but my preparations were finally complete. I had no reason to waste any more time with his words.

"**[Cracking]**."

The Null spell known as **[Cracking]** was a spell that completely overwrote elements related to artifacts and their primary configurations.

For example, think of someone that had an artifact that looked like a bathroom faucet. If they turned the handle, water came out by magical means. I could use this spell to either prevent the flow of water entirely, cause a massive gush of water to come out of the faucet, or just make it a miserable trickle.

It was a magic that I discovered in Babylon's library. If I used it in conjunction with my [**Analyze**] spell, I could easily pinpoint the exact functions of an object, and modify them to my will.

This did, however, exclude things I couldn't comprehend due to lack of knowledge. I had to take care not to tweak anything unnecessarily complex, lest I cause a major issue.

Even the Submission Collar was a bit much for me. I couldn't nullify the effects it had like absolute obedience, or forcing people to move.

What I did manage to do, though, was delete the magical wavelength and replace it with my own. I'd experimented using the collars I'd gotten from the slavers back when they were on my island.

In layman's terms, I changed the owner of all the slaves in Sandora.

More specifically, I transferred ownership of all the slaves in Sandora from the king... to me. Which meant...

"What are you fools doing?! Off with his head!" The battle slaves turned their blades to me on his order, and then stopped in their tracks. They suddenly glanced at one another, somewhat confused.

That was only natural. They weren't moving by force, after all. Their lurch toward me was just their own muscle memory reflex. They realized they didn't have to do it at all.

"Come on! Cut them to ribbons!" The king of Sandora started screaming and shouting at them, snarling even. But the slaves didn't respond at all. They merely brought their hands up to their necks, as if to check for their collars. They were still there, but they no longer restrained them.

"What... What is this...?"

"Filthy pissants! Obey me!" The retainers in the area also began looking around uneasily.

"They won't obey you, fatty. Slaves with those Submission Collars won't accept orders from anyone other than the one designated as their master. And, as of a few moments ago, that master is me."

"N-Nonsense!"

"About two-thirds of Sandora's population are slaves, right? That means I have control of the oppressed majority. Do you want me to put it into simpler terms, you idiot? I own your country now."

"Wh... What...?!" The king of Sandora sat there, stupefied. But then he began attempting to channel magical power into a golden bracelet on his wrist. I got the feeling that the bracelet was the artifact he used to register ownership.

It would be no use for him, though. Try as he might, I was the one with all the control. His orders would reach slaves further away, but I saw no reason to tell him that.

"Nonsense...! The Slave King's Bangle can access every Submission Collar in the world! I-It can't be overwritten... U-Unless... Unless you're part of my family line...?"

"Don't be so damn disgusting, you bastard." The thought of being related to this slimy lardass sent shivers up my spine. No way in hell would I be related to a pigman like this.

The warrior slaves glanced between me and the king, seemingly unable to grasp their situation.

"Now, slave ladies and slave gentlemen. I won't be giving you any orders today. I promise to release all of you from your captive bonds, provided you aren't criminals. If you were brought from outside of Sandora, you'll also be free to return to your homes." I stood up from my chair and addressed the armed men around me. They'd already dropped their weapons. Some of them were crying.

"W-We… We're really free…?"

"I promise you, yes. You're really free. I won't let this nation keep you bound anymore." I spoke to the slaves around me with an understanding smile on my face. One by one, they began to murmur amongst themselves. Pretty much all of them were crying at this point.

"F-Freedom… a-at last…?"

"We're slaves no more…"

"…A-A normal life… for all of us…?"

"Back to my home… to my family…"

The trembling men began to wipe at their eyes. They probably had a massive buildup of emotions welling inside them.

"My slaves… No… How…?!"

"**[Apport].**"

"Huh?" The gaudy ornament on the Sandora king's wrist suddenly vanished and found its way into my hand.

Nice, got me a Slave King's Bangle.

"G-Give me that back!"

"Nope, you don't need it anymore." I grinned at the wobbling bastard as I dropped it to the ground and sliced it to bits.

It fell into two clean pieces. The slaves didn't need to obey the bearer of it anymore. It was true that there were still many slaves with individual owners out there, but I planned on releasing them one by one anyway.

"You wretch! How could you?! Who gave you the right to come in here and judge my culture! Who gave you the right to impose your morality upon my people!"

"Look who's talking, pig. Who gave you the right to impose your slavery upon the people of this land, and others' lands?"

"Ughgh…!" The slaves around me suddenly turned their attention to the king, and the tears in their eyes gave way to unbridled fury. Their lives were stolen away, their dignity as people were robbed from them. Their anger was a natural outcome.

At the same time, a large amount of noise came from the outside. I heard the roaring of wild animals, and a series of thuds as various things fell to the ground. It was about time for that to begin.

"What was that… What's that sound?!" The retainers flew into a panic, unable to understand what was going on. The robe-clad man who had brought us to the room charged in through the door, clearly in a panic.

"Your brilliance, it's awful! The magical beasts under the control of our knights have gone on a rampage! They're not obeying at all!"

"Wh-What did you say?!" That was only obvious, too. Enslaved people would still have their wits about them. They had their collars around their necks so they'd still know to be cautious. Animals were a different matter entirely. They were released, so they were just doing what was instinctive. It made me wonder if they could ever be tamed in a non-forcible way.

"Didn't I tell you? The Submission Collars are mine now. They only obey me, and I've given no command."

"Hgngh…!" I did issue one silent command, though. I told the creatures not to harm anyone, and to get out of the city. Nobody else knew that, hence the frenzied panic.

"You bastard… You… You bastard! Silence, silence damn you!"

"I asked you over and over, didn't I? I asked you if you wanted to start a war. I'm a pacifist, but that doesn't make me foolish or naive. If you hit me, I will hit back. You declared war on us, fatso. When will you learn? When will you learn that your actions have consequences?"

"Shut up, shut up, shut up!" The king of Sandora glared at me, fire in his eyes. All I had to do now was arrest him and find out where the collars were being made.

I took a step forward to begin doing that, when… The slave girl, who had still been hiding behind the throne, unsheathed the gaudy blade by its side and drove it deep into the side of the fat man's neck.

"Whhh…" I heard a squelch, and then a stupid sounding wheeze. And then, I watched a fat pigman-like head soar through the air in an arc.

I blinked and it had happened, it was all over in a few seconds. I could've perhaps intervened with [Teleport], but I barely had a chance to register what she was doing. Even at the last moment, my body refused to move. I didn't have any will to save him. In the end, I might have just allowed him to die.

I shrugged my shoulders slightly and watched as his head flew over and landed by my feet.

"Augh, gross!" I reflexively kicked the head away from me.

Ah, crap! I didn't mean to disrespect the dead or anything, it was just a gross head! I was surprised! Anyone that gets a head thrown at them would be surprised, right?! The flying head rolled to a slow bounce and hopped on the ground, landing by the prime minister.

"Eeek!" He was overcome by horror and collapsed on the spot. The king's body then slumped forward as blood gushed from its neck stump.

A whole body's worth of blood made a glopping sound as it flowed out of the king's neck.

I was just looking down at my shoes, which were now completely ruined by the sticky red liquid coating them.

Aw maaan... I didn't even get to use [**Slip**]*...* This time the guy I would've used it on ended up dying without me doing anything. I wanted to hit him at least once, but I figured a kick on his severed head was good enough as a middle ground.

"Alright, now that's over with... [**Paralyze**]."

"Hngh!"

"Gwaugh!" I used a paralyzing spell on the retainers and the prime minister, preventing them from moving. Then, I asked the former slaves to help me tie them up with rope.

The slave girl, who had already fallen to her knees as if exhausted, slowly turned toward me.

"...Thank you. Thank you so much... I... I finally managed to avenge my sisters..." I wondered what she meant, so I asked her. It seemed that she and her sisters were adventurers, but during a mission in Regulus they were attacked by slavers and captured.

She and her sisters were extremely beautiful, so they were brought to the king as pleasure slaves. They were brutally treated as his playthings, but both of her sisters somehow managed to upset the king. He had them slowly tortured until they mentally broke and then died. She went on to say that she had gone on living, waiting for the opportunity to take vengeance on the one responsible for something so heinous.

In the end, that man was garbage. He had many sins to atone for, and I was glad she'd been the one to stick him like a pig.

I didn't know what to do with her, though. From an objective standpoint, she was a criminal who had murdered her monarch. But the monarch was an enemy, and frankly, from Brunhild's perspective, she was probably a hero.

I figured there'd probably be no issue if we had her emigrate to Brunhild. Ultimately, what had happened was that a war had broken out between Brunhild and Sandora. Within fifteen minutes, Sandora's war potential was massively reduced, and then the king of Sandora was killed in action, kind of... Then, the war ended. That was it.

That was what would have basically happened if a formal war was declared, so it was close enough to me.

They started the fight, anyway... I wasn't really looking forward to explaining that to Kousaka, though.

I just decided not to do that for the time being. That was the best thing for it. Yep, you couldn't convince me otherwise. The best way to deal with problems you don't want to address was to just bury them down.

I removed the prime minister's paralysis and had him guide me to the place where the Submission Collars were created.

It was located beneath one of the spires on the western side of the castle.

The country produced the collars, which were then sold to the slavers, bandits then captured people for the slavers, and the slavers bought them as slaves. The enslaved people were then brought back to Sandora and sold to the citizens... A horrid cycle indeed.

There were a lot of slaves at work in the facility, but that work had since stopped.

An artifact that vaguely resembled a microwave sat at the center of the facility. Apparently, by feeding regular collars into it, the configuration of the device enchanted it with the properties that made them into Submission Collars.

Next to this one sat two artifacts that looked similar. They looked a lot newer. Apparently, they were exact replicas that had only been recently created. The replicas were the result of decades of research into the original one.

The mages that created it were apparently incredible magitechnicians from Felsen, who were promptly enslaved in a tactical operation and whisked away to Sandora.

They all died due to the severe exhaustion brought on by hours of constant research and no rest. And because of that, nobody left alive could replicate the device. From what I heard, Sandora planned on doing another raiding run into Felsen, but that wasn't happening now.

"With this, the well should be cut off at the source." I used [Gravity] on all three devices, crushing them under their own weight and destroying them entirely.

With that, no more Submission Collars could ever be created again. That wasn't actually true, as both I and Doctor Babylon could use [Analyze] to reconstruct them, but we weren't going to do that.

Now all that was left was the freeing of the slaves. The only issue was there'd probably be a rebellion all across Sandora if I did that. The formerly oppressed would be free to get their revenge. That being said, they could still be forced into indentured servitude if they committed a severe crime, so part of me hoped that they'd be a little more rational.

I didn't want to free the slaves who had been enslaved for committing crimes in the first place. It was better to leave them as they were in order to set an example. I didn't know how many there were, though.

Sandora was largely desert, so thankfully it didn't have a massive population…

I wondered just how many days I'd end up spending on carting slaves back and forth.

"Guess there's nothing for it… Gonna need to ask the alliance for help." I didn't really want to deal with Sandora any longer, but a war was a war no matter how small. I would make the government cough up and pay for their deeds. At the very least, they'd pay reparations to the people they enslaved.

If the country collapsed as a result, then that wasn't my concern. They were free to rebuild Sandora again, just without slaves.

They'd have to do it all themselves, though. No more free labor. Well, except for criminal slaves. I figured they could still use those.

I wondered if it'd be another Yulong situation where a bunch of self-proclaimed rulers ended up appearing. I wondered if it'd break into city-states or just be a bunch of people vying for full control.

I doubted it'd happen, though. Anyone with any kind of claim like that had relied on slaves all their lives. They wouldn't know hard work if it slapped them in the face. I was fairly sure that Sandora was on the path to extinction… That did make me wonder, though… If the king of Sandora had kids or not.

It had nothing to do with me, either way. The country lost its grip over slaves, so I wondered if anyone left around would even respect a birthright claim at this point.

I was a little bummed out, since ultimately I ended up doing what the other world leaders wanted me to do. I didn't intend to crush Sandora at all, I just didn't expect the king to be this much of a dumbass. I'd have had a better job of negotiating with a chimp, seriously.

Man… War… War never changes…

Several days had passed since the Sandora situation, and I'd just about dealt with the aftermath.

I gathered all the slaves in the capital, criminals aside, and gave each of them a sum of money from Sandora's treasury. Then, I sent all those with a place to return to through individual [**Gate**] destinations. I used my magic to look into the memories of those from places I'd never been to before. I readily informed members of the alliance so that they'd be prepared for an influx of people returning home.

I also returned the people from the Sea of Trees back to Pam. I made sure not to miss any of them.

"Form an orderly line, please. From here to here." Before sending them through the portals, I used the secret weapon that Doctor Babylon had developed along with Tica in the research laboratory. It was capable of de-powering their collars around their neck.

Tica brought an object that resembled a syringe without a needle and zapped the collars with it, one by one. It was an artifact we called the Initializer.

In short, it was an artifact that eliminated magic effects from anything it was used on.

After that, I used [**Apport**] to pull the collars off safely. [**Apport**] was a magic I could use to call any item in my sight into my hands. It was limited to items the size of a softball, but collars were the right size for that. I didn't really mind, even though it was a little time-consuming.

The Initializer was a pretty terrifying artifact in terms of strength. Artifacts from the old days were incredible, and we could even make amazing ones now. The Frame Gears were just big devices in comparison to the complex tools that could be developed.

To be more specific, the Initializer was a magical device that overwrote any magical device with a command of "do nothing," so to speak. Obviously, I was the one who had to charge it up, too. It'd take a full year for an ordinary mage to charge this device up. It was basically that extreme in terms of effect and power necessity. The Babylon Gynoids all helped with disabling the collars, and then the slaves went through the portals back home.

There were many people who didn't want to give up their slaves, but we had our knights suppress them, arrest them, and throw them into the very cages they had their slaves live in. I thought perhaps some of that treatment would make them think a bit about their attitudes.

We even had some people who didn't want to be liberated from slavery, but those people were few and far between. Some of them seemed to be fine with the lives they had, and the people they served, so... even if it was weird, I didn't want to judge that. I did make sure to confirm they weren't being forced to say anything against their wills, though.

We disabled their collars just in case, however. Didn't want to leave any stragglers. Everything after that depended on their feelings. If a person legitimately wanted to live in servitude... It was a weird lifestyle choice, but not one I felt like shaming.

Several days after liberating the capital city, we continued making our efforts in other Sandora settlements.

A lot of the people who ruled over those towns ended up resisting us, but they typically relented after we surrounded their settlements with a few Frame Gears.

We ended up spreading the rumor that the king of Sandora declared war on Brunhild and promptly lost his head, which wasn't technically incorrect. We simply threatened anyone who resisted with the same fate as their king.

I didn't really want to threaten people like that, but it helped smooth things over as far as freeing the slaves went.

The slave girl that decapitated the king of Sandora didn't have a home to return to, so I asked her to come to Brunhild. She was a former adventurer, so she'd fit in just fine.

People who had no places to return to were given their choice of nations to live in. Some people went off to new lands, while others said they'd prefer to remain in Sandora.

There were some who wanted to come to Brunhild, and I invited them with open arms. There was still land to tame and other jobs that needed to be filled, so they'd be able to scrape by just fine.

Kousaka ended up chewing me out big-time for what happened, but the influx of immigration was an unexpected boon in terms of new labor forces. He didn't say a word about that, though... He told me I should've squeezed more reparation money out of Sandora, but that was my mistake.

All in all, it took over a month to settle all affairs in Sandora. A lot of the Sandoran government associates attempted to hide their slaves from us, some even pretending to help us in the search. They were mostly slave traders, and we sorted them out with little issue.

The slave traders were stripped of their property and, ironically, enslaved themselves for their crimes. They'd been going from country to country, hurting people and taking people, so it was only natural they'd get their just desserts. We decided they'd work in the mines for the rest of their lives. I was the one with the authority over their collars, too.

There were... more proper slave traders, I guess if you could call them that. They didn't dirty their hands by raiding other nations, and they operated within Sandoran law at the time. I overlooked their crimes, but I was still on the fence about whether or not to make them do some forced labor in the mines.

To be honest, I wouldn't have been surprised if the liberated slaves went back to Sandora in order to exact revenge on their oppressors.

I wasn't about to stop them, either. Vengeance was a personal choice at the end of the day. If they had the resolve to be killed, arrested, or enslaved again, then I believed they should just go for it. I did kind of hope they wouldn't be hasty, though. They'd just gotten their freedom, after all.

It was also possible that some of the criminal slaves had been imprisoned on false charges, so I decided to give them all individual polygraph tests to determine whether or not they were innocent. I did try asking them all as a crowd to raise their hands if they were innocent, but they all ended up raising their hands shamelessly.

There were many crimes that one could be arrested for in Sandora, but I wasn't really in a position to judge. Honestly, it was kind of a complicated situation, judging all their lives and the circumstances that might have forced them into leading a life of crime.

In the end, I asked Yumina to use her Mystic Eye to determine the innocent from their personalities.

I didn't really have to go that far, but I wanted to obliterate slavery as much as was reasonably possible.

Frankly, I wanted to eliminate slavery being used as punishment, too... But that'd take more work down the line.

Still, what mattered was that my hard work was finally over. I was basically done, and I could finally head home. In all honesty, I was almost a slave... A slave to work!

Freedom, sweet freedom...!

"Sweet freedom... Wasn't I supposed to be done with this crap?" It seemed that I had celebrated too soon.

Alas, I was standing in the Sandora royal castle once more, sighing to myself.

I was looking over at a man sitting on the throne. It was the king of Sandora, Abdul Djerba Sandora III. Or rather, the former king.

"Guhuhuhu... Wretched Grand Duke... I see you've come again! Ohoho!"

"Geez..." His rotten, severed head started chatting to me. The pigman king sat atop his gaudy throne, head literally in his hands. His entire body looked pale, and his once-beautiful clothes were all worn and dirty.

Basically, he was a Zombie. He was buried in a Sandoran graveyard, and apparently he just up and rose right out of it. I thought maybe it was the work of the wicked god, but no. He seriously just came back as a Zombie. He just straight-up had so much of an attachment to the material world that he rose right up out of the dead.

The Zombie king attacked the prime minister first and turned him into one as well. As is the typical rule, those bitten by a Zombie would typically rise as a Zombie themselves.

Apparently, the Zombies started multiplying like rabbits after that. We were just so busy dealing with the slaves in the other settlements that none of us noticed the capital city becoming a Zombie settlement.

The king wasn't the only one here. There was a line of Zombie generals and Zombie retainers, too. They all stood there, staring at me with vacant eyes. Their mouths drooped open.

Gross, gross... Something's coming outta your mouths...

"Guhuhuhu... I have a new power... I have new slaves... I'll enslave you too...! Oink, oink, squeee!"

Did he seriously just oink? He's transitioned entirely into a Pigman Orc, holy crap.

I sighed slightly as three men and one... What looked like a woman... appeared from behind the throne. They all had pig-like faces.

"Oink, oink... Father's goal is our goal! Father's grudges are our grudges!"

"Snort, snort... Let's eat him!"

"B-B-Brains... L-L-Let me e-eat b-braiiiiiins..."

"Oink, oiiink! Let's kill him...!"

Goddamn. Pigmen princes and a princess, huh...? He seriously zombified his own kids? They're the spitting image of him... Were they ever even human to begin with? Well, whatever. They're Zombies now.

"Oink, oink, oiiink! See, fool? How can you defeat us now? We're immortal! We'll use this new power to enslave those foolish runaways!"

You're really saying that again? Well, as the saying goes... Once a fool, always a fool. I guess even death can't cure stupidity. I can see that pretty clearly in front of me.

"I guess I'll have to put you down for good, huh."

"Silence! Kill him, Zombies!" I sliced at one of the Zombie generals with Brunhild, severing his arm, but he just came charging at me again. Then, I shrugged, realizing I didn't need to hold back. Zombies were rotten... Though, these people were rotten even when they were alive.

"Oink oink oiiink! Fool! We have immortal bodies! Bodies that know no pain! Any attack you launch at us is futi—"

"Come forth, Light! Soothing Comfort: [Cure Heal]."

"Hnghuh! O-Ow! I-I-It hurts! I-It burns!"

"Looks like you were wrong."

Damn, that really worked. Nice. The Zombie general started screaming and writhing in pain after I cast Healing magic on him. For the undead, restoration magic was a natural ward.

I took a small bottle out of [**Storage**] and sprinkled it over the Zombie. It was the perfect finishing move.

"Auuugh! My body! I'm melting! I'm meeelting! What was that?!"

"Holy water, duh. I boiled the hell out of it."

"H— Ugaaah!" The Zombie general writhed in pain as he melted and vanished into nothingness.

Pass on in peace... Man, the holy water from Ramissh is some crazy strong stuff... Crazy strong...

"Bastard... Where did you get that?!"

"Huh? Are you stupid? I heard I'd be fighting Zombies, why wouldn't I bring holy stuff? Also, I'm adept at purifying magic."

"Wh-What'd you say?! Gwaugh!" The pigman rose from his throne and tried to run away. The other Zombies ran after him, too. They were surprisingly fast, given their state...

"[Slip]."

"Hngh?!" Their feet all gave way below them, and the Zombies went tumbling down. Blood, guts, and gore splattered everywhere as their rotting bodies burst open on impact. Zombies couldn't regenerate, but they could go on living for as long as their brains weren't destroyed.

"Alright, enough of this crap. **Come forth, Light! Shining Exile: [Banish]!**" The Zombie retainers standing by turned to particles of light and vanished. They were done.

"Gyaaah!"

"I don't wanna die agaiiin! Guyahaaah!"

"I'm meltiiing!" They all screamed out in agony as they vanished. The only ones left were the pigman king and his family.

The princes and princess all left their father's side and shambled over to me. They leaped up into the air before crumpling down at my feet in a haphazard bow. I'd never seen a jump turn into a bow before... It was kind of gross because they broke their legs on impact.

"O-Oink! We were only following orders!"

"We're not even his real children, honest!"

"P-P-P-Promise!"

"Just forget you saw us...!"

"Y-You brats! How dare you disregard your father!" The pig king screamed, his head rolling around on the ground. The four of them looked back at him and tilted their heads.

"Oink... Who were you again?"

"You little shiiiiiits!" The pigman clenched his teeth to the point where I thought his blood vessels would explode. I took advantage of the situation and poured a bucket of holy water over the heads of those little oinkers.

"Gyaaaaaauuugh!!!" The four piglets screamed as smoke rose from their bodies and they vanished into nothingness. The pigman king looked on, his expression of fury transforming into a full-fledged grin.

"Oinkahahaha! Serves you right, traitors! Little shits!"

You and your whole damn family are disgusting... There's no way the slaves you've all killed could rest in peace while you're still chattering.

"Strike true, Light! Sparkling Holy Lance: [Shining Javelin]!" I fired a lance of light into the king's chest. His entire body caught fire and burned away to ashes in a matter of seconds.

"M-My bodyyy!" He squealed in shock as his rolling head looked at what was going on. I was tired of his nonsense, so I decided to put an end to it all.

I took out a tank of water from **[Storage]**. Unlike the previous containers I'd taken out, this one didn't contain holy water. It was just plain old river water.

I invoked **[Gate]** and summoned several living creatures from the Great Gau River. They appeared inside the tank. They were long and thin, around ten centimeters in length. I enchanted them with Light magic.

"What... What is that thing?"

"Fish native to the Great Gau River. They're called the candira. They exclusively eat meat, and have a particular preference for rotten meat."

"W-Wait, then you...?"

"[Gate]." I created a portal beneath the pig of a man, and his head fell into the tank with the fish. All the fish in the tank immediately began nibbling at his face.

"Hiagaugh!! N-No! No! My e-eyes! My eyes! They're e-eating... Nghn!!!"

"Oh man, they sure are hungry..." The candira were a funny type of fish. They greatly resembled the candiru fish from my former world.

The candiru fish lived in the Amazon rainforest, and they were fierce. They were a parasitic species that burrowed inside larger fish and ate them from the inside.

They were supposedly related to catfish, but they were more deadly than piranhas. They also attacked larger creatures in groups. Humans weren't even an exception to this creature's horrific menu. They were even known as the vampire fish to some people.

I was pleased to see that the candira fish were just as horrible.

"S-Save me!"

"Hell no. If I spared you now, the people you've hurt would never forgive me. I guess if I did let you out, I'd just put you back in your grave as a head." I watched him writhe in torment as I recalled the faces of the slaves we'd recovered from the castle dungeons. Most of them were dead and bound. Tortured, and abused. Not just the men, but the women and children too.

My only regret was that he couldn't feel more than the disgusting sensation of his own death creeping toward him. In a sense, I was glad he came back. He didn't deserve a regular, clean death. I wondered if he came back to the world of the living so the dead would find peace knowing he truly regretted his deeds.

"Ohhh god! Please, please! It's horrible, m-make them stop! They're… They're burrowing, oh, oh god!" The fish had been enchanted with light, so once they entered his body they created a burning sensation. He was a Zombie, so he wouldn't suffocate. It would probably take a full day for the fish to pick the flesh from his face entirely.

"Think about the vile deeds you've done up until now. Think about it, and know nobody will ever forgive you."

"O-Oink! Auuuuuugh!" He'd die after losing part of his brain, since he was a Zombie. I was happy to wait for it to happen.

I used [Banish] on every Zombie in the capital city… except the king, and called it a day.

The royal capital, much like Astal before it, became a city of the dead. There was no way Sandora would recover. I used Earth magic to weaken the city's foundations, hoping that the sands would reclaim that cursed place.

The dead slaves might find peace now, I hope... I left the desert capital with those feelings in mind.

"...Hm?"

"What is it, Touya?" I was in Regulus with Lu, since we hadn't been there in a while. We didn't want to just head home empty-handed, so we dropped by the market on the way back. Lu said she wanted to get some fresh ingredients for dinner, too.

Gallaria was a massive city, even by western standards, and it had a little bit of everything in it. There were all kinds of foods available, including stuff I'd never seen before.

A variety of smells drifted around the bustling marketplace. One of these smells was one that I remembered quite fondly.

"That smell..."

"What smell...?" Lu tilted her head in confusion as the fragrance gently sailed in on the breeze. I wondered where it was coming from. I followed my nose around the market and finally found it. Without a doubt, it was a smell I recalled from my old world.

It wasn't too expensive, either. I picked some up, looking forward to enjoying it after dinner.

"What is this, Touya-dono...? It smells interesting, but..." Yae sat and brought the object up to her nose, and sniffed it. When I found them at the stall, they were being properly roasted and sold to customers, but it didn't smell so strongly when it was raw beans.

"Is this some kind of... nut?" Leen looked at it with a raised brow. Back on earth, the coffee bean was the seed of a plant. It was probably the same thing here. I hoped it wasn't some kind of evil plant or some kind of creature.

At any rate, it was a coffee bean. I'd found coffee. I had no idea coffee existed in this world. From what I was told, it only grew in certain areas, and it wasn't particularly popular, so not many people knew about it.

Elze shrugged slightly after looking at the bean in Yae's mouth, then took one for herself and popped it into her mouth. That was sudden.

"...It's kind of tough, and not exactly tasty..."

"You're not really meant to eat it raw..." I'd confirmed via [Search] that it wasn't poisonous, at least... Given that the vendor in Gallaria was brewing and roasting it himself, I figured that it was prepared in the same way in this world as it was in mine. It certainly wasn't the kind of bean that you just ate on its own, though.

"Sorry to keep you waiting."

"Sorry for the wait!"

"The deed is done." They were finally here.

Three of our maids, Lapis, Renne, and Cesca, brought cups of coffee into the room. I'd looked up how to properly brew coffee on the internet and shown them all.

"Oh... It smells nice."

"That kind of bean smells nice when it's roasted, yes." Yumina and Lu seemed enchanted by the scent that started drifting through the room. I personally didn't think it was that magical, but I was pleased to smell it nonetheless.

"Uhm... Touya? Is the drink supposed to be black like that, or...?" Hilde tilted her head slightly as she looked over the cup. She'd clearly never seen coffee before.

"It's a spooky black drink...."

"Smells good... Smells good..." Sue seemed curious about the drink. I had no idea why Sakura said exactly the same thing twice, though.

"This is coffee. It's a drink beloved by many people in the world I came from. You guys should try it. If it's too bitter, then you can add milk and sugar until it's better suited to your needs."

"Ah... Hm... It's... bitter?" Linze's expression seemed a little downcast as I spoke. She didn't seem very impressed, but I hoped she'd give it a go anyway.

I took in the pleasant scent as I brought the cup to my lips.

Mhm, just as I thought. Not as strong as the coffee on Earth, but quite pleasant. Oh... Maybe it is a little bitter though, we probably roasted it a bit much.

"Mm... It's been a while..." I brought down my cup with a content sigh and saw that everyone was staring at me.

Hey, c'mon! What am I, a poison tester?!

"Blegh!!!"

Everyone tried their coffee, and they all had the same response. I wasn't too surprised by their reaction. After all, if you weren't used to coffee, it was a natural response.

"Th-This must be liquid charcoal, it must…"

"Grand Duke… This drink can't be good for you… I'm sure of it…" Yae didn't seem very impressed, and Sakura cited health concerns. If I recalled correctly, it was said that the caffeine in coffee wasn't good for you.

But I also remembered hearing that it promoted fat burning because of something or other with lipids. There were a lot of fad coffee diets, too. Drinking too much was definitely unhealthy, though.

"The taste will change as you add more sugar and milk. It'll become less bitter." After I said that, everyone scrambled for the sugar and milk. It wasn't that much of a surprise, all things considered…

I couldn't drink it when I was a kid. My father always drank black coffee, so I just gradually got used to it as time went on.

I was incapable of enjoying non-black coffee at this point. Even canned coffee was a little too sugary for my tastes.

"I think I'll manage if I have sugar…"

"The milk makes it change color, interesting… I think I can enjoy it better now." Everyone seemed to take their coffee differently.

"You're amazing, Touya… To enjoy something so bitter…"

"Where I come from, coffee is considered a drink for adults. I guess I wanted to be an adult so much that I just stuck with it." I laughed a little at Hilde's bewilderment, remembering being just as amazed by adults who could drink straight black coffee when I was a kid. Still, just being able to handle it didn't necessarily make you an adult.

"Ah… That makes sense…"

"Hm, Renne? What does?" Renne nodded slightly as she held her silver serving tray across her front.

"When I tasted it in the kitchen, I couldn't enjoy it at all. But boss-lady and Missus Cesca could drink it fine. It's because they're grownups and I'm a kid, right?"

Well, I wonder... Lapis is an adult, sure... But sometimes I wonder about Cesca's sensibilities... I guess it's just a matter of taste.

"Ohoh... I am in fact an adult... Very adult. Today I drink black coffee as I wear black lace beneath my dress." My stupid idiot of a robomaid chimed in with an uncalled for comment. Hadn't she ever heard of the concept of TMI? Was she even listening? Who the hell decided that wearing black made someone more adult, anyway?

"I thought it was delicious. I've tried many deliciously bitter things in the past." I laughed quietly and nervously at Lapis' words, desperately mulling over what else she might have had.

She used to work for Belfast's intelligence agency, so I wondered if she was candidly referring to poison... It wasn't unreasonable to expect that she'd have been trained in identifying them, after all. She might have even built up an immunity.

"I'm not really sure why a drink so bitter exists... Sweet things are much better..."

"It's just a matter of taste. Also black coffee is good if you're tired, it helps keep you up. I used to drink it when I studied at night." I shrugged toward Sakura as she dumped more sugar into her cup.

You shouldn't put so much in... You're gonna have a yucky pile at the bottom at this rate...

"It reduces sleepiness, huh...? I wonder if I'll feel any effects." Elze muttered as she poured a little more milk into her coffee. The sugar and milk wouldn't actually reduce the caffeine content, so it'd probably have an effect. I should have had them drink coffee in the morning, rather than after dinner.

Well, I figured they hadn't really had too much so it'd be fine. Plus, I had no idea if the coffee beans of this world were the same as the ones from my old world.

The guy I bought them from didn't say much, and it was entirely possible that there was no sleep deprivation effect. I didn't really care, so long as it tasted the same.

I smiled gently as I melted away into a coffee-scented wonderland.

"Hey, I can't sleep! What about you?!" Elze came to my room in the middle of the night. She was grumbling.

"I mean, I'm a little sleepy, but…"

Hmph…

I wondered if this was because of the coffee, but I didn't really feel tired at all.

"You should be able to sleep if you get under your blanket and count sheep."

"There aren't any sheep in my room."

They're not real sheep…

I knew that there were different levels of tolerance to caffeine in different people, so I wondered if the effect was just stronger on Elze.

Hmm… I guess I'm calling it coffee, but it's still something from this world. I know from stuff I've been through so far that it doesn't need to follow a conventional logic or at least the kind I'm used to… I guess I shouldn't have brewed it up without researching it properly.

As I was pondering to myself, Elze moved a little closer to me. Her face was red.

W-Whoa there!

"I-It's your fault I can't sleep… s-so take responsibility until I can!" She was insanely cute. In all honesty, I could have just made her fall asleep instantly using **[Sleep Cloud],** a Dark magic spell I'd learned in the library… But the mood didn't quite feel right for that. I was a little sleepy, but I felt like staying up all of a sudden.

"So, what should we do?"

"I think I can sleep if I exhaust myself… Let's go spar at the training field."

"W-Wait just a minute! We can't just go out there in the middle of the night!"

What kind of logic was that?! That wouldn't be sleeping, it'd just be draining your batteries until you can't function anymore!

"Then what should I do?" Elze bit back with a growl in her voice. I had no idea what to say… but I gave it a go anyway.

"…Read a difficult book or something?"

"That could make me sleepy, but… it's boring, isn't it?"

That's exactly why you should do it! Boring stuff makes you fall asleep! It's why I slept through the classes I didn't enjoy.

"Nothing else…?"

"Hmm… Let me think here. Oh, wait a sec…" I picked up the smartphone from the side of my bed and started flicking through it.

"You could stretch… Listen to music… Have a hot drink…"

"Stretch?"

"Uh… You know, like moving around lightly to loosen muscle tension."

"I already did all those things. Is there nothing else?"

You even listened to music…? Oh, right… The mass-produced smartphones have mp3 players.

I wondered what there was left to do.

"Oh, wait! How about a movie? That might make me sleepy." That didn't exactly seem unreasonable to me. I'd fallen asleep watching TV several times in the past. But that was basically the same thing as reading a book when you thought about it…

Well, there wasn't really any harm in watching a movie with her. I wasn't sleepy, but I was down to do that with her.

I chose a movie from my smartphone and started casting it. It was late, so I turned the volume pretty low.

The movie started up. It was a movie adapted from a video game series back on earth, about a prince in Persia. The setting included a vast desert. It was completely different from the game's plot, though.

"Wow… This is an interesting one." Elze leaned forward toward the screen. This movie had a lot of parkour-style movement in it, and a lot of high-tension action. It made sense that it'd appeal to a fighter like her.

Thus, we ended up watching a movie together. Elze didn't get sleepy at all, she just got really engrossed in the movie. I wasn't too surprised, since it was definitely to her taste.

"That was great!" Elze spoke with excitation in her voice. Her eyes were glittering with joy. It was a lot of fun, but I wasn't as excited as she was... Probably because I was used to that kind of Hollywood stuff.

"Didn't get to sleep, huh?"

"Ah... Well, it was a lot of fun..." I had a feeling she just wanted to spend time with me. I didn't really mind, though. She could be incredibly cute at times like this. I laughed a little when I thought of her gentle face, but she seemed to misinterpret it as me mocking her.

"C'mon! I usually sleep like a log...! Linze is usually the one who doesn't sleep as well..."

"That's because Linze is girly."

"...Linze isn't the only girly person... I-I am too..."

"Ah, wait! I didn't mean it like that! I'm sorry!"

Elze stared at me with a pout. All I could do was apologize, as I didn't know what else to say.

I knew well enough that Elze was delicate and gentle. She had traits that were more traditionally masculine, but behind that was a very pleasant and gentle young woman.

"Were there ever times when you couldn't sleep so well?"

"Well, uhm... Wh-When I heard scary stories... But that was only when I was a kid, I swear!" Elze grumbled a little bit. I didn't quite believe her, but I didn't wanna tease her anymore.

I sighed quietly, then smiled over at Elze... But I suddenly heard a noise from the hallway outside.

We both noticed the sound and turned our heads toward the door.

"What... was that...?"

"I'll check it out." I left Elze's side and headed into the hall with my smartphone.

I opened the door and went into the dark. This area was private, and we didn't even have guards patrolling... The only people around here could've been my other fiancees...

There was nobody in sight. The moonlight came through the window, but that was about it. I wondered if it was a trick of the night, but then...

"Hm?"

I noticed something on the floor, illuminated by the light of the moon. There were pieces of pottery scattered across the floor. There was a little vase that had fallen from a table. It must've been the source of the noise.

Still, it was a pretty big stand, and we had placed the vases there in a way that'd make them hard to fall on their own. I wondered if someone had bumped into it and made it fall. On top of that, I found something suspicious mixed in with the debris. I picked it up and brought it close to my eye.

"Coffee beans...?" There were roasted coffee beans on the ground. I looked up and glanced along the floor. There was a trail of yet more beans along the ground. I followed the trail, and the beans continued further into the darkness of the corridor. I had no idea what was going on.

"T-Touya, wait! Come back... Where are you going?"

"Wait there, Elze. Something weird's going on." Elze tried to call me back into the room, but I couldn't ignore these beans. There could've been a robber about.

"Run search. Robber."

"Search complete. No results." It seemed like there weren't any results, but that was fair. I had no clear mental image of a thief, unless you counted a guy in white and black striped clothing with a burlap money sack over his shoulder.

I tried searching for intruders, but that got no results either. In other words, the one responsible wasn't an intruder. It had to be someone that lived in the castle. I wondered if it was Yumina or one of the other fiancees. But what would they be doing with beans in the middle of the night?

"I'm gonna check this out. Go back inside, El—"

"No way! If you're going around, I am too!" Elze scuttled out of the room and grabbed the hem of my nightshirt... She was totally scared. We followed the trail of beans down the dimly lit corridor.

On the way, we passed by a painting. I suddenly remembered we had a security system.

"Hey, Ripple?"

《...Yaaas? Oooh, hey maaaster!》

"Eeek!" A pretty girl appeared within the painting. She had a beautiful ribbon in her pink-colored hair. Elze clung to my side when she appeared.

Her name was Ripple. She was an artificial lifeform created by Doctor Babylon long ago. She currently lived in my castle as a sort of living security system.

"Do you know who broke the vase in the other hallway?"

《Nooope. My eye in your private space is gooone. I don't know who broooke it.》

That was surprising. Ripple constantly monitored us, so I was shocked she'd been disabled like that.

"Are we under attack?"

《Ouuut of the questiooon. I'd have told the security guaaards if that was the case.》 Ripple puffed out her chest with a prideful nod. She wasn't wrong, to be fair.

"C-Could it be a g-ghost..?"

"I don't think so. The castle has a [**Banish**] effect around it, so it can't be anything like that…" I realized Elze was looking nervously toward Ripple.

Damn it, Elze, she's just a painting.

Either way, someone was skulking around our castle. It was definitely not a thief, but I had to figure out who it was.

Ripple couldn't leave her frame, so Elze and I continued through the dark. I turned on my smartphone's light, but it actually kind of made the dark castle interior even spookier…

"T-T-Touya… could you cast [**Light Orb**]…?"

"I could, but it might make things a bit more complicated, you know?"

That spell created a small orb of light that radiated in all directions, it wasn't one-directional like my smartphone light. I didn't really want to confuse any patrolling knights with a mysterious orb walking around the castle. I didn't even know who I was looking for, so I didn't want to get the guards involved.

The bean trail continued onward. I wondered if there was a hole in the bag or something. Could it seriously have been a bean burglar? The bean trail carried on until a certain door, and then it stopped. That meant the thief had to be in this room. But this was an unused guest room…

Light leaked out from behind the door. I could hear a voice from within. Multiple voices…

"Mm… It's bitter, you know? Super bitter…"

"I don't really like it… Ehhh… It's not bitter, though."

"You ought to be ashamed if you can't drink this… Don't you have pride as a woman?!"

"Your metric for pride is pretty unusual… Well, I can drink it just fine either way."

"This is delicious... The fruits of the earth's soil're truly somethin' else."

"Gimme some with sake, yeah?! With sake!"

I peeked through the door and saw the goddess of alcohol acting like an idiot, then I saw the others. As usual, the god of music didn't utter a single word. He simply strummed his guitar merrily. It was late, so he was playing more quietly than usual.

The drunk idiot had a sack filled with coffee beans. It had a hole in it. The source of the trail, no doubt. They'd taken the beans straight from the kitchen, and took the makeshift coffee mill that I'd made as well. Those idiots...

"Ah... It wasn't a ghost..." Elze sighed in relief. I was sure it wasn't a thief, but I was also glad to know for certain.

"Seems like there's no harm, so let's leave them be. The little drunk broke the vase, so I'll make her help in the kitchen tomorrow." Even gods weren't free from judgment. Vases weren't free. Neither was coffee.

Coffee was valuable in this world and fairly uncommon. Still, now that I recognized it clearly, I'd be able to find the beans with my search magic.

I decided I'd get the god of agriculture to cultivate some for me.

Still, coffee needed certain environments to grow well in, so I'd need to figure that out. It was probably doable in the Babylon garden. I'd talk to Cesca or Doctor Babylon about it later on.

When I got back to the room, I heard voices coming from my room. *What the...?*

I opened up the door and found Yumina and the other girls all in their PJs.

"We can't sleep very well... It was probably that koffey drink we had at dinner..." Linze mumbled quietly, it seemed like the girls had been waking up all night. I wondered if the beans in this world had more to them than mere caffeine...

Either way, they were all up. There was nothing I could do about that.

"Let's play, let's play! I got cards!" Sue cheered merrily. She came over to stay with Yumina.

Cards...?! I mean, I guess, but...

We played board games, we goofed around and even watched another movie. However, nobody showed any signs of sleepiness. I had no idea what was going on.

In the end, I secretly cast **[Sleep Cloud]** to send everyone off to the land of rest. This world's coffee wasn't magic-resistant, at least.

I carried each and every one of them back to their rooms and tucked them gently into bed. I wondered what was up with this world's coffee... The next morning, fresh coffee was served for us all. Nobody drank any except Karen, who was remaining conspicuously quiet. Oddly enough, from the corner of my eye... I saw her give me a shit-eating grin.

Here we are at the end of another volume of In Another World With My Smartphone. That marks eleven now.

Just like volume seven, we have ourselves a short afterword. My interaction went kind of like this...

"If there's no mecha design commentary this volume, then the afterword should be three pages!"

"Tsk... Let's just make it one!"

Time to give my thanks!

To Eiji Usatsuka, thanks as usual for the illustrations.

Tomofumi Ogasawara, your Frame Gear designs just keep getting better and better. Thank you.

Thanks as always to K and everyone else in the editorial department at Hobby Japan. Thanks to everyone involved in the publication of this series!

And as always, thanks to everyone who supported my story when it was just a web novel.

Alright, everyone! I hope you have a great year.

Patora Fuyuhara

Schwertleite

Developer: High Rosetta
Maintainer: High Rosetta
Administrator: Fredmonica
Height: 17.5m   Weight: 8.2t
Primary Color: Purple

Bone Frame Designer: Regina Babylon
Affiliation: Duchy of Brunhild
Compatible Pilot: Yae Kokonoe
Maximum Capacity: 1 Person
Armaments: Crystal Odachi Katana, Crystal Kodachi Shortsword

A new special-model Frame Gear designed specifically for Yae. One of the Valkyrie Gears. This particular Frame Gear was designed for close-quarters combat.

This Frame Gear was specifically designed to make use of blades in melee range. It has an emphasis on mobility, with a focus on offensive output rather than defensive potential. Its armor has been bolstered by Phrasium material.

Siegrune

Developer: High Rosetta
Maintainer: High Rosetta
Administrator: Fredmonica
Height: 17.8m   Weight: 9.5t
Primary Color: Orange

Bone Frame Designer: Regina Babylon
Affiliation: Duchy of Brunhild
Compatible Pilot: Hildegard Minas Lestia
Maximum Capacity: 1 Person
Armaments: Crystal Broadsword, Greatsword, Mace

A new special-model Frame Gear designed specifically for Hilde. One of the Valkyrie Gears. This particular Frame Gear was designed for close-quarters combat.

This Frame Gear was specifically designed to make use of a sword and shield in melee range, with high defensive potential. Its armor has been bolstered by Phrasium material.

In Another World With My Smartphone

12

Patora Fuyuhara
illustration・Eiji Usatsuka

VOLUMES 1-15
ON SALE NOW!

Sakon Kaidou

Illustrator: Taiki

Infinite Dendrogram

11. The Glory Selector

NOVELS 1-11 ON SALE NOW!

4

Author
F U N A

Illust.
SUKIMA

I SHALL SURVIVE USING POTIONS!

NOVEL VOLUME 4
ON SALE NOW!

J-Novel Club Lineup

Ebook Releases Series List

A Lily Blooms in Another World
A Wild Last Boss Appeared!
Altina the Sword Princess
Amagi Brilliant Park
An Archdemon's Dilemma:
    How to Love Your Elf Bride
Arifureta Zero
Arifureta: From Commonplace
    to World's Strongest
Ascendance of a Bookworm
Beatless
Bibliophile Princess
Black Summoner
By the Grace of the Gods
Campfire Cooking in Another
    World with My Absurd Skill
Can Someone Please Explain
    What's Going On?!
Cooking with Wild Game
Crest of the Stars
Deathbound Duke's Daughter
Demon Lord, Retry!
Der Werwolf: The Annals of Veight
From Truant to Anime Screenwriter:
    My Path to "Anohana" and "The
    Anthem of the Heart"
Full Metal Panic!
Grimgar of Fantasy and Ash
Her Majesty's Swarm
Holmes of Kyoto
How a Realist Hero Rebuilt the
    Kingdom
How NOT to Summon a Demon
    Lord
I Refuse to Be Your Enemy!
I Saved Too Many Girls and Caused
    the Apocalypse
I Shall Survive Using Potions!
In Another World With My
    Smartphone
Infinite Dendrogram
Infinite Stratos
Invaders of the Rokujouma!?
Isekai Rebuilding Project
JK Haru is a Sex Worker in Another
    World
Kobold King
Kokoro Connect
Last and First Idol
Lazy Dungeon Master
Mapping: The Trash-Tier Skill That
    Got Me Into a Top-Tier Party

Middle-Aged Businessman, Arise in
    Another World!
Mixed Bathing in Another
    Dimension
Monster Tamer
My Big Sister Lives in a Fantasy
    World
My Instant Death Ability is So
    Overpowered, No One in This
    Other World Stands a Chance
    Against Me!
My Next Life as a Villainess: All
    Routes Lead to Doom!
Otherside Picnic
Outbreak Company
Outer Ragna
Record of Wortenia War
Seirei Gensouki: Spirit Chronicles
Sexiled: My Sexist Party Leader
    Kicked Me Out, So I Teamed Up
    With a Mythical Sorceress!
Slayers
Sorcerous Stabber Orphen:
    The Wayward Journey
Tearmoon Empire
Teogonia
The Bloodline
The Combat Butler and Automaton
    Waitress
The Economics of Prophecy
The Epic Tale of the Reincarnated
    Prince Herscherik
The Extraordinary, the Ordinary,
    and SOAP!
The Greatest Magicmaster's
    Retirement Plan
The Holy Knight's Dark Road
The Magic in this Other World is
    Too Far Behind!
The Master of Ragnarok & Blesser
    of Einherjar
The Sorcerer's Receptionist
The Tales of Marielle Clarac
The Underdog of the Eight Greater
    Tribes
The Unwanted Undead Adventurer
WATARU!!! The Hot-Blooded
    Fighting Teen & His Epic
    Adventures in a Fantasy World
    After Stopping a Truck with His
    Bare Hands!!

The White Cat's Revenge as
    Plotted from the Demon King's
    Lap
The World's Least Interesting
    Master Swordsman
Welcome to Japan, Ms. Elf!
When the Clock Strikes Z
Wild Times with a Fake Fake
    Princess

Manga Series:
A Very Fairy Apartment
An Archdemon's Dilemma:
    How to Love Your Elf Bride
Animeta!
Ascendance of a Bookworm
Bibliophile Princess
Black Summoner
Campfire Cooking in Another
    World with My Absurd Skill
Cooking with Wild Game
Demon Lord, Retry!
Discommunication
How a Realist Hero Rebuilt the
    Kingdom
I Love Yuri and I Got Bodyswapped
    with a Fujoshi!
I Shall Survive Using Potions!
Infinite Dendrogram
Mapping: The Trash-Tier Skill That
    Got Me Into a Top-Tier Party
Marginal Operation
Record of Wortenia War
Seirei Gensouki: Spirit Chronicles
Sorcerous Stabber Orphen:
    The Reckless Journey
Sorcerous Stabber Orphen:
    The Youthful Journey
Sweet Reincarnation
The Faraway Paladin
The Magic in this Other World is
    Too Far Behind!
The Master of Ragnarok & Blesser
    of Einherjar
The Tales of Marielle Clarac
The Unwanted Undead Adventurer

Keep an eye out at j-novel.club
    for further new title
    announcements!